ROBERTS &

THE
A **TOM WAGNER** ADVENTURE
LIBRARY
OF
THE
KINGS

Thriller

Translator: Edwin Miles / Copyeditor: Philip Yaeger

Imprint: Independently published / Paperback ISBN 9798577863845 ,
Hardcover ISBN 9798711473176

Cover Art by reinhardfenzl.com

Cover Art was created with photos from:
depositphotos.com (steveheap, czuber, tribal, y6uca, dleindecdp,
iLexx) and https://www.neo-stock.com

www.robertsmaclay.com

office@robertsmaclay.com

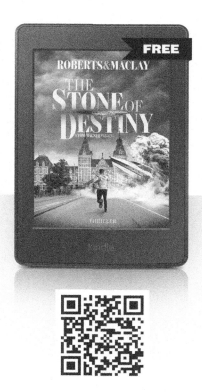

"The more perfect, the more pain."

Michelangelo (1475-1564)

1

THE VILLA OF NIKOLAUS III, COUNT PALFFY VON ERDÖD, IN A SUBURB OF THE HAGUE

The man watched the beautiful black woman for a few moments as she strolled away. He knew her name, of course—Ossana Ibori—and followed her, keeping his distance.

He watched as she climbed into her car, which was parked two blocks away, and drove off. He waited five minutes, wanting to be certain that she did not return and take him by surprise. Only then did he return to the villa. In contrast to Ossana, he did not have to climb over the wall. He had a key. With gloved hands, he unlocked the wrought-iron gate and, as Ossana had done some fifteen minutes earlier, he walked three hundred yards up the tree-lined, cobblestoned driveway until he reached the villa. The garden around him was pitch black. Ossana, presumably, had switched off the old London street lamps that would otherwise have lit the well-tended grounds.

The villa also lay in darkness. The man unlocked the entrance door, crossed to the alarm system and typed in the seven-digit code. He went into the study and snapped on a light. He looked down at the floor and nodded appreciatively: Ossana had done a thorough job. She had closed the safe that was set into the wall above the chimney, hidden behind a Kandinsky painting. But the safe was not what interested him. He left the study, crossed the entrance hall and went up the large marble staircase to the floor above. He made his way along the first-floor hallway to the last bedroom and switched on the light. A closet stood open, and clothes lay on the bed and the floor. A closed suitcase stood on the floor, an open one lay on the bed. Someone had certainly been planning a quick exit from the country. The man smiled grimly: he could understand the impulse only too well. He walked around to the side of the antique oak bed that faced the window and pushed aside the heavy old nightstand. One had to look very closely to see the irregularities in the wood grain of the bed frame. He pressed against a part of the base where the wood was a little lighter. With a soft click, a section about twelve inches long and four inches high moved a fraction of an inch inward. The man pushed the loose board to the side, opening up a gap about the size of a mail slot. He reached inside and retrieved three loose hand-written sheets of paper. He fished a pair of reading glasses out of his jacket and rapidly scanned the pages, then nodded. He closed the compartment and pushed the nightstand back into place, then exited the bedroom, switching off the light as he went. On his way back to the entrance he paused, then returned to the study.

So far, he had acted calmly and without haste, but now his actions betrayed a sudden disquiet. His eyes strayed

8

nervously around the room. He went to the desk, opened the drawers and cupboards, searched the document trays and papers lying on the desk. Then he looked up at the Kandinsky, pushed it aside and opened the safe. Empty. The man sighed. Apparently she had taken it with her. He did not like that at all; it should never have found its way into anyone else's hands. But he knew he would get it back. All in good time. He left the villa and got into his car. He twisted around to the back seat and picked up an envelope that lay there, addressed to "Hellen de Mey." The man slipped the three loose pages into the envelope and sealed it. He checked that there was enough postage, then got out of the car again and walked to the next intersection, where one of the red post boxes so typical of the Netherlands stood. He slipped the envelope through the slot and returned to his car.

2

WASHINGTON D.C., USA

Thomas Maria Wagner squinted against the blinding sun. He could not afford to lose his orientation, not now. There was too much at stake. He swung the aircraft hard to the left to get out of his adversary's firing line. The incessant beeping, now getting faster and faster, told him that his pursuer was hard on his tail and trying relentlessly to get a lock on him. Tom knew that if the beeping merged into a continuous tone – like a heart monitor flatlining – it would mean the end for him, too.

He swung the F4 Phantom hard again, now in the opposite direction. The airplane tipped one hundred degrees onto its side, rattling every bone in Tom's body. A flick of the joystick sent it back the other way at punishing speed. The plane flipped upside down, tipped to the left, to the right, and barrel rolled several times. Any normal person would have left their lunch all over the console, and would most likely have blacked out by now. But Tom found it all . . . fun.

He was an adrenaline junkie of the purest kind, enthusiastically tackling every absurd or dangerous pursuit ever invented by God or sponsored by Red Bull. The tedium was also the reason he'd left his old job. Originally, he'd thought that line of work would keep him supplied with the necessary dose of action, but he had been monumentally disappointed. Being an officer with one of the world's best antiterror units had sounded exciting, but it had turned out to be one big letdown. His last official assignment with Cobra, as the unit was called, had been as an in-flight security officer, an air marshal—by far the most boring task associated with the job. He had earned it on account of his being prone to a certain . . . creative re-interpretation of his orders.

A shrill warning signal ripped him out of his maudlin thoughts.

No way, Tom thought. He simply could not shake off his pursuer, let alone turn the tables on him. He had only one chance left.

With no time to think, he shut the throttle down and leaned straight back on the joystick. The result was a kind of midair emergency stop: the Phantom's nose tipped up almost ninety degrees, and for a brief moment his speed was cut in half. But his pursuer didn't shoot past underneath, as Tom had expected. Guiding the nose back down, he opened the throttle wide.

Where the hell did he go? He was right on my tail, Tom wondered.

The next moment, the high-pitched signal sounded again. This time, however, it was not the intermittent beeping, but the continuous *beeeeeep* that Tom had feared. He clenched his eyes shut and released the controls, surrendering himself to his fate.

"Game Over. Please exit the simulator to the right. Thank you for visiting the Smithsonian National Air and Space Museum. We hope you enjoy the rest of your visit," he heard through the speakers inside the small cockpit.

He climbed out of the simulator and trotted down the steps, where his uncle, Admiral Scott Wagner, was waiting for him.

"Beers are on you," the admiral said, smiling victoriously. He threw an arm around his nephew's shoulders and gave him a quick hug. Uncle Scott was Tom's uncle on his father's side. After Scott had helped him out of a life-or-death situation about six months earlier, Tom had decided it was time to pay him a visit.

"So you really used to fly an old tin can like that?" Tom asked.

"Sure did. Desert Storm. The F4s may be fifty years old, but they've still got it," Scott replied.

"So do you. There was no way I could shake you off."

"Your PlayStation experience ain't enough to outfly me."

"When are you going to take me up for a spin in the real thing?" Tom asked optimistically.

"I'll ask around, see if I can swing it. But keep in mind that one hour in a fighter jet sets the U.S. taxpayer back a solid thirty thousand dollars."

Tom's eyes widened.

"Thirty grand? For one hour? That's a pricey joy ride. Maybe I'll stick to the PlayStation."

The two men laughed as they made their way out of the simulator room at the Air & Space Museum and ambled on through the enormous halls.

From the Wright Brothers' first plane to every kind of flying machine imaginable, and onward to modern space flight, the entire history of aerospace technology was documented in meticulous detail, in one impressive display after another. Aircraft were suspended overhead, and Tom had spent the last few hours moving through sections of the space shuttle and admiring space suits, scale models and thousands of other things.

An announcement droned through the museum's PA system: "Ladies and gentlemen, the museum will be closing in a few minutes. Please make your way to the exits. Thank you for visiting the Smithsonian National Air and Space Museum. We hope to see you again."

"Thanks for the guided tour, Uncle Scott. It's been a blast," said Tom as they left the museum among the last to exit.

"My pleasure."

They walked westward along the National Mall parallel to Jefferson Drive, heading back toward their car. The immense national park was strewn with the buildings of the Smithsonian complex, spread across 150 acres and with a breathtaking view of the Washington Monument, the enormous obelisk that was just one of the city's famous landmarks. Behind them, the majestic United States Capitol shone in the late-afternoon sunlight. And although the two structures might look very close on a cinema screen, the impression was misleading: the Washington Monument stood a good mile and a half from Capitol Hill.

Off to their left, the Smithsonian Castle, the main building and present-day information center of the Smithsonian Institute, appeared between the trees. Tom and his uncle stopped at a hot dog stand—and then watched, hot dogs in hand, as two black SUVs screeched to a halt across the road and eight men jumped out. They were dressed in civilian clothes, but their movements were unmistakably military. Each man carried a black sports bag. They did not run, but strode rapidly toward the rear entrance of the Castle, pulling masks over their faces as they went. They reached into the sports bags, pulling out automatic weapons fitted with suppressors, and marched into the building.

3

AMOUN HOTEL, ALEXANDRIA, EGYPT

Hellen de Mey's sleep that night was more restless than it had been for a very long time. Her gut feeling had never let her down. As young as she was, she had taken part in a surprising number of excavations. Since giving up her job with Blue Shield—a subsidiary of UNESCO charged with the protection of heritage around the world—her feelings had become less frequent, but they were still never wrong. When they came, they unfailingly meant the discovery of something special. Adventures weren't really the norm for archaeologists and historians, but in recent years it had been a different story for Hellen—and she liked tackling history this way. Tomorrow was a big day; she was about to follow up on a lead that had reached her in a very unusual way: someone had sent her an actual letter. An anonymous letter to boot, about a subject that had preoccupied her father all his life: the Library of Alexandria.

No ancient object was more wrapped in myth and legend than the Library of Alexandria, except perhaps for the

Holy Grail or the Ark of the Covenant. The entire knowledge of antiquity, both Eastern and Western, was said to have been collected within its walls. Though the actual number is no longer known, the library had accumulated an enormous number of scrolls by the standards of the day, including both literary texts and a large number of scientific treatises from many different fields. Since its founding by Alexander the Great, at the start of the third century B.C. in the city of Alexandria, the collection was said to have become practically unmanageable down through the ages. However, the location of the treasures once housed in the library was a mystery: at some point the library had simply disappeared from the public record. The actual date of its demise was unknown, although estimates range from 48 B.C. to the seventh century AD.

Hellen's father had told her all about it when she was still a child, and about the many myths surrounding its disappearance. There were many theories, but none had ever been proven, and so far no remains of the actual library had been found. Clues lurked in the works of many ancient writers, but none had led to a definite location. Hellen smiled sadly as she remembered the enthusiasm with which her father had told her about the treasures in the library, and the countless antique riddles whose solutions were said to be found there—Atlantis, for example, and the secret of the pyramids.

Tomorrow, perhaps, a huge step toward locating the fabled library would be revealed to her. The handwritten letter she had received contained unprecedented clues. It claimed knowledge of hidden passageways in the

Necropolis of Anfushi, close to the historical port of Alexandria. One of the many legends surrounding the city told of a system of underground canals that had been used in the battles against Gaius Julius Caesar during the Siege of Alexandria. Ganymedes, a eunuch and educator under the Ptolemaic king's daughter Arsinoë, sister of Cleopatra, had ordered the passages flooded, drowning many of Caesar's men. The letter claimed that treasures from the library were hidden in the canal system; now it was up to Hellen to verify the truth—or otherwise—of the information.

She had quickly found a sponsor for the excavation: still dreaming of Alexandria, she glanced at the man who lay beside her in bed. She smiled, because for the first time in a long time she felt protected. Arno embodied everything she wanted in a man: he was intelligent and good-looking and, most importantly, reliable. He strived for stability and security, and she appreciated that quality in him very much. He opened his eyes. The calm he radiated was like a heavy, warm, woolen blanket enveloping her. Without a word, Hellen kissed him. She had to forget that other man once and for all. She was with Arno now.

"Excited about tomorrow, babe?" Arno asked sleepily.

"Of course. I really hope we find something."

"I hope so too, for your sake. I'd love for you to be able to carry through your father's legacy and finally rediscover the library. And I'm happy that I'm able to help you with it, at least a little."

One agreeable advantage to being with Arno was that his father happened to own a South African diamond mine;

the family had more money than the Sahara had grains of sand. Hellen had wasted no time getting him excited about the excavation.

4

SMITHSONIAN INSTITUTE, WASHINGTON D.C.

Scott dragged Tom back from the street. Tom, on autopilot, had been heading toward the two SUVs parked on Jefferson Drive, and had almost been hit by a car.

"Tom, look out!" Scott cried as they stumbled backwards. The car flew past honking its horn, the driver gesticulating furiously.

"Did you see those guys?" Tom said, still in his trance. He threw his hot dog in the trash and ran across the street. Scott took a final bite of his own, and followed him.

Construction of the Castle, as the impressive structure had been nicknamed, had begun in 1847, a year after the Smithsonian Institute's founding. It had been completed in 1855, the first building erected as part of Institute. Today, the Smithsonian was the biggest museum complex in the world, with more that 142 million items officially in its possession, although no more than two percent of that was on display in its nineteen museums.

Tom and Scott could hear the first cries from inside the Castle as they approached, and a few hysterical people came running out of the building.

"They killed a security guard," a distraught young woman sobbed, pointing inside.

Arriving at the entrance, they peered cautiously through a gap in the door. A few visitors crouched fearfully in one corner, not daring to move. A guard lay dead on the small staircase to the left, beside the elevator for disabled visitors. The unfortunate (and probably woefully underpaid) man hadn't even managed to get to his radio to report the intruders.

Ducking low, Tom and Scott entered the foyer; Scott crossed immediately to the guard. He checked for signs of life, then took out his phone and tried to dial 911, but the line was dead. "They're blocking the mobile network," he said to Tom. He reached for the guard's radio. "Hello? Central?" he said. The radio returned nothing but crackling static and humming. "Shit!" He searched the guard for weapons, finding only a taser, which he took. He shook his head angrily, and Tom understood that the man was dead, and there were no other weapons to be had.

"Where did they go?" Tom whispered to the group cowering in the corner.

An elderly man pointed to the right and said, "That way, down to the basement."

Tom nodded his thanks and signaled to them to get outside fast.

"Reinforcements could take a while," Scott said to Tom. "These guys are pros. They've blocked everything."

"What are they after?"

"Looks to me like they're heading for the secret archive."

"I thought that was a myth."

"That's the idea." Scott smiled.

"Well, then, let's go. What are we waiting for?"

"Tom!" Scott hissed after his nephew, who was already heading down the stairs to the basement. *Hothead*, he thought, taking a deep breath and going after him.

At the bottom of the stairs, Tom heard a distant noise. He dashed onward, following the long white corridor until he reached the end. He could feel the adrenaline surging through him: he was in battle mode. It had been a long time since he'd been in action. *But it's like riding a bicycle*, he thought.

At the end of the corridor, Tom saw a sign on the wall, describing an underground tunnel linking the Castle with the National Museum of Natural History on the other side of the Mall.

Tom edged the door open until he had a gap wide enough to see through. About five yards away, one of the intruders stood next to a small stairway, which led down to a narrow, rusted gate. Behind it was a tunnel leading into darkness.

Meanwhile, Scott had caught up with him. Tom used hand signals to indicate *stop, one man, right side, five yards*.

Scott handed Tom the taser, then crouched beside the door and grasped the handle. Tom positioned himself to spring.

The soldier never saw it coming. Scott swung the door open as Tom launched himself toward the man. He fired the taser, then slid between the man's legs and brought him down. Back on his feet, Tom booted the convulsing man hard beneath the chin, taking him out of action for good.

"Clear," Tom whispered to his uncle as he began taking the soldier's weapons and other gear.

"There's supposed to be an entrance to the archive in the middle of that tunnel," Scott whispered, nodding toward the gate.

Tom handed the pistol, a Glock, to Scott and kept the tactical knife and a silenced FN P90 for himself. He slung the strap of the small machine pistol over his shoulder, tested the flashlight, handed two spare magazines to Scott and pushed two for himself into the back pocket of his jeans. He cocked the machine pistol, smiled encouragingly at his uncle and disappeared into the darkness.

"Tom, this isn't a simulator. You screw up here and it's game over for real," Scott said behind him. He glanced down at the Glock, then ducked his head and followed his nephew into the tunnel.

Scott was right; the archive was the soldiers' target. Halfway down the 250-yard-long tunnel, a modern security door with a retinal scanner stood open. A man in a white coat lay motionless on the floor, blocking the door.

Tom checked the man's pulse and sighed, shaking his head. The man had probably been forced to open the door before he'd been killed. Keeping low, Tom and Scott stepped over the lifeless body and pressed on into the secret archive that lay beneath the Smithsonian Institute.

5

13TH CENTURY B.C., MOUNT SINAI, EGYPT

The man stood on the summit of the mountain and gazed down into the valley. He listened to the whistling of the wind and contemplated the rugged landscape all around him, nothing but rocks and sand. There could be no life up there, and yet he had come to the summit to hear the word of God. Who was he to be chosen to hear His voice? Who was he to lead the chosen people into the Promised Land? For he alone had been permitted to climb the mountain and to meet his God once more.

He was Moses, the son of a Levite family, set adrift on the Nile in a reed basket and then found and raised by the daughter of the Egyptian Pharaoh. Why had God revealed Himself to him and given him the task of freeing the Israelites from slavery? Whatever challenge Moses might face, God was on his side: the Israelites had been spared the plagues, the sea had parted before them, the desert could do them no harm, the battle against the Amalekites had been won. And every time, it was because God had protected Moses and his people. When they realized that they were the chosen ones, they had rejoiced, but had then become overconfident, neglecting to show the necessary humility. Some had become angry that they were not all allowed to meet their God at the summit, that only Moses was allowed to ascend. Now, here he stood to hear the commandments of the Lord— commandments that were new not only to him, but which he knew would not be accepted by the people. But they were the commandments of the Creator, the Ten Commandments that represented not only moral law, but also regulated the civil life of the people.

It was not the Ten Commandments that frightened Moses, nor the two stone tablets upon which were inscribed the ten rules by which his people were now supposed to live. It was the third tablet that troubled him, for it represented the true test of God. If the Ten Commandments were the rules of God the people had to obey, the third stone tablet was the temptation that showed how faithful they were, and whether they deserved to be the chosen race. Long after God had spoken to Moses, he remained where he stood on the summit. He was troubled by the message that had just been revealed to him, but a paralyzing fear consumed him when he thought of returning to his people with the rules of the Lord and the tablet of eternal temptation.

Finally, he summoned his courage. Placing the three tablets carefully in the linen bag he had brought, he began the descent to the valley, where his people would be waiting impatiently for his return and God's message. With every step that brought him closer to his people, his doubts and fears increased. Would his God continue to help them pass the tests they faced? Was the worst behind them? Would the Creator continue to shelter him with His hand, or would He turn His back? Would He watch to see if they could manage to follow the commandments and resist temptation?

Moses knew, of course, that he would not be alone. Many of the people were behind him. Many of those busily assembling the Ark of the Covenant and erecting the Tabernacle trusted him blindly. They would follow him and humbly accept the rules of the Lord, first among them his brother Aaron and Joshua, the commander of the army. But there were many who looked at Moses' role with resentment, who neither saw the true God nor wanted to follow Him. Could his people really have turned to a false god while he had climbed Mount Sinai to receive the commandments, as God had prophesied they would? These reflections and doubts, this responsibility weighed heavily on Moses—and when he reached the valley, he saw the sad truth: the people danced around a golden calf and prayed to the graven image. They had gone astray in no time at all.

A feeling of wrath overcame Moses, and driven by his anger, he took the first of the stone tablets he carried and smashed it against a rock. The songs of the people grew louder and louder, in rapturous tribute to their false idol. Moses felt that none of them deserved to see the true God's laws even once, and he shattered the second stone tablet as well. Then Joshua came to him and reassured him. The Levites had proved they were faithful to God; as for the credulous folk, they would be led back to the true faith by the sword. Moses and Joshua set to gathering the broken pieces of the two stone tablets. The Ark of the Covenant was finished and the pieces would be stored inside it, alongside the intact tablet—the one that shimmered emerald green.

6

BENEATH THE SMITHSONIAN INSTITUTE,
WASHINGTON D.C.

"Go on, get in!" the leader of the mercenaries ordered. One of his men pushed the last of the seven archivists into one of the glass book vaults that stood inside the Smithsonian's hangar-like secret archive. The hall was the size of several football fields and equipped with thousands of yards of high, heavy-duty shelving. In the center were three of these book vaults—hermetically sealed glass containers, each with its own atmospheric controls and an airlock through which the archivists could enter. The air supply, temperature and oxygen levels of each vault could be regulated individually, to protect the ancient documents inside from decay. An overhead crane, with which heavy objects could be transported throughout the cavernous hall, hung just below the ceiling.

Tom and Scott entered the hangar through a gallery at the far end, and Tom stood awestruck for a moment. He had never seen anything like it in his life. Grinning ear to ear, he turned to Scott and whispered: "Is the Ark of the Covenant somewhere in here?"

"Sure. Back there on the left, row three, shelf four," Scott murmured back, smiling grimly.

"I imagine your friends will have about ten minutes left after we shut off the air supply, at most. Then you can watch them all turn blue," said the leader imperiously, his silenced pistol pressed to the kneeling archivist's head. The man looked fearfully at his colleagues inside the vault, hammering on the glass wall, their plea written on their faces. "Where can we find this?" The leader held a sheet of paper in front of the kneeling man's face. The elderly archivist squinted at the image and shook his head. His entire body trembled.

"I don't know. I've worked here for forty years, but I've never seen—"

He didn't even hear the hissing sound of the pistol when the mercenary leader, irritated, pulled the trigger. His blood poured across the floor, and his lifeless body slumped to the side.

"Find it. Now. Go!" he snapped at his men, and they ran off in all directions.

Tom and Scott looked at each other in dismay. They had crept down from the gallery and closer to the scene, and had overheard everything. Along the way, they had run into another of the mercenaries and had wasted no time in taking him out.

I know that voice, Tom thought. "The guy. It's Isaac Hagen," he whispered to his uncle.

They retreated a short distance to avoid detection.

"You know that madman?" Scott asked.

"Yeah. Two years ago, Madeira. I told you about it."

"That stunt on the cable car?"

Tom nodded. "The guy's a total maniac. We've got to get the hostages out. If we don't act fast, they'll suffocate." Tom looked at his watch and set a timer for eight minutes. "Wait here." Quietly and cautiously, he climbed to the top of one of the rows of shelving to get a better view over the hall. Only the emergency lighting was switched on and he couldn't see the far end, but the three vaults in the center glowed like gold ingots in the dim light. The overhead crane was parked not far from the front of the first of the glass vaults, into which the archivists had been herded. The crane had a cable hoist with a heavy hook dangling from it. Tom could also see a control room overlooking everything, at about the level of the vaults. Only one mercenary was inside. Tom ducked out of sight when the man turned in his direction.

Back at floor level, he whispered to his uncle: "I've got an idea. There's a control room over there with one guy inside. Take him out, and try to activate the air supply to the vaults. That will win us a little time."

"Okay. I'll do my best," Scott said with a nod. He seemed a little out of breath. "Just a bit rusty."

Tom explained the rest of his plan, and the two men

bumped fists. "Wait for my signal," Tom whispered, and they crept off in different directions.

Turning a corner, Tom almost ran into the back of a mercenary standing in front of a shelf. He acted instantly: leaving the P90 dangling on its strap, he rammed his fist into the man's kidney and followed it up with a choke-hold. Within seconds, the man fell unconscious. Tom dragged his body around the corner and stowed it under a shelf, then crossed two more rows of shelves to reach the center aisle. The rest of the men were searching in the other half of the hall, and didn't seem to be expecting any trouble from the police just yet. Tom was able to move with relative freedom. Reaching his goal directly beneath the crane hook, he climbed the shelves and lay flat on top. From there, he could see the control room; he watched as his uncle expertly took out the mercenary inside. Now Scott had a P90, too.

So much for rusty. He's still got it. Tom smiled.

A few moments later, Scott signaled that he couldn't control the air supply from there, and gave Tom the sign for Plan B. Tom nodded. He took the rope he'd taken from an emergency box earlier, tossed a loop over the crane hook and hauled the crane toward him. He let the two ends of the rope fall to the floor and climbed back down. At floor level, he pulled one end of the rope around an upright of the shelf on the left and the other around its counterpart on the right, then knotted them together in the exact center of the aisle. The rope formed a taut triangle between the hook and the two shelves.

Now Tom crept toward the glass vault. Two of the hostages inside were still knocking weakly against the thick panes of their glass prison, but no sound penetrated outside. The rest were sitting on the floor, exhausted and frightened. They had already resigned themselves to their fate, and were waiting for death. Tom looked around cautiously, then approached the glass wall. He signaled to the people inside to take cover. Then he took a few steps back and looked over his shoulder, checking he was still in the clear.

He raised the P90 and aimed at the vault. Shocked faces inside stared back at him. They shook their heads in bewilderment. "NOW!" Tom yelled as loudly as he could, and fired the P90. At the same moment, the crane started to move. Scott steered it forward, letting its hoist out a little as it went. They only had a few moments to carry out their plan; Tom's shout and the shooting had naturally not gone unnoticed.

Drawn by the noise, Hagen called his remaining men together.

"Go and find whoever that is. Bring him to me," he ordered, and the men rushed off. They were at the far end of the hall, but they were highly trained and could probably manage 150 yards in under twenty-five seconds, even in combat gear.

The glass walls were too thick for bullets to penetrate, but the pane had been weakened and destabilized by the shots. When the crane came to a halt just above the vault holding the hostages, Tom turned and fired at the rope that held the hook back. The bullets shredded the knot and the hook swung on its cable like a wrecking ball, striking it at precisely the spot that Tom had weakened. The glass wall shattered.

The four men at the far end of the hall were now sprinting back toward the center. Scott, with a view of almost the entire hall, shouted a warning: "Heads up, Tom. You're about to have company." Then he aimed his P90 at one of the men and opened fire. The man went down. Scott ducked into cover, escaping the return fire from one of the soldiers. He crawled out of the control room and ran down the stairs to help Tom.

Hagen's fury grew. Had he overlooked someone? How could the police already be there? They had shut down every network in a two-mile radius. Who dared to throw a wrench in his foolproof plan? For now, he held back and stayed out of sight.

The hostages could hardly believe their good fortune. As they clambered out of the destroyed vault, Tom pointed them toward the exit at the back of the hall. They ran the length of the center aisle and escaped over the walkway where Tom and Scott had come in. Tom put a new clip in his P90, then lay down in a dark corner and waited. He spotted one of the mercenaries, who had slowed down and now peered cautiously around a corner. The bright light from the vault gave Tom a clear shot at the man, and he took him down with a single bullet. Scott took out another.

"Is that all of them?" Scott shouted through the hall.

"There's one more," Tom replied.

They ran through the hall, looking for the last man. Hagen, well hidden, watched them search and was stunned when he realized who he was up against. He opted for discretion, for now.

After a few minutes of searching, Tom and Scott met again at the destroyed vault. Tom was carrying a mask and one of the tactical vests.

"I found this back there. Looks like Hagen got away."

While Tom and Scott were tying up the last of the mercenaries still left alive, Tom noticed a Iban-style tattoo on the man's forearm. The A and F worked into the design were all too familiar. When an organization like "Absolute Freedom" was after something, it didn't bode well.

He sat down with his uncle, both of them exhausted but satisfied. *I need to contact Noah as soon as possible*, Tom thought. It was the first time since Barcelona that he had a new lead. A short time later, a team of FBI officers and local cops stormed the hall, but there was nothing left for them to do.

7

NECROPOLIS OF ANFUSHI, ALEXANDRIA

It didn't look promising at all. After visiting the Necropolis of Anfushi for the first time a few days earlier, Hellen's hopes had all but evaporated. The small excavation site didn't look like it could possibly be hiding a sensational archaeological find. The area was run-down and unimpressive, and around the small necropolis were schools, sports fields, a harbor building, and one of the many public beaches. The excavation site itself was deserted, untended, and partly overgrown with vegetation. The tombs were from the third century—the right era, at least—but that was the only ray of hope.

"Are you sure this is the place the letters were talking about? It looks more like an abandoned construction site," Arno had said. And Hellen also had to admit that she would never have thought to look here for clues to the magnificent Library of Alexandria, or for anything valuable at all. The letter, however, had been crystal clear. Still, there was another problem: when she applied for permission to examine inside the tombs and corridors of the necropolis, she was immediately denied.

"The excavation site is located too close to the sea, and most of the passageways and tombs are partially flooded or unstable due to the ingress of seawater. Exploration is therefore far too dangerous to be authorized." —so ran the official rejection letter from the Egyptian Ministry of Culture. Even Arno's more-than-generous attempts to offer *baksheesh* hadn't succeeded in changing their minds.

"Then we'll go in anyway. We'll just do it at night, when nobody will see us. And we'll need diving equipment to get through the flooded corridors," Hellen said matter-of-factly.

She no longer recognized herself. Not so long ago, she would not have accepted a flat rejection from the authorities and would have got caught up in a lengthy bureaucratic to-and-fro. But she had changed. She knew who was responsible for that change, and she would remain eternally grateful to him for it . . . but that was not important, not now. Now she had to delve into the clues in the letter. It was shortly after midnight when Arno stopped the SUV directly in front of the necropolis, across the road from a military hospital.

"We can't stop here. Not right under the noses of the military," Hellen said. "Let's see if we can get in from the other side."

Arno agreed. Pulling away slowly, he noticed that the soldier guarding the hospital entrance had noticed the SUV and its occupants. They drove farther down the road and turned left into a narrow alley running along the side of the excavation, where they found a small grove of trees that would give them the cover they needed to scale the wall.

Arno lifted the two backpacks with their equipment from the trunk and handed one to Hellen. They tossed the backpacks over the wall and clambered over after them.

It was a clear, moonlit night, and they were able to cross the open section of the excavation easily without using their flashlights. They used the pry bar Arno had brought to break the padlock on the wooden door, then slipped into the first burial chamber. Hellen switched on her flashlight.

"So far, so good," Arno said, sliding the pry bar back into his pack. He looked over at Hellen. In her olive-green tank top and cargo shorts, and given the setting, the similarity to Lara Croft was undeniable.

"Look!" Hellen pointed at the paintings on the wall. "Clearly pre-Ptolemaic. These cartouches are from the 26th Dynasty, the reign of Pharaoh Apries—they're rare. I don't understand why they're letting the place fall apart like this."

"Over here's an image of Horus," Arno said.

Hellen smiled. She liked being with a man with whom she shared so many interests.

They passed through several burial chambers until they reached a larger room, its walls covered with simple geometric patterns and a representation of the god Osiris. At the far end of the room, a stone stairway descended. Arno shone his flashlight down the steps: about ten feet below, they could see the shimmer of water.

Hellen's heart began to race. She turned pale.

"Hellen? Are you all right?" Arno had seen the fear on her face.

"All . . . all good. It just reminds me of . . . of a time when I almost drowned," she said, her voice faltering.

She had known all along that they would have to dive, but it was only now that the reality hit home. The sight of the steps disappearing into the pitch-black water brought back all the memories, sapping her strength. She closed her eyes, breathed deeply in and out, and quickly recovered. "But we didn't have any diving gear back then," she said mostly to herself, trying to allay her fear. Her voice was back to normal.

Arno took the two air bottles out of the backpack and passed one to Hellen. The bottle was barely twelve inches long and held enough air for ten minutes; a mouthpiece was attached directly to the top end. Hellen sat on the steps at the edge of the water, pulled her swimming goggles on, slipped into her fins and fitted the mouthpiece between her teeth. She also took a handful of glow sticks out of her backpack and slipped them into a pocket of her shorts.

"Remember: we only have enough air for ten minutes," Arno reminded her as he sat down beside her and put his own gear on. Hellen gave Arno a thumbs-up, then slid down the steps and dived. Arno followed close behind. The descent was short, and the stairs soon opened into another room. They dropped glow sticks at intervals to find their way back quickly. According to a sketch Hellen had made on a white plastic card with an underwater marker, they had to find a narrow corridor and follow it for about 200 yards. At the end, they would find a false door of the kind often found on ancient Egyptian structures. They swam on and found everything exactly as it was on the map. The outer frame of the false door was decorated with hundreds of hieroglyphics; a checkerboard pattern of yellowed dark- and light-colored stones flanked it to the left and right. They dropped a few glow sticks on the floor, giving themselves enough light to keep their hands free, and set to work.

Twelve stones wide and twelve high. Hellen had memorized the instructions in the letter and gone through them with Arno a dozen times. From her side, Hellen counted four stones to the left and three up, while Arno counted six stones up and two to the right on his side.

They pressed simultaneously on their respective stones. Nothing happened. The stones seemed to be fixed in place. They tried again, and again nothing moved. After a few attempts, Arno pointed to his diving watch. Their efforts were consuming more air than planned; they only had enough for five more minutes. They had to hurry or the air would run out too soon.

Hellen took out her pocketknife and scraped some gunk out of the joints around the stone. Arno did the same. They pressed once more—and finally the stones slid back about four inches. At the same time, a stone block about two feet on a side abruptly jutted out from the center of the false door. Air bubbles rose. *A hollow space,* thought Hellen. They took hold of the block and tried to haul it farther out of the wall. It was heavy work, but they managed it. The block slid out completely, and Hellen saw that there was indeed a hollow behind it. Inside were two amphorae, each bearing a symbol that she recognized instantly. Arno tapped his watch again: two minutes of air left. Hellen's fear returned. Her last diving experience had been traumatic enough, and she had no desire to experience anything like that ever again. She grabbed one of the amphorae and swam back the way they had come, following the glow sticks. Arno took the other one under his arm and swam after her.

Hellen's head broke the surface. She gasped loudly—her air bottle was empty, and she had swum the last few strokes holding her breath. Arno surfaced seconds later. They had made it.

"I know this symbol." Hellen pointed enthusiastically at the amphorae. "I've seen it in my father's papers countless times." She was breathing quickly and smiled happily at Arno. "These two amphorae are from the Library of Alexandria. I'm sure of it!"

8

BLUEJACKET BAR, WASHINGTON D.C.

"How did you find me?" Tom asked, narrowing his eyes at the young man in the black suit who appeared beside the piano where Tom was sitting. He had just launched into "The Blue Danube" when he saw Jakob Leitner heading in his direction.

Leitner nodded to Scott then turned back to Tom. "When an Austrian citizen—and a former Cobra officer—is involved in a terrorist attack in the heart of Washington D.C., the local authorities tend to ask questions at the embassy," Leitner explained confidently in his broad Viennese accent. "Your uncle is with the Navy. The rest was basic research," he added proudly.

"So you checked out every Navy bar in D.C. till you found me, did you?" Tom asked mockingly. He stopped playing, and Leitner shrugged and grinned sheepishly. "Looks like you've healed up. How have you been?"

"Good, thanks. I'm reporting directly to CKL now!"

Tom nodded, but he was less than thrilled to have

Leitner walk in on such a private moment. Playing the piano had always been a meditative pursuit for him, and above all a solitary one. Even among those close to him, only his uncle and his best friend Noah knew, and had heard him play. He preferred to play in the anonymity of small bars, where nobody knew him. It made him feel vulnerable, but at the same time more alive than in practically any other part of his life. It was his secret, one he hadn't even told Hellen about. The brief thought of her was like a stab to the heart. It felt like an eternity ago, as if the time with her had been in another life.

His uncle raised his glass to Tom, interrupting his sentimental frame of mind, and downed his whiskey. They felt they had earned a drink after hours of FBI questioning. He approached the piano and held out his clenched fist; Tom briefly bumped it with his own.

"You take care. And call her!" Scott said.

He nodded goodbye to Tom, ignoring the outstretched hand of the young man, who said nervously to him in German: "It was nice to meet you."

"*No hablo alemán*," Scott said in flawless Spanish. He gave Tom a wink and left the bar.

"So I'm guessing *he* wants to talk to me, right? What's up?" Tom asked, standing up from the piano and glaring at Leitner.

The younger man cleared his throat and stammered uncertainly. "He . . . I don't really . . . he wants . . . there's a car waiting out front."

Tom laid a few bills on the piano, clapped Leitner on the shoulder with a bitter smile and headed for the exit. "Then let's go. Don't want to keep His Lordship waiting."

As they drove over the Arlington Memorial Bridge, Tom realized where the Austrian chancellor would be waiting for him. Konstantin Lang had majored in history and had a flair for the dramatic. Meeting at night on the steps of the Lincoln Memorial would be just his style.

Tom didn't really feel like being part of CKL's drama though, not now. His mind was more occupied with the young FBI agent who had given him her card. After the questioning was done, they'd had a great conversation. And if even his uncle had seen the sparks flying, then he wanted to grab the opportunity.

He took out his phone and tapped out a quick message.

The car curved into the traffic circle surrounding the monument, then stopped where the traffic circle met Henry Bacon Drive. Tom and Leitner got out and walked to the memorial steps. The chancellor, CKL to his friends, was already sitting on the steps.

Jakob Leitner was a former Cobra colleague of Tom's. They had been through quite a bit together, and now it looked as if Jakob had taken over Tom's old job. *Well, good for him*, Tom thought. Leitner went to where the chancellor's bodyguard was standing off to the side, sent him back to the car with a word and took up his post.

The chancellor beckoned, and Tom took a seat on the stairs. For a moment they both remained silent, enjoying the view. From where they sat, they looked over the two-thousand-foot-long Lincoln Memorial Reflecting Pool to the Washington Monument, on top of which a red signal light flashed. On the horizon was the Capitol building.

"The seat of power. Impressive, wouldn't you say?" Konstantin Lang said, breaking the silence. "I know I have no right to ask you this, but I need your help. I need you to come with me to Egypt."

Tom said nothing, but a choked laugh escaped him. Ignoring it, Lang continued: "I can't explain it, but for some time now I've felt like things are slipping. Everything our parents and grandparents built up after World War II, all the ways we've managed to open up society . . . it seems like it's worth nothing anymore. We're back to medieval conditions, and the only politics that seems to get any traction is the politics of fear. The Ibiza affair, Brexit and Putin in Syria ... you start to wonder if the forest fires in Australia were arson, or if it's really Mother Earth kicking our ass."

Tom thought about whether he should say something, but decided to let his friend talk for the time being. Just then, his cell phone buzzed. An unknown number. He declined the call and put his phone away again. In any case, it reminded him that he still hadn't contacted Noah, and that he should call him again when he was finished with Lang.

"Austria is a divided country now, and the same thing is happening everywhere. You see extremes developing all over the place. I'm attending an economic conference in Cairo in two days and I'd like you to accompany me, just on this one trip. There haven't been any direct threats, and I have no concrete suspicions, but I'd feel a lot safer if you were with me."

"I'm sorry, but—"

"I don't even know if I can trust Cobra anymore," the chancellor said, quietly enough that Leitner wouldn't hear him.

Tom thought for a moment, then said: "Konstantin, I'm sorry, but I'm done with that life. I've got myself a nice little place in California now, and believe it or not, I just started college there, too. I don't want all that anymore." Tom got to his feet and moved two steps lower. "I'm sorry. Really. But Leitner's a good man." He nodded in Jakob's direction.

"There's no need to answer right away," replied Konstantin. "Sleep on it and let me know tomorrow. The driver will take you to where you're staying."

Tom held out his hand, and the chancellor shook it. "Sorry. Don't count on me," Tom said. "But I do wish you all the best," he called over his shoulder as he reached the bottom of the stairs and walked back to the car. He took out his phone and was about to check the missed call when a new text message caught his eye. He smiled happily.

This might turn out to be a nice evening after all, Tom thought as he wrote a short reply. Again, he'd forgotten to call Noah.

9

THE WHITE HOUSE, WASHINGTON D.C.

"You can go in now," said the secretary to the graying gentleman in his mid-fifties. He was sitting in an armchair in the anteroom of probably the most famous office in the world, calmly waiting for his appointment. He entered the unmistakable office and was met by a man about the same age, with a grave expression on his face. They shook hands and sat down across from one another on the beige sofas.

It wasn't every day that he had to brief the president of the United States. But here he was, in the Oval Office, at his feet the Presidential Seal with its imposing bald eagle, sitting across President George William Samson, the 46th president of the United States.

"Sir, there is no doubt at all: last night's incident at the Smithsonian was AF-related. With the help of the Austrian Cobra officer, all of the surviving mercenaries, except their leader"—he glanced at the dossier in his lap —"a man named Isaac Hagen, were taken into custody. If Mr. Wagner hadn't happened to be there, we would have no idea who was behind it, and we would be dealing with many more casualties." He handed the dossier to the president.

"An Austrian? I just met with their chancellor. Always thought they were only good at skiing and waltzing." He smiled.

"Cobra is one of the finest antiterrorist units in the world. Their training is rock solid. Our guys fly over there regularly to train with them."

"I'm impressed," said the president. "So who were these mercenaries?"

"Former members of various special ops teams. English, German, South African . . . one or two Americans, too. Sir, they all have one thing in common: they're all dead."

The president looked up in confusion from the dossier, a collection of files on the individual mercenaries.

"I thought they'd been arrested?"

"Yes, sir. I apologize. I meant to say they were all declared dead years ago, all officially killed in action. And these 'ghosts,' as we so affectionately call them, offered themselves as mercenaries to the highest bidder. In this case, AF."

"And have the interrogations produced anything?" asked President Samson, although he knew that such men were unlikely to give up much.

"Nothing, sir, as expected. They're professionals. They don't talk."

The president was now holding Tom's file in his hand.

"Tell me, this Tom Wagner—isn't he the same fellow who had a run-in with one of our aircraft carriers in the Mediterranean, what, six months ago?"

"The same, sir," the man answered with a smile.

"He certainly gets around," Samson murmured and smiled.

"Since I've been in charge of the AF project, this is the first confirmed incident since Barcelona. What we don't know is why they broke in at all. The Smithsonian staff told us that the head of the facility was interrogated by the leader of the mercenaries before he was murdered. Unfortunately, they have no idea what it was about—but apparently he was either unwilling or unable to give the man an answer, and was summarily executed. Both we and the FBI are still in the dark about what they were after."

The president stood up and paced across the Oval Office. He stopped by the window and gazed out over the Rose Garden. "What I'm about to tell you is known only to a handful of people," he said. "I think I know what AF was after in the Smithsonian," he added in a more subdued voice. The CIA man looked at him in surprise. From beneath his shirt, President Samson withdrew a silver card dangling on a chain around his neck, and slipped it into a narrow slot on his desk. A small panel slid sideways to reveal a palm scanner. He laid his hand on the scanner and typed a twelve-digit code into the adjacent keypad. Around them, all the doors locked, the windows went dark, and the painting of George Washington, hanging above the fireplace opposite the president's desk, swung aside to reveal a wall safe.

The CIA man was taken aback, to say the least. President Samson crossed to the safe, opened it and took out a file and a small box. He handed the file to his astonished guest; *Project Hermes* was printed on the cover.

"Not even Congress knows about this," the president said. "They'd think we'd lost our minds, wasting money and resources on this. The project was initiated by Franklin D. Roosevelt at the end of World War II. Since then, this information has been passed only from one president to the next. And every president has had a confidant—I want you to be mine." He opened the small box and removed a chain and card identical to the one he wore around his neck. He handed it to his guest.

"Project Hermes is incomplete. I would like you to obtain the remaining parts. If an organization like AF is after them, we have no time to lose. Read the file. You will find all the information you need inside. I already know what you will think—I thought the same at first, that my predecessor was making a bad joke. But believe me, it's all true."

The leader of the free world saying things like this? Unbelievable, the CIA man thought. He had already skimmed a few pages of the file and could hardly believe what he was looking at. It read like something out of a bad movie.

The president continued: "A CIA team in Brazil recently became aware of a new lead. I want you to take charge of it personally. We can't trust anyone on this. Bring Project Hermes to a successful conclusion, whatever it takes, and we'll all be able to sleep a little easier."

President Samson returned to the desk and removed his

key card. The safe and the sliding panel on the desk closed immediately, and the doors unlocked.

Departing, the CIA man saluted and shook hands with the president.

"I will not let you down, sir."

He already had the door handle in his hand when the president spoke again.

"This is about more than just national security. The fate of the entire world is at stake."

10

ANFUSHI NECROPOLIS, ALEXANDRIA

As Hellen and Arno made their way back along the passages, Hellen chattered away like a wind-up toy.

"I'm so incredibly curious to find out what's inside these amphorae. I mean, Arno, can you imagine? What if we really find the crucial clue to the Library of Alexandria inside? It's hard to imagine what that would even mean for science. For archaeology, it would be unprecedented. We've been searching for this library for centuries. I can't wait to open them and find out what's inside. But we have to find somewhere we can open them properly, with as little damage as possible. They've been sealed tight, too, to survive the passage of time. My God, I hardly dare to dream what we might find inside. Lost knowledge from ancient times, things we can't even imag—"

The word hung in Hellen's throat. They had stepped out of the passageway into the open yard only to find themselves face to face with a squad of Egyptian soldiers, three of whom had their AK-200 rifles leveled at them. Arno looked at Hellen with horror.

"Fuck!" he muttered. Hellen looked at him in surprise. Until now, she had known Arno as a man of culture, not someone who ever used that kind of language. But his emotions seemed to have run away with him— presumably their joint project had become as important to him as it was to Hellen.

"You have no permission whatsoever to be conducting archaeological investigations on Egyptian soil," said one of the soldiers, obviously the ranking officer among them, judging by the amount of gold decorating his shoulder. He paused for a moment to give his next sentence even more weight. "Dr. Hellen de Mey, the Egyptian Ministry of Culture explicitly denied your application to carry out any exploration or research at the Necropolis of Anfushi. You are not allowed to be here, you certainly have no permission to remove artifacts of any kind from the necropolis and under no circumstances are you allowed to examine them. All this" —he made a sweeping gesture—"belongs to the Egyptian people. That includes the plundered goods you are holding in your hands."

The man snapped out an order, and two soldiers hurried to Hellen and Arno and took the amphorae from them. Hellen resisted briefly, but one of the soldiers held his gun to her forehead and she panicked, almost dropping the amphora. Tears clouded her eyes, but when she saw the determined look on the soldier's face, she backed down and, trembling, handed it over. Arno looked petrified.

"You can't do this!" Hellen cried. "We discovered these. Without us, these amphorae might never have been found at all. We have a right . . ."

"You have no rights here at all!" the man giving the orders barked at her, and Hellen was taken aback by his intensity—he was truly starting to frighten her. But she had made up her mind not to give in, not yet. She took a step toward the commander.

"I am an employee of Blue Shield, a UNESCO organization. I'd be happy to show you my credentials."

The commander nodded. Hellen rummaged in her backpack and finally dug out her old UNESCO identification card. She handed it to the commander. "This provides us with diplomatic immunity and a scientific right to our find."

The captain smiled grimly.

"Dr. de Mey, please do not take me for a fool. As you have no doubt noticed, I know exactly who you are. I also know that you have not been with UNESCO for some time. This ID isn't worth the plastic it's printed on. As for diplomatic immunity . . ." He laughed and shook his head.

Hellen's hopes of wriggling out of the situation vanished, and her face drained of color.

After a long pause, the commander continued: "But I am in a good mood tonight, and I would like to spare myself the paperwork that arresting you would mean. So I've decided not to take you into custody at this time, despite the fact that you have just lied to an officer of the Egyptian army."

Hellen was about to say something, but Arno tugged at her sleeve.

"Hellen, it's probably best if we just get out of here, before he changes his mind."

Hellen nodded in resignation and watched as the soldiers wrapped the two amphorae carefully in blankets and placed them on the back seat of their car. As they drove away, Hellen felt her chance of fulfilling her father's dream—of getting just one step closer to the Library of Alexandria—burst like a soap bubble.

11

THE MAYFLOWER HOTEL, WASHINGTON D.C.

Tom luxuriated in the refreshing shower. He had needed it. When he'd arranged to meet the young FBI agent Jennifer Baker at his hotel bar the previous night, he hadn't expected them to end up in his room an hour later.

"It's highly . . . unorthodox for me to . . . get involved with a . . . witness," she had managed to gasp through a flurry of kisses. They had practically attacked each other in the elevator. They had hardly arrived in Tom's room before pieces of clothing were falling to the floor as they made their way to the bed. "I could lose my job," she said, unbuttoning her blouse and casting it to the floor. They tumbled onto the bed, and there was no more talking.

She was as untamed a creature as any Tom had ever known, but she was the right woman at exactly the right time. After what Tom had been through, he needed to celebrate life.

Now, in the shower, he decided to forego his usual five miles on the treadmill and his daily circuit training in the hotel's fitness center. Jennifer had worn him out enough already. He got out of the shower, slung a towel around his neck and went back to his room. It was not a bad thing at all to find a ravishing woman in his bed in the light of the morning sun.

He got dressed and kissed Jennifer on her naked shoulder. "Good morning," he said. She stretched and smiled up at him. "I just need to call my uncle, then we can go find some breakfast." He stepped out onto the small balcony, taking in the view from the luxury hotel. Behind him, Jennifer slipped out of bed and disappeared into the bathroom.

Tom didn't go on vacation often, but when he did he liked to treat himself a little. That meant a decent hotel with a pool, a fitness center and good food. That wasn't always possible, of course—the remote corners of the world to which his action-and-adventure jaunts took him didn't usually offer such luxuries. But he could get by with a sleeping bag, too, when he had to.

Tom took out his cell phone to call his uncle, and then remembered the call from the unknown number the evening before, during his meeting with the chancellor. He clicked on voicemail and lifted the phone to his ear, and his face instantly drained of color. His hands trembled, but he forced himself to listen to the message a second time.

"Tom, you gotta help . . . they've got me . . . Osa . . . I'm in —" The choppy, fragmented words in the short message made Tom's guts twist. Immediately, he called the number on the display, but all he heard was: "The number you have dialed is temporarily unavailable."

What could he do? Noah's call had come hours ago. Tom had tried to call Noah himself the evening before, to tell him about AF turning up in Washington. In fact, it had been more than two months since he had actually spoken to his best friend. Noah had been on permanent loan to Cobra from the Israeli secret service, Mossad, and had decided to return to Israel after the events six months ago.

A few years earlier, on a joint mission with Tom during which they had saved the Austrian chancellor's life, Noah had been seriously injured. He'd been confined to a wheelchair ever since. To this day, Tom blamed himself. The physical distance between them, and the fact that they hadn't worked together for a long time, were already putting their friendship to the test— and now that his friend really needed him, he hadn't been there.

Calm down! Think! he told himself, trying to put his thoughts in order. *There was nothing you could have done anyway, the call broke off almost immediately.*

Would his uncle be able to help? Scott's contacts at the Pentagon could find out where the call had originated. Or should he go to the embassy? With the chancellor in the U.S., Tom would surely be able to use the embassy's resources—after all, Noah had been one of them. He chose the embassy, packed his things and was about to leave the room when the phone on the nightstand rang. He snatched the receiver off its cradle.

"Mr. Wagner?" Tom heard the concierge's voice. "You have a visitor. She would like to meet with you immediately."

"A visitor? What's her name?"

"I'm afraid I cannot answer that, sir. The lady is waiting for you in conference room 302," the concierge said, and ended the conversation.

Tom replaced the receiver. *Who the hell is this now?* he wondered. *Someone from the embassy? Is Konstantin sending that cute PA of his to persuade me to fly with him to Cairo?*

Tom left the room. He'd banished the young FBI agent in the shower from his mind. He took the elevator to the conference center on the third floor and hurried down the hallway in search of room 302.

When he found it, he threw open the door and his heart almost stopped. His hand reflexively flew to his hip, but there was nothing there: he was on vacation and wasn't armed. Facing him, at the far end of the long conference table, stood a young and beautiful black woman—with a silenced pistol pointing back at him.

Ossana Ibori.

"Have a seat, Mr. Wagner." Taken by surprise, he hesitated for a moment, then did as she bade and sat down on one of the comfortable chairs at the head of the table.

Tom was rarely speechless, but this was one of those times. Ossana Ibori was an agent of AF, the terrorist organization responsible—not least—for the death of Tom's parents. AF also employed Isaac Hagen, the man who just the day before had broken into the Smithsonian with his men. Ossana and Hagen in the same city, and then the emergency call from Noah? That couldn't be a coincidence. *What the hell is going on?* Tom asked himself. The answer came soon enough.

"No doubt you are wondering why I am visiting you here in your hotel," Ossana said in her crisp South African accent. She placed the gun in front of her on the table, beside an open laptop.

Tom's tension grew. He clenched one fist under the table and racked his brain, trying to figure out how to gain some advantage on the bitch, but she was holding all the cards.

"You see, Mr. Wagner, we are in a difficult situation. We are facing a small problem in the Middle East and have come to the conclusion that you are the man to help us. Knowing you as I believe I do, I'm sure you can't be bought, so we've come up with something special." She pressed a button on the laptop and an image appeared on the huge screen suspended on the side wall.

At the sight of his best friend's bloodstained face, Tom sprang up from his chair. Noah was sitting bound and gagged, in what looked like a dark basement room.

"You—" Tom didn't get far with the sentence. The cocking of Ossana's gun, once again trained on him, made him fall silent.

"Mr. Wagner, please. Let us talk like professionals. We have a problem, and you are the solution. If all goes well, you'll get your crippled Israeli back unharmed in one piece . . . well, almost in one piece," she said malevolently. She pushed a file across the table to Tom.

12

AMOUN HOTEL, ALEXANDRIA

"I've got to ask UNESCO for help. We have to get the amphorae back before they vanish forever into some warehouse at the Egyptian Museum," Hellen said as they entered the hotel room. Her hotel was only a few minutes from the necropolis, and she had decided to let her frustration settle a little before deciding what to do next.

"Why would they take the amphorae to the Egyptian Museum? They could take them anywhere."

"We're in Egypt. Anything that gets dug out of the ground here goes to the Egyptian Museum in Cairo, at least at first."

She reached for her phone and scrolled through her contacts, until she found the number she needed. Her finger hovered a few millimeters above the display.

"What's wrong?" Arno asked.

"You know who the new boss of Blue Shield is these days," said Hellen, fighting her frustration.

"Damn. I hadn't thought about that," Arno said sheepishly. He went over to her, wrapped his arms around her and kissed her. "You know, you've made it through so many dangerous situations in the past, and these amphorae mean so much to you. You can do it. You *will* come through. Besides, can a call to your mother be so bad?"

"You don't know her. She drove my father up the wall. Although, to be fair, he drove *her* up the wall, too. Things were never that great between us, even when I was little, and when papa disappeared they got worse."

Hellen's voice had grown quieter. Arno squeezed her again, and she pressed her cheek against his shoulder. They remained like that for a minute, unmoving, and Hellen felt a sense of security she hadn't known for a long time. Arno was a good man. He was there for her and she could rely on him—in moments like this, she felt it most of all.

"Oh, to hell with it. What the worst that can happen?" Hellen said suddenly, pulling free of Arno's embrace. She tapped the number on the display, lifted the phone to her ear and waited.

"Hello, Mother," Hellen said, and Arno was astounded how different Hellen's voice suddenly sounded. Hellen noticed him watching her and turned away.

"Hellen! How nice of you to call. We haven't spoken in, well, forever. Let alone actually met. The last time was when you—"

"Yes. When I quit Blue Shield."

"Which I still don't understand, frankly. But you always have to have your way. You get that from your father.

"Mother, please. Don't start. You know I had my reasons."

"Yes, because you lost your mind over that Austrian soldier."

"He wasn't a soldier. He was with Cobra."

"Doesn't matter. They're all the same. But why have you called? Not just to ask me how I've been, I imagine."

Hellen sighed and summoned up her courage.

"I need ... " She was struggling hard to get the words out. "I need your help. UNESCO's help, actually. I'm in Egypt, and I've found something sensational in the Necropolis of Anfushi."

"The Necropolis of Anfushi? That dump? What are you even doing in Egypt?"

"That's beside the point. Listen, I found two amphorae that, I believe, contain something of exceptional importance. It's just ..."

Her voice faltered.

"Just what?" her mother pressed.

"It's just that some Egyptian soldiers took them away from me."

"Why would they do that? Oh my God, don't tell me you were poking around without permission."

Hellen said nothing.

"Dammit, Hellen! You used to be such a responsible

person. Ever since that Tom Wagner turned your head, I don't know you anymore. He had such a terrible influence on you."

"Mother, please. Tom and I are done."

"So tell me, what's so exciting about these amphorae? What do you think is inside?"

"I can't say for certain," Hellen had to admit.

"Then what makes you think their contents are so sensational?"

Hellen took a deep breath. She had to lay her cards on the table. She had to tell her mother the truth.

"Well, there was a symbol on them."

"What kind of symbol? Honestly, Hellen, getting anything out of you is like pulling teeth."

"Well, it's the symbol of . . . of the Library of Alexandria."

There was silence on the other end. Hellen's mother was saying nothing, and Hellen could picture her struggling to contain her outrage.

"The Library of Alexandria? Have you completely lost your mind? Your father tortured me with that for decades, and here you come with the same old fairy tales?"

"Mother, they're not fairy tales."

"Yes, your father used to say that, too. And you know what happened to him."

"No, Mother, I don't know. No one knows."

"Of course not. Because he went looking for the library and disappeared without a trace. And now you want to follow in his footsteps. Never! I forbid you! Don't you dare pursue this fantasy any further. I don't want to lose you too, like I lost him. That's final. Don't expect any help from me, or from UNESCO."

The line went dead.

"That went better than expected," Arno said grimly, and he gave Hellen a crooked smile.

"It went exactly as expected," Hellen replied sourly.

"Then we'll just have to do this ourselves," said Arno firmly.

———

Theresia de Mey ended the call without saying goodbye, then paced back and forth in her office. Hellen had raised a subject that Theresia thought had been closed for years. After the disappearance of Hellen's father, it had taken her a long time to return to a normal life. She had hoped that Hellen would never follow in her father's footsteps. But now it seemed her worst fears had come true.

13

AUSTRIAN EMBASSY, WASHINGTON D.C.

The car hurtled along Connecticut Avenue, heading north. Tom's mind was racing. Where was Noah? What had they done to him? How could this happen? Where was he being held?

After Ossana had presented her conditions and instructions, she had simply walked out, leaving Tom alone in the conference room. He had a lot to digest. Ossana had left a file with the details of his assignment on the table and given him a disposable cell phone, with one number stored in it: the number he was to call to work out Noah's handover, once the job was done.

He sat in the large room no more than five minutes, but it felt like an eternity. Then he jumped to his feet, went back to his room, grabbed his duffel bag and checked out. He did not even notice that Jennifer was no longer there; he had simply forgotten all about her. He had the valet bring his rental car around—a Mustang, of course —and he roared off toward the Austrian Embassy. It was in a small embassy district in Van Ness, just behind the

University of the District of Columbia. Austria, Egypt, Ethiopia and thirteen other countries kept embassies in the area.

Tom turned onto Van Ness Drive, then International Drive. At the end of the cul-de-sac was the embassy. Cul-de-sacs in America usually ended in a circle that made turning around a breeze, and this was no exception. *Smart*, he thought, and it surprised him that such a banal thought would enter his head now. He steered the Mustang into the embassy driveway and pulled up in front of the main entrance. The unattractive concrete block looked more like a Bond villain's headquarters than an inviting embassy, and was surrounded by a small forest of trees and bushes. In the center of the circular entrance was a red marble sign ten feet long inscribed with "Embassy of Austria"; the Austrian flag and the blue flag of the EU rippled from the northern tower of the concrete castle.

He had made it clear to the embassy staffer on the ground floor who he was and who he wanted to speak to, and two minutes later Jakob Leitner picked him up in the foyer and led him upstairs to a small break room among the offices.

"What's so urgent that's got you charging in here like you've been stung by a bee?" Jakob asked his former colleague.

"Noah's been kidnapped. He left a message on my voice-mail, from a number I don't know. Can you find out where the call originated?" Tom snapped out.

"Kidnapped? Who'd do something like that?" Leitner asked. He feigned sympathy, but he was grinning on the inside. "Yeah, sure. Give me the number. I'll get it checked."

Tom scribbled the number onto a sheet of paper and Jakob disappeared with it into an adjoining office. "Be right back. Make yourself at home."

Tom paced back and forth in the break room. He took out his phone and called his uncle's number. Voicemail. He was probably in another one of those tedious meetings at the Pentagon that he often complained about. Tom put the phone away and made himself a black coffee on the oversized espresso machine.

Leitner was back in twenty minutes, a computer printout in his hand. He signaled to Tom to sit, then pulled up a chair beside him.

"What have you got?" Tom asked.

"Okay, well, the number you gave me belongs to a mobile phone that's been inactive since yesterday. The guys in Intelligence have assured me that when the call was made, the phone was in Cairo, but they weren't able to narrow it down any further."

Tom's eyes widened. Cairo. That's where Ossana's errand was sending him.

"That's not all," Leitner continued. "I called a contact in Israel who told me that Noah resigned two months back. It looks like some software company cherry-picked him. They haven't heard a peep from him since."

Tom's amazement grew. Noah had quit Mossad? Was it

even *possible* to quit Mossad? He had to smile: that must have been the big surprise Noah had announced that last time they'd spoken.

"That's all I've got so far. Maybe with more time . . ."

"I didn't know he'd given up his job," said Tom a little sadly. It seemed they had really grown apart in the last six months.

"What makes you think he's been kidnapped? Maybe he's just got normal problems and had bad reception."

"I just know." Tom had made up his mind. He stood up and exited the break room. Leitner, surprised, followed him out.

"Where are you going? You can't just wander around here these days."

"Is he in the building? I have to talk to him," Tom said. Leitner still trotted close behind.

When Tom reached the door of the office reserved for the chancellor's visits, he knocked and entered without waiting for a response. He closed the door behind him, shutting Leitner outside.

"Okay. I'm in. I'll go to Egypt with you."

Konstantin Lang looked up from his desk, and when he saw Tom he shook his head and said, "Can't you ever do things like normal people? A phone call would have done."

· · ·

Half an hour later, after they had talked through the details of the job, Tom went and found Leitner at his desk.

"I need a suit, a service pistol, and a bug-proof cell phone," Tom barked. Leitner gaped, stunned to find himself suddenly relegated to the bench.

Tom didn't wait around, but turned and went back to the break room. He still had an important call to make. He needed support in Egypt, both for the search for Noah and for the assignment Ossana had dumped on him. Noah's life was at stake. There was only one man who could help, only one man that had been through enough with him that Tom could trust him with his life.

14

ROUTE 75, THE ALEXANDRIA DESERT ROAD, HEADING TOWARD CAIRO

"Don't torment me like this," said Hellen, and she punched Arno in the side. He sat behind the wheel of the Toyota Landcruiser they had rented in Alexandria and smiled happily. "Tell me what you're up to."

Arno laid one hand reassuringly on Hellen's thigh. He exuded composure and warmth, and Hellen calmed down. "As you know, my father is not only very well off, but also has friends in some very high places. Through our businesses, many people in many countries owe us favors."

"But what does that have to do with the amphorae?" Hellen said, her impatience returning.

"Isn't it enough for me to assure you that in a few hours we'll have the amphorae back in our hands, and you'll be able to take your time examining them?"

Hellen was torn. On the one hand, that was exactly what she desperately wanted. And to be honest, she didn't care how Arno made it happen. But on the other hand, she was dying to know what he had in mind.

"First, tell my why these amphorae matter so much to you" said Arno decisively. Hellen couldn't refuse him.

"I was still a child, maybe six or seven, when my father first told me about the Library of Alexandria. He told me that all the knowledge of the antique world was collected there, and that it was safe to assume that a lot of that knowledge would still be useful today. Old recipes for medicines, the calculations and formulas they used to build the pyramids, the secrets of ancient places like Atlantis, that are still so mysterious today."

Arno's eyes were filled with fascination.

"And that's just the things we know about. There might be treasures in the library that we can hardly dream of, things that could explain all the myths that have been handed down over the last four millennia."

"I see. And your father wanted to find it."

"Mystical artifacts have intrigued my entire family for generations. But the Library of Alexandria, for my father, was the crown jewel of them all. He used to say that the Holy Grail, the Philosopher's Stone, and Excalibur paled in comparison to the Library of Alexandria."

"Now I understand why this absorbs you the way it does. But why does your mother have such a problem with it?"

Hellen turned away and gazed out the window. Seconds passed in silence, as the harsh desert landscape rolled by. Arno could sense how difficult it was for her to go on.

"Because when he was searching for the library my father suddenly disappeared. I was eight when we heard that he was missing.

Arno nodded.

"My father was obsessed with the library. Everything else in his life took second place, even my mother and I. That's what hurt my mother so much, and that's why she doesn't want to hear anything about it these days."

"And you? Why do you want to find the library?" Arno asked.

"I . . . I believe it will bring me closer to my father. When I recognize, when I understand what fascinated him so much about the library, I feel . . . closer to him." Her voice broke a little and she looked away again. "I never even got to say goodbye."

Arno abruptly braked and pulled off onto the shoulder on the right. He took Hellen's hand in his and gazed into her eyes. It felt like an eternity before he spoke.

"As I said, through our business we know many people in Cairo who owe us favors. I made a few phone calls. Tonight, a member of staff at the Egyptian Museum will meet us, and you will have the opportunity to examine the amphorae and whatever they contain."

Hellen's eyes opened wide. "How?"

"He'll smuggle us into the museum tonight and deactivate the alarm system for a while. He'll tell us where they're keeping the amphorae and you'll have time to examine them."

"And this is legal?"

"Of course not, but no one will find out about it. Don't worry. We walk in, you look at the amphorae, and then we just walk out again."

Hellen hugged Arno and snuggled against him.

"You don't have to do this," she said. "You don't have to put yourself in danger for me. We can find another way, something less risky."

"There is no other way. And the risk is negligible. My contact is trustworthy. Everyone's attention is on the construction of the new museum near Giza, he says, so security is even more lax than usual. A lot of the staff have been sent home for a while. We've got this. Easy-peasy."

Hellen planted a dozen kisses on Arno's face. "You really don't have to do this for me," she said.

"I know. But I want to."

Hellen was endlessly grateful. Still, she felt more than a little guilty for dragging Arno into this.

15

CURITIBA, BRAZIL

The American had spent the entire flight pondering the assignment the president had given him. He had not yet been able to fully digest what he had been asked to accept. He knew, of course, about the CIA's Special Projects Division, which worked with projects beyond the normal confines of comprehension. And he also knew that Area 51 was just an elaborate lie, created to distract people from the real truth: the CIA really did operate underground bunkers, where the most absurd and irrational things were collected and investigated. There were three such bunkers, spread around the United States. Personally, he had always felt that the research they did was crazy. But now that the president himself had ordered him to obtain this particular artifact, the status quo had changed.

During the flight, he had studied the top-secret file that Langley, on the president's orders, had sent him. The CIA had recently recovered the long-lost Capri files: Capri was a company that had been founded in Brazil after

World War II. It had been set up by former Nazi VIPs who had found refuge in Argentina and Brazil. Even today not much was really known about it, except that the war criminal Adolf Eichmann had been involved in a big way.

The American strode through the arrivals hall. From the corner of his eye, he spotted his CIA contact man. He approached him.

"Got a match?"

The man looked at him and answered: "Sorry, Señor, but smoking is forbidden even in South American airports."

"Where can I smoke?"

"Outside, by the taxis. I'm sorry I can't give you a match. I always use my lighter." The man paused, then added; "And I'll use it till it breaks. What brand do you smoke?"

"Nothing but Lucky Strikes. I hate the Marlboro Man."

The conversation sounded harmless enough, but it contained the necessary code words, more trustworthy for the two men than any ID card.

They left the terminal, got into a car that looked like a regular taxi, and drove in the direction of the town center. As soon as the car doors closed, the façade fell away.

"My name is Will Jimenez. I'm your liaison here. We can talk freely—the driver is Jerry. He works at the embassy."

"I'm the one who always gets to play the taxi driver. Shitty job, but it pays well," the driver joked.

Will got down to business. "We stumbled onto this file by accident. With the help of the DEA, we pulled apart the headquarters of a drug kingpin who called himself El Azul. We found a lot of files in the guy's vault; the Capri files were among them. They were thought to have disappeared."

"Do the Germans know about this? They'd be very interested."

"We're not crazy! The Germans have no idea. Why should we tell them anything? Since they discovered that the NSA have been listening in on them 24/7—and that we have too, of course—relations have been a little frosty. They don't tell us anything anymore. We are not at war, exactly, but things are definitely chilly. So they don't get anything from us."

"Okay. When can I see the files?"

"We're going to our safe house in Santa Felicidada at the other end of the city. It will take a little while. The traffic jams here are hell. What exactly do you hope to find in the files?" Jimenez asked, although he knew even as he did so that he was asking too much. The man frowned and looked at him with disapproval. Jimenez answered his own question: "Let me guess. Top secret. National security. Above my clearance level."

"Bingo," said the American. The rest of the drive passed in silence.

The car stopped in front of a shop with a sign over the door that read "Multiciclo Bike," a cycling accessories store. They climbed out, went inside, and passed through the shop and the workshop behind. At the end of the workshop was a door; the stairs beyond it led down to a shabby basement. Once they had passed through another door, the shabby basement was quickly revealed for what it was: the front for a CIA base. The fingerprint scanner at the entrance was the first sign that there were no old bicycle tubes stored down there.

Jimenez handed the American the Capri file. "Where can I read this in private?" was all he said. Jimenez opened the door to a small, windowless meeting room. The American nodded, pulled out a chair and began to comb through the papers.

The first fifteen minutes didn't yield any significant results. With the money they had been able to smuggle out, the Nazis had set up a construction company—Capri —in which every Nazi war criminal who had made it out of Germany clearly had a part. There was a lot in the files about the company's projects. The Germans had apparently managed to set it up as a legal business, and one that offered the legendary German craftsmanship at that.

The man was beginning to think that all he held in his hands were the facts and figures of a construction company run by ex-Nazis. He was about to close the file in resignation when he came across a few sheets of paper that, although part of the file, obviously didn't fit with the rest of the documents. He read the name "Jörg Lanz von Liebenfels" and suddenly his interest returned. The Nazis had founded a new Templar order in Argentina with the aim of reviving Ariosophy, a Gnostic-dualist religion based on their racist principles. Before the two world wars, Liebenfels had taken the lead in establishing this so-called religion, and had fundamentally influenced the worldviews of Heinrich Himmler and even Hitler himself. Himmler's fascination with occultism could also be traced back directly to Liebenfels's Ariosophy.

There was a lot of nonsensical stuff about the Holy Grail, Atlantis, the Ark of the Covenant, cabalism and black magic in the pages. None of it brought him any further, except for a few notes penned by an anonymous writer. Attached to the pages, there was also an interrogation transcript, and in that he found the key word he was looking for. He reached for his phone and booked a plane ticket to Vienna.

16

A HOSPITAL IN THE AL-QAHIRA DISTRICT, CAIRO

Farid Shaham left the hospital. He felt as if he was carrying the weight of the world on his shoulders. His wife, Armeen, looked at him in despair. He would have done or given anything to be able to console her, but he had no idea how to go about it.

"Farid, what are we going to do? Shamira has been given a death sentence. Allah will call her, and I don't know how I can live after that."

"I will find an answer," said Farid.

His wife looked at him in anguish.

"How? We have no money for the treatment! And your pride about your father's money has only caused us more problems. We can hardly afford food and our apartment as it is. How are we supposed to pay for Shamira's cancer treatment?"

Farid knew that she was right. His father's death had fundamentally changed Farid's life. Farid had never approved of his father's schemes and had always tried to get his own family through by legal means, a choice that his father had always scoffed at. Farid had steadfastly refused to have any part in his father's business and had never accepted money from him, but this was different. To save his daughter's life, he would take any kind of money, he didn't care how dirty. But that spring had dried up for good when his father was murdered.

"I will find a way," Farid said emphatically.

"And how will you do that?"

"I will go and get what we are owed. Nor for myself, but for Shamira!"

Armeen embraced Farid, but she had a bad feeling. She already knew what her husband was planning, and though she didn't like it, she knew that it was the only way to save their daughter.

"My father's boss, François Cloutard. He is to blame. He alone is responsible for my father's death."

Farid did not know many of the details, but at his father's funeral he had learned that he had been murdered by a contract killer who worked for some kind of terrorist organization, and that the killer turned out to be Cloutard's own mistress. Cloutard had gotten his father into this. He was still alive, and had no doubt gotten richer. Farid's father was dead. Armeen stopped and looked at her husband hopelessly.

Farid knew she wouldn't be able to cope with her daughter's death. She might take her own life. He was on the verge of losing the two people dearest to him.

"Farid, I don't want you to put yourself in danger. We did not distance ourselves from that part of your family for nothing. We wanted nothing to do with that world." Her tone swung between accusation and despair.

"I have no other choice. I have to take this risk. For Shamira." Farid knew some of his father's former cronies, of course, other men who earned their money by illegal means. He would have to find the courage to ask them for advice. Armeen shook her head anxiously.

"And how are you going to get money from Cloutard? Are you going to find him and hold a gun to his head?"

Farid nodded imperceptibly. Yes. That was exactly what he was going to do.

17

13TH CENTURY B.C., EAST OF THE JORDAN RIVER

The stone crashed hard against the side of Moses' head. The chilling crunch of rock against bone frightened even Joshua, though he was the one who had struck Moses. The old man fell to the ground, instantly dead—the stone had caved in his skull. Joshua turned away. It was not that he regretted his action, for he knew that this was about something more important—more important than Moses, more important than himself, more important than the people of Israel.

He left Moses's tent. He knew what he had to do next. Moses had been too trusting; he had told Joshua everything. Not only about the ten laws of Yahweh, but also about a third tablet: one that didn't enslave people, restricting their actions with commandments, but which gave them power: power to perfect all things deserving of perfection, and to destroy the things deserving of destruction. When Joshua heard this, he had known immediately that this was his destiny. God had not entrusted the tablets to Moses for no reason, and now

Joshua knew that he had to possess them. Moses was not the one. He was God-fearing and weak.

Joshua made his way to the Tabernacle. The two men standing guard were known to him. He had commanded them in the war against Amalek. He knew they would obey him.

"Moses is dead. He has been betrayed by heretics and murdered."

The two guards looked at Joshua with dismay. Neither had the slightest suspicion that he was lying.

"Before his death, Moses charged me with ensuring the sanctity of the Holy of Holies. You will help me with that."

At first, the two guards looked at each other, unsure of what to do. But Joshua's gaze was relentless. He stared both of them down, leaving no doubt as to who would lead the Jewish people now. A few seconds passed and their decision was made. They would stand by Joshua.

Joshua stepped past the guards and entered the Tabernacle, where the Ark of the Covenant stood. Until now no one but Moses had dared look inside the Ark; no one knew what it contained. Joshua once again summoned his courage and pushed aside the lid, then took a torch that flickered in the corner and held it over the Ark. Inside, he saw a row of stone fragments, upon which he could decipher various words and phrases. He knew the commandments well, of course. They were the same commandments that Moses had revealed to the people on his return from Mount Sinai. The broken tablets contained the word of the Almighty himself. But there was more inside the Ark. There was another stone tablet, one that seemed intact. It had to be the one that would bring perfection and destruction. The thought of being able to call the tablet his own made Joshua tremble. At first he hesitated, but then he lifted the tablet out of the Ark. He slipped it under his robe and hastily left the tent.

"Follow me!" he ordered the guards. "We must gather the faithful and avenge the death of Moses. I am your leader now."

18

AUSTRIAN EMBASSY, WASHINGTON D.C.

The three black SUVs stood in the curved driveway in front of the embassy building. Tom Wagner and his colleague Jakob Leitner each stood in front of one of the vehicles, waiting for their passengers. Tom was impatient and looked repeatedly at his watch. He couldn't get to Cairo fast enough. He had spent the entire afternoon preparing for this trip, but not for the chancellor's assignment: he had spent every free minute working on how to rescue Noah. He had studied the dossier Ossana had given him down to the minutest detail, and had also sent a copy to his contact in Egypt.

He was only using the chancellor as a means to an end, a way of getting to Cairo as quickly as possible and with the fewest complications. And he didn't even feel guilty about it. It all came back to the same mission, after all— the one that had ended with the chancellor being saved, and Noah spending the rest of his life in a wheelchair. *Konstantin owes Noah that much*, he told himself.

Tom was not sure, however, if the chancellor still owed him. Konstantin had helped him out of a few holes, to be sure. Considering the messes he'd got himself into while working with Cobra, anyone else would have been fired many times over.

When Konstantin appeared from the embassy building, Tom opened the door of the car for him. Then he got in beside the chancellor and closed the door. His leg jiggled nervously up and down, and he checked his watch yet again.

"Are you all right?" the chancellor asked him.

"Yep, all good." He turned impatiently to the driver and said: "Can we go?"

The other members of the economic delegation flying to the talks in Cairo had climbed into the second and third cars. The construction of the new capital, thirty miles out of Cairo, was a big chance to secure international contracts, and Austria wanted to be part of that. The three cars set off for Dulles International Airport, where the luxurious private jet of an Austrian industrial magnate was waiting for them—it was he who had arranged the talks. If everything went as Konstantin Lang hoped, it would mean a huge economic boost for Austria. After extensive reforms, the economic upswing in Egypt was obvious to anyone who was watching; international donors were investing hundreds of billions into the new but highly controversial construction project. Lang wanted a piece of that pie for Austria.

Apart from one or two stretches of turbulence, the flight was largely uneventful. As the journey progressed, spirits inside the cabin warmed up to match the weather in Egypt. Most of the delegation were certainly enjoying themselves: the magnate's jet offered every luxury imaginable, including a bar, à la carte food worthy of a 3-star restaurant, a living-room atmosphere and a separate cinema. But Tom wasn't interested in any of it. He was sitting apart from the others and reading through Ossana's file again when Konstantin Lang, a glass of wine in his hand, came and sat down opposite him in one of the huge upholstered chairs. The chancellor had rolled up his sleeves and loosened his tie.

"Come on, Tom. Put that away and relax a little. This is a business trip, not a study trip," Lang said. He seemed more relaxed today than he had two days earlier, when he had first asked Tom for his assistance.

"If the danger's already been neutralized, you don't need me anymore," Tom joked, although it came out a little snide.

"What's going to happen up here? We're among friends," Lang said, spreading his arms wide and looking around. It looked as if the wine had already gotten to him, Tom thought.

"Konstantin, I'm going to be up front with you," said Tom, closing the file. "I'm only here because Noah needs my help. He's caught in some serious shit and I'm the only one who can help."

"And that means . . .?"

"That means that I needed a fast, uncomplicated flight to Cairo, and you happened to be offering just that. I'm sorry."

"But Tom, you can't do that. We've got a deal, and I expect you to keep up your end of it." The chancellor suddenly sounded more formal.

"So Noah doesn't mean anything to you? Think back. Think about why he's in a wheelchair."

"That may be. I am extremely sorry, and I will be eternally grateful to him, but I need you there. A deal is a deal. You do what you're supposed to do for me, and when I'm back at the embassy you're free to do whatever you want." Shaking his head, the chancellor stood up and rejoined his colleagues.

Tom wanted to say more, but thought better of it. He decided to keep his mouth shut for now and make the best of the situation. The chancellor's errand would only take up a few hours tomorrow, and in the meantime Tom's ally could take care of all the necessary preparations before they met in Cairo. In the evening, when the chancellor was safely back at the embassy, Tom could devote himself to Ossana's job.

After a while, Tom put the dossier aside and used the rest of the flight to grab a little sleep. Tomorrow would be a long day. He leaned the luxurious recliner all the way back, stretched out and snapped off the light. When Tom closed his eyes, the party in the front section of the plane was still in full swing.

The plane landed in Cairo early the next morning. Once they had completed the diplomatic formalities and were led away to their waiting limousines, Tom excused himself for a moment and walked over to a man waiting for him outside the VIP parking lot.

It was none other than his old friend François Cloutard.

19

CAFÉ CORNICHE, BESIDE THE NILE, CAIRO

"Tom thinks it is so easy," Cloutard muttered to himself as he wandered through the back alleys of Cairo. "Does he really believe I can just snap my fingers and make all the crooks in Cairo come running to tell me what they know?" In his light-colored, somewhat rumpled seersucker suit, creased white linen shirt and a Panama hat, François Cloutard looked at first glance like an exceedingly elegant and worldly Frenchman. His hair, already starting to gray, was combed back stiffly, giving a neat but not oily impression. Smoke rose from the cigar tucked in the corner of his mouth. What was not visible on the outside, however, and what made his friendship with Tom so extraordinary, was the fact that he had run the largest art-smuggling ring in the world until six months ago.

Cloutard and Tom had gotten to know each other under very unusual circumstances, and they had shared a common nemesis ever since: Ossana Ibori, who had been Cloutard's mistress until she brought his empire crashing down. She had also murdered his confidante and right-hand man Karim. Since then, Cloutard's luck hadn't been the same. Once fallen from grace, it was not easy to regain his former status—that was as true in criminal organizations as it was in politics. Building trust took years, but one mistake and you could lose everything in the blink of an eye. But perhaps working with Tom would restore a little of his karma. When Tom had called and asked for his help, it was the tonic Cloutard had needed. After his last adventure with Tom, he had discovered for himself that one could never know what would happen next. Shortly after arriving at the airport, they had talked through their next steps.

Cloutard had not been to Cairo for almost two years and, although he still had plenty of contacts in the city, he did not know how cooperative they would be after his loss of power. Cairo was one of his former hubs. He had recruited many a grave robber and smuggler there in the past, so he knew exactly where to start his search: Café Corniche, on the banks of the Nile in what was by far Cairo's best neighborhood. The Ritz-Carlton Hotel, the U.S. Embassy and the Egyptian Museum were around the corner, and it was where the rich and beautiful of the Egyptian capital came to play. It was a district where one could expect to meet all kinds of people, though perhaps not the movers and shakers of the international grave-robber mafia. Still, it was one of these that Cloutard was looking for.

As he entered the café, which at first glance looked like an old Viennese coffee house, his mind turned automatically to Tom. He would no doubt feel at home in here. He walked confidently through the café, heading for the bathroom at the back, and opened an unmarked door along the way. On the other side stood a six-foot-six guard with a wrestler's build and a Kalashnikov dangling from his shoulder. He recognized Cloutard immediately, nodded and stepped aside. Cloutard descended the stairs behind him.

It was like a gateway to another world, another time. The bar at the bottom of the stairs was beyond run-down—it was a complete shithole. Plaster crumbled from the walls, and the furniture was a random assortment of aging wooden chairs and tables. It might be called "retro-shabby-chic" in other latitudes, but here it was authentic: time had created the look. Low music oozed from an ancient jukebox. At the bar sat a drunk, trying to cajole the bartender into giving him another drink. A handful of other guests occupied a few tables. A ceiling fan turned slowly with a low, scratchy squeak, making no difference whatsoever.

As Cloutard descended the stairs, all eyes were on him. He walked slowly to the bar. A few of the patrons leaned close and whispered, but most quickly returned to their own business. The bartender had a glass of cognac poured for him before he reached the bar. Cloutard nodded his thanks, briefly inhaled the bouquet and took a sip. Much had remained the same. Cloutard handed the bartender a fifty-dollar bill.

"Where is the Welshman?"

The man took the bill and pointed toward a doorway hung with a bead curtain at the other end of the bar.

Cloutard thanked him. He went along the bar and pushed the curtain aside. Cigar and cigarette smoke filled room. The air was motionless. A huge, ancient light globe dangled above a small, round poker table. And there sat Berlin Brice, known to all as the Welshman, the *grand seigneur* of Egyptian grave-robbers.

"François Cloutard. You've got some nerve, showing up here out of the blue." The voice was like a whisper and matched perfectly the small, frail figure who had just laid down his cards and was gathering the chips he'd won.

"I need your help," said Cloutard, ignoring the Welshman's remark.

"He needs my help," the Welshman croaked, and the rest of the poker players broke into laughter.

"It is not for me. A friend of mine has been kidnapped. He's being held somewhere in Cairo."

"And you thought you'd toddle down here after all that's happened and just ask me if I knew anything about it?"

The old man had stood up from the table and now approached Cloutard. A silence had suddenly fallen over the room. Every eye was riveted on the Welshman, who glared unflinchingly at Cloutard.

Seconds passed before the old man's stern gaze transformed into amicable warmth. The Welshman threw his arms around Cloutard for a moment, then asked him to sit and join them. "It's good to see you again, old friend," the Welshman said, and he patted Cloutard's hand. "And I have heard a thing or two, as it happens. Someone's signing up diggers and grave robbers as if they've found a new Tutankhamun's tomb. Every man in Egypt with a pick or shovel's been hired, though nobody even knows yet where the dig is supposed to be. Now, I can't say whether this is tied to your particular problem or not, but if you ask me, AF is behind it. They're looking for something really big. As for the kidnapping of your friend, we'll ask around and find out what we can."

The Welshman looked around at the others at the table. They nodded.

"I'll know more in a few hours. Cairo is a big city. But for us, it's a village."

Cloutard thanked him and exchanged a few more friendly words with the old man before saying a warm goodbye. The Welshman waited until Cloutard had left.

"Call Farid. He'll be happy to hear that his search for Cloutard is over," he said to the shaven-headed man beside him at the poker table. "Send one of our men to follow him. I don't want him getting away."

20

STREETS OF CAIRO, CLOSE TO THE SARAYA GALLERY RESTAURANT

Cloutard had been doing the rounds for several hours, checking every bar and café he could think of. None of his old cronies had been able to help him directly, and in some places he'd been promptly brushed off. He decided to put his trust in the Welshman and wait a little. In the meantime, he would treat himself to an early dinner before he met with Tom again. Cloutard was looking forward to their evening operation. It had been a few years, but he was a professional. Nothing about that had changed.

"Do you have a reservation?" asked the man at the entrance to the Saraya Gallery, one of Cairo's top restaurants, but after a moment's hesitation he recognized Cloutard. "*Excusez-moi*, Monsieur Cloutard, of course we have a table for you."

The man led him through the restaurant, and Cloutard took his place at his usual table. *At least this hasn't changed*, he thought.

As the first course was served—*Escalope de Foie Gras de Canard a la Mangue*—and Cloutard let the duck melt on his tongue, he was in seventh heaven. Several months had passed since his downfall, and he had missed this. He raised his glass in a toast to himself and solemnly promised himself that he would take his old life back. He had to seize the reins again and lead the life that destiny had ordained for him. But to do that, he needed the necessary capital—and a lot of it. It was not yet clear to him how he would get it, but he would not be François Cloutard if he could not come up with something. He had been letting himself down for too long, and that annoyed him.

"Stuffing your face with duck in a place like this? You should spend your money on more important things."

Cloutard froze and looked up from his table, straight into the eyes of Farid Shaham, Karim Shaham's son. In recent years, Karim had been responsible for the finances of Cloutard's smuggling imperium, and he had been murdered on the job.

Farid sat at the table and leaned across to Cloutard.

"You have my father's blood on your hands. You lost your power through your own incompetence, and my father was murdered for the same reason. You will pay for that."

Farid opened his caftan and Cloutard saw a pistol underneath.

"Money will not bring my father back to life, but it will save my daughter. Half a million dollars is a fair price to pay to ease your conscience and save the life of a young girl. You have 72 hours. Deliver, or you will be keeping my little angel company."

Cloutard looked at Farid in disbelief. He tried to say something, but Farid cut him off.

"You have seen how fast I can find you, and I will find you wherever you go." He stood up. As he left, he said: "If you do not pay, you're a dead man."

21

EGYPTIAN MUSEUM, CAIRO

They had to park the car in a nearby side street; behind the museum there was only an enormous interchange, where the masses of traffic rolled slowly on multi-lane roads through the capital of the former kingdom of the pharaohs. Egypt, the pinnacle of ancient culture, was today a morass of poverty, overpopulation and smog. Hellen and Arno, on foot, squeezed between the columns of cars slowly creeping through the city along Meret Basha. It was late in the evening, but the run-down, stinking city was as bustling as ever. Just across from the rear entrance of the museum, they waited for the next opportunity to cross a major intersection. When it came, then ran across the street and hammered at the big gate at the back of the museum. A few moments later a small, bearded man with a hearty, gap-toothed smile opened the gate, looked around furtively and hastily waved them in, then led them across the small, dusty courtyard.

They had no way of knowing, of course, that they were being observed from across the street, from the balcony of the Hotel Tahrir Plaza Suites.

"I am already waiting, Sidi. Come, come," said the elderly man with a heavy accent, inviting them inside. He wore grey trousers, a grubby button-down shirt and worn-out black shoes. "You are lucky, today is no one here, everyone is gone home." He held the door open for them and Hellen and Arno slipped inside the museum building.

Another world revealed itself when they entered the security center of the 120-year-old museum. The antiquated security system and the handful of black-and-white screens made it clear that the new museum near Giza could not be completed soon enough. The unimaginably valuable treasures housed in the world's largest museum of Egyptian art urgently needed a safer, more modern home.

Almost casually, Arno placed an envelope on the man's desk. The man saw it out of the corner of his eye and smiled. The money inside would be more than welcome for his family; he could finally bring a little joy to his children and his wife.

The night watchman went over to a wall, hung with plans of each floor of the museum, and began to explain. "We are here." He tapped his finger on his office in the northeast corner of the building. "You go here, here, here, then down—not there, never there—then this way, then here."

Hellen and Arno did their best to remember the man's instructions. Hellen took her phone out of the pocket of her cargo pants and photographed the wall. *Better safe than sorry*, she thought.

The night watchman tapped excitedly on a room in the basement.

"Here. Here is amphoras from Anfushi. First bring today." He pressed a worn, old keycard into Arno's hand. "For open door. You have one hour. Bring card back after."

Suddenly, all three heard a loud, metallic pounding. It was coming from the rear gate.

"Alarm is off one hour. Don't forget, one hour! Go, go!" The man shooed Hellen and Arno out of his office with his cheerful, mostly toothless smile. He waited until they had disappeared around the corner. The metallic hammering came again, and he ran outside to see who it was.

Hellen turned back and watched the night watchman doubtfully for a moment. Could they really trust the old man, charming as he was? Or had the police already arrived to arrest them, and he and the cops would share the money Arno had left behind on the table?

"What are we waiting for? Let's go! The clock is ticking," said Arno, tugging Hellen along by her arm. She hesitated for a moment, then followed after him. They followed the guard's instructions to the letter, careful to follow the path he had shown them on the map. Hellen had already visited the museum several times; places like this enchanted her. The smell always made her feel good, and it was doubly exciting to walk through the immense halls at night and all alone. The museum's most famous artifact appeared in her mind's eye: the golden death mask of Pharaoh Tutankhamun, dead for 3343 years. It was among the most famous works of art in the world, up there with Leonardo da Vinci's "Mona Lisa," although Tutankhamen's only real claim to fame, in fact, was that his tomb had been discovered almost intact by Howard Carter in 1922 in the Valley of the Kings. As a pharaoh, he hadn't been anything special, but the contents of his tomb were among the most spectacular archaeological finds ever made. If such riches had been found in the small tomb of a relatively insignificant king, what treasures must have been lost over the millennia, plundered by grave robbers? Hellen thought of Cloutard and wondered whether any of it had ended up in his hands.

But there were also more illustrious personalities within this museum's walls. For instance Rameses II, once the most powerful pharaoh and one of the longest-reigning heads of state in recorded history, had now found his final resting place in a refrigerator at the Cairo Museum. Hellen remembered how her father had once taken her there as a child, and how she had had the honor of actually seeing the mummy of Rameses II for herself. They were in luck: an American film crew had been making a documentary, and the mummy had been taken out of its climate-controlled vault. That was one of Hellen's fondest memories of her father.

Finally, she and Arno reached the basement. She stood at the door for which the night watchman had given them the keycard, let out a little squeal of glee and inserted the card into the card reader. The door buzzed, clicked and opened. They passed through into the cool laboratory and Hellen turned on the light. In the center of the lab was a large steel table, upon which rested a dark wooden box. Hellen and Arno looked at each other, wide-eyed with eagerness.

Hellen kissed Arno on the cheek. "Thank you for doing this for me," she said.

She found a small pry bar on a rack beneath the table, cracked open the lid and set it aside. And there they were, lying on a bed of wood shavings: the two amphorae. The clay vessels were each about eighteen inches long, and were in almost perfect condition. Being exposed to seawater for the two minutes it took Hellen and Arno to swum back to the surface seemed to have done them little harm. The cavity from which Hellen had taken them must have been completely airtight, which would explain the air that had escaped when they pulled the stone block out of the wall, and also why they hadn't been able to press the trigger stones at first: whoever put them in the hidden compartment had sealed it well. Hellen lifted an amphora from the box, admiring the texture of the simple vessel. But what interested her the most was the symbol pressed into the clay. Hellen lifted out the second amphora and began her examination.

22

TAHRIR PLAZA SUITES HOTEL, CAIRO

Cloutard sat on the small, covered balcony, sipping a glass of cognac—Hennessy Louis XIII. The Tahrir Plaza Suites was a three-star hotel; he was used to better, but he was pleasantly surprised that they at least kept a supply of his favorite cognac. For now, however, location mattered more than luxury. The balcony had an excellent view over the entire area, and every now and then he peered through binoculars, looking at the back entrance to the building and the people hustling through the crowded streets. He watched until the sun began to set, and the staff had all left the complex. Now, the only one left was the elderly night watchman, whom he had been watching for a couple of hours—but for the moment, he was enjoying the last gleams of the sunset over the Egyptian metropolis. He sipped with relish at his expensive cognac. He wanted nothing more than to banish the surprising and disagreeable encounter with Farid—and the unexpected threat—from his mind. But he knew he would have to find time for it later.

Cloutard glanced at his watch. His friend was due any time. It was already very late: apparently his official duties were taking longer than expected. But this situation was important, too; it was literally a matter of life and death. Finally, he heard a knock at the door. He got up and walked across the small but clean and pleasantly lit room. He opened the door to an athletically built and exhausted looking man in a dark gray suit and loose tie: Tom Wagner. The two embraced warmly and Tom said, "Thank you, François, for doing this. For Noah and me."

"That goes without saying, my friend. Come in, come in," Cloutard said. He closed the door behind Tom and both men went out onto the balcony. "Drink?"

"No thanks. I have to keep a clear head," Tom replied. He picked up the binoculars that lay on the tiny table next to Cloutard's glass of Louis XIII.

"The security center is at the northeast corner. There is only a night watchman on duty," Cloutard explained. Tom swung the binoculars to the left and saw the watchman's window. "I cannot believe we are forced to work for that woman," Cloutard said angrily, as he slumped onto the chair beside the table. "It is gutless to target a man in a wheelchair, but Ossana will stoop to anything. She has no criminal's code of honor."

"But the file she gave me has been a big help. This ought to be a walk in the park." Tom looked around a little with the field glasses until he had the binoculars trained on the iron gate at the back of the complex. "I see someone," he said, but he was looking at the newcomers from behind and could not make out who it was. There were two, a man and a woman, and when the gate opened, the woman glanced back over her shoulder for a moment. Tom recognized her instantly.

"Hellen?" What was Hellen doing in Egypt? And what was she doing here, now?

"*The* Hellen? Your ex-girlfriend?" Cloutard was as bewildered as Tom.

Tom's brain was already in high gear. Could this really be a coincidence? She was an archaeologist, after all, and the building below was a museum. But why in the world was she sneaking in at the back gate in the middle of the night? No way was this a fluke. They had to be here for the same thing. What could interest both Hellen and Ossana—desperately enough that she would kidnap Noah to get it?

"Grab your things, let's go. We're doing this now!" Tom snapped at Cloutard, who jumped up from his chair and drained the last drops of his cognac.

Minutes later, they left the hotel at a run and dodged across the road, still jammed with traffic, to the museum's back entrance. Tom pounded on the iron gate.

"Tom, we had a detailed plan. What are we doing?" Cloutard asked.

"Improvising," Tom said. He hammered against the gate a second time and drew his pistol.

"*Merde*," Cloutard muttered. "This is not good. When it comes to this woman, your judgment is still, shall we say, impaired. Tom, please, we should—"

Just then, the gate opened a crack and the cheerful smile of the night watchman appeared.

"*Nem min fadlik?*" he asked. Then he saw the gun that Tom was casually pointing at him at waist level. "What you want?" he said in broken English, startled. He retreated as Tom and Cloutard pushed into the yard.

All three quickly entered the museum. "Take us to your office," Tom ordered the fearful man. When they reached the security center, Tom ordered him to sit down. "You let two people in here five minutes ago. Why? What are they doing here?"

The man could not help himself as his eyes drifted to the envelope on his desk. "I no understand," he said. But Tom had followed the man's gaze. He snatched up the envelope and opened it. Inside was five thousand dollars. The man looked at Tom in despair.

"Ah. A private after-dark tour, something like that?" He put the envelope back on the table. The man's relief was palpable.

"*Madha yurid alrajul walmar'at hna?* What do the man and woman want here?" Cloutard asked.

To Tom, it sounded like the purest high Arabic, and he nodded at François, impressed. "Not bad," he said.

"Excuse me?" the man said tentatively. He pointed to the map on the wall and indicated that he wanted to stand up. Tom nodded. The man went to the map and tapped on the room in the basement.

"Amphora from Anfushi here. Here going man and woman."

"Thank you. Sit down again," said Tom, and he pointed at the chair.

"*Shukraan. Waljuluws*," Cloutard translated, and the guard returned to his chair.

Tom began rummaging through drawers and cupboards. "What are you looking for?" Cloutard asked.

But Tom had already found a roll of electrical tape in a cupboard. "Sorry," he said to the man, as he bound him to the chair. He taped his mouth closed, too.

"*Eadhar, eadhar*," Cloutard said. "Alibi."

Tom picked up the envelope of cash and laid it demonstratively in a drawer. "So that no one steals it when they find you."

The man nodded gratefully. Tom left the office, and Cloutard followed a few seconds later. Before he left, however, he removed the envelope from the drawer, shrugged apologetically at the night watchman, and slipped it into his jacket pocket.

23

CAFÉ CENTRAL, VIENNA, AUSTRIA

The American stepped inside Vienna's most famous café, located in the former stock market. To call the Café Central stylish was a gross understatement: the columned hall, with its Tuscan neo-renaissance design, was peerless.

Many years earlier, the American had read a description of the venerable Viennese institution that he had found particularly apt:

The Central is not a coffeehouse like other coffeehouses, but a way of life. Its denizens are, for the most part, people whose loathing of their fellow humans is as intense as their desire for companionship with people who want to be alone, but who need company to do so. The guests of the Central know, love and scorn one another. There are creative types for whom nothing comes to mind only in the Central, and far less anywhere else.

As soon as he entered, the American spotted Ruben Steinberg. He was seated far in the back of the café, and the American wound his way through the usual crowds that frequented the café every day. He pushed past the tuxedoed waiters, referred to as "*Ober*" in Vienna—as in the Emperor's day, the staff of the Central still considered the tuxedo to be the only conceivable and proper uniform of a waiter—and sat down opposite Steinberg.

Steinberg was a spy. That was all the American knew. He had been a spy for a very long time, and had probably switched allegiances many, many times in his career. The American had no idea who Steinberg was working for now, and he didn't want to know. The Agency had simply named him as the best source of information in Vienna, especially for the World War II era.

The American wasted no time. He told Steinberg what he'd found in Brazil, naturally taking care neither to say a word about what he was really looking for, nor to reveal that he was actually on a mission personally assigned to him by the president of the United States.

"The Nazis conducted countless interrogations. The Austrian resistance grew strong quite early, so it will be difficult to find the man you are looking for. Perhaps the Documentation Centre of the Austrian Resistance can help, or we might have to visit the Austrian Archaeological Institute."

"The Archaeological Institute? Why would they be involved?" The American's curiosity had been piqued.

Steinberg raised his hand, the *Ober* nodded, and within moments two cups of *Wiener melange* arrived at the table —arranged on a silver tray with a glass of water, naturally, as was customary in Vienna.

The American was astounded. Steinberg smiled mildly. "Have you heard of our writer, Peter Altenberg?" he asked. "They used to say that if he was not in the Central, then he was on his way here. He actually gave out the café as his home address. It's almost like that for me, too."

The American glanced impatiently at his watch, a message not lost on Steinberg, who continued: "But getting back to the topic, you said that the Capri file contained all kinds of information about occult and mystical artifacts. The Nazis, Himmler and Hitler above all, were fascinated by that stuff." Steinberg leaned closer and lowered his voice: "They say that's why the Austrian Archaeological Institute was annexed in 1938 and converted into the Vienna Department of the German Archaeological Institute—because it possessed many, many objects that fascinated the Nazis. I will arrange for us to visit both institutions privately." He winked at the American, drank his *melange* and stood up.

"I'll be in touch as soon as I know more. I assume I can expect the usual fee from the Agency?"

The American nodded, although he had no idea what Steinberg's usual fee was. He paid for the coffee and strolled toward the open plaza at Michaelerplatz. He did not realize, as he left the Central, that he was being watched by someone who knew him only too well.

24

EGYPTIAN MUSEUM, CAIRO

The clay lid had probably been sealed with pine resin. Hellen had managed to open the first amphora quickly and had discovered a few tightly rolled scrolls inside, but the second was proving more stubborn. Was there a surprise waiting for her inside? Something big? Her excitement was almost painful.

These containers had been used thousands of years earlier to store all kinds of things: oils and wine, but also meat, salted fish and beans were sealed and transported in them. They could be closed with lids of animal skin, cork, or clay, and made airtight with resins. To waterproof them completely, they were coated with pine resin. Embossed symbols were used to label them, identifying the contents, origin, producer or year.

But the symbol these two clay vessels bore was not something normally found on an amphora: the ankh.

"In the ankh symbol, people usually see the cross of life, the symbol of eternal life. But it had other meanings,"

Hellen explained. "It was also known as 'the key to the maturity of spirit and soul' and 'the key to wisdom and knowledge of the secrets of life.' My father believed that it was literally the key to the secret of the library, and when I saw it on that letter, it was clear to me that, somehow, it had to be the answer." She traced the tip of her thumb gently over the embossed symbol and felt certain that she had finally found the clue she'd been looking for. Maybe one day she would even be able to discover why her father had disappeared, but right now, she dared not dream of that. Carefully, Hellen scraped the sealing material out of the gap around the lid of the second amphora.

"Careful!" Arno said. He was standing behind Hellen, watching anxiously over her shoulder. But Hellen was in her element. With gloved hands, she treated the fragile artifacts as she would a raw egg. She gave Arno a shove with her hip because he was standing too close, literally breathing down her neck.

"Please, Arno. Give me a little space. Make yourself useful and see if you can find something we can use to transport the scrolls."

"What do you mean, 'transport'? We can't take them with us."

"We *have to* take them with us. I can't simply unroll the scrolls and analyze them here. They'd fall apart on the spot. We don't have the time or the equipment to do it properly. They have to be hydrated for a few days before you can even try to unroll them, and you need a properly equipped lab for that."

"But . . ." Arno started to say, but then shrugged in defeat and began searching the cupboards that lined the walls.

"There is no other way," Hellen said. "I'm so close, closer than ever before. There's no way I'm leaving here without these scrolls."

"Found something," Arno said, proudly holding up a cardboard roll.

"Got it!" Hellen cried, then briefly hoped her happy outburst hadn't been too loud. And then both of them suddenly heard a sound and fell silent. For several seconds, neither dared to move at all.

"That came from outside," Arno whispered.

"Go see what it was," Hellen said.

Arno crept out of the room and Hellen immediately turned back to her work. She lifted the lid carefully off the second amphora and set it aside, then moved the magnifying lamp toward and looked inside. A moment later she pulled away, mystified, before peering inside again. She tried different angles, she tried adjusting the lamp, but nothing changed. At first glance, and even at the second, the amphora seemed to be empty. But something was off. Hellen rolled up the sleeve of her blouse and, with great care, reached into the opening. Yes! She had not been mistaken: the amphora looked deeper from the outside than on the inside: it had a false bottom! She ran her fingers over the inside base of the amphora and felt irregular holes. At a point on the side she felt an indentation of some sort. She looked inside again and then she saw it: a tiny ankh symbol stamped into the edge of the false base.

A loud blast from outside shocked Hellen so much that the amphora slipped out of her hands and smashed on the floor. *A gunshot*, she thought, her mind suddenly blank. "Arno!" she cried. Ignoring the fact that she had just destroyed an ancient, priceless artifact, she ran out of the laboratory into the corridor. She heard voices, and they grew louder as she ran toward them.

"Put the gun down and your hands up!" a man shouted. "Now!"

She knew the voice, but it wasn't Arno. Then another shot rang out just as Hellen turned the corner of the corridor.

It took her a moment to realize what had happened. Arno had his back to her. He seemed to be standing without moving. Then a pistol slipped from his grasp and clattered to the floor. He collapsed on the spot and lay motionless on the floor.

Hellen let out a piercing, horrified wail. Farther back she saw Tom lowering his gun.

"Arno!" she cried in despair. She ran to her lover, sliding the last few feet on her knees. Tears already welled from her eyes. "Arno! Arno . . ." she sobbed. She turned him over, but could only stare into his dead eyes. She lifted his head onto her lap. "What have you done? Why??" she screamed tearfully at Tom.

"I . . . he had a gun. I warned him," Tom stammered, running his hands nervously through his hair. Cloutard, looking grim, pushed Tom aside a little, and Tom understood that it would be better if Cloutard tried to comfort Hellen.

"I'm sorry, Hellen. I'm sorry," Tom said. He turned away and smashed his fist against a wall.

Cloutard knelt beside Hellen and did his best to console her. He knew it was hopeless, but he checked the fallen man's pulse. Nothing. Arno was dead.

Cloutard lifted Hellen to her feet, put his arm around her and walked her a few paces away from the body. Tom, who had stayed in the background until now, went to Arno's body, knelt beside him and searched his pockets.

Had he been mistaken? The man had been about to shoot him dead. If Cloutard hadn't pushed Tom out of the firing line in time, the first bullet would have struck him. Another thing: the man had not reacted at all to his warning—he had been about to fire again. They had been facing each other, as if in a duel, and Tom had been left with no choice but to shoot.

Arno Kruger, Tom read from the man's ID card. South African. Apart from the ID card, his pockets held only a money clip with a few bills, a business card for a company that seemed to trade in diamonds, and the key to a rental car.

"Leave him be! Get your hands off him! Why did you do that?" Hellen, in tears, screamed at Tom. Cloutard gently turned her face away and she buried her face in his chest. After a few moments, they moved slowly back toward the laboratory. Tom followed a few steps behind.

Cloutard sat Hellen down on a stool and gave her his handkerchief. She dried her eyes and mechanically passed the handkerchief back to Cloutard. Tom looked around inside the lab and saw the papyrus scrolls lying on the table. He stepped over the remains of the second amphora on the floor, kicking a few clay shards aside, and approached the table. He picked up the small tray holding the delicate scrolls and turned to Hellen.

"Is this what you found?" She raised her head and nodded apathetically. Tom turned away. He picked up the cardboard document roll that lay on the table, carefully slipped the papyruses inside and closed the roll. Hellen, who had spent the entire time staring at the floor and sobbing, suddenly came back to life. She had seen something among the shards on the floor: the false bottom of the amphora.

All at once, an ear-splitting siren cut through the silence, and Tom and Cloutard almost jumped out of their skin. The alarm!

25

EGYPTIAN MUSEUM, CAIRO

"One hour, no more. He warned us," Hellen said disinterestedly, looking at her watch.

"We can't go back the same way. We have to find another way out," Tom said. "Let's go!"

He grabbed the document roll, opened the lab door, glanced out into the corridor to check that they were in the clear, then moved off quickly to the left. Cloutard was right behind him. In the lab, Hellen quickly crouched and picked up the round clay disk that Tom had revealed when he kicked the shards aside. It was about six inches across, just small enough to fit into a pocket of her cargo pants. Then she followed them out of the room. Outside the door, she stopped for a moment and looked to the right, in the direction Arno lay. For a moment, time seemed to stand perfectly still. A single tear welled from her eye. She wiped it away, then turned and went after Tom and Cloutard.

Tom stopped at a junction of corridors. "Which way?" he asked.

Cloutard slid his backpack from his shoulder and began rummaging through it. There had been a museum plan in Ossana's file, he remembered. "Give me a just a second," he said, still digging in the backpack.

Tom frowned. "Could it be that the master thief is getting rusty? In case you hadn't noticed, the alarm is screaming its head off. We've got to get out of here."

"Go right," Hellen suddenly said from behind. "Then take the stairs up and go right again at the top." Tom and Cloutard looked around to her in surprise. Hellen's face was lit by her phone's display. She looked up and held it out for them to see, and they found themselves looking at a picture of the plan on the nightwatchman's wall. They looked at each other, nodded, and headed to the right. When they turned the corner, they were suddenly confronted by two security men. The security men had their weapons at the ready, but they were just as surprised as Tom, Hellen and Cloutard.

Unlike Cloutard, Tom was anything but out of practice. He did not hesitate for a fraction of a second. Throwing himself at the man on the left, he rammed his elbow under the man's chin, at the same time slamming his foot into the gut of the second security guy. The second man groaned, doubled over, dropped to the floor and lost his grip on his pistol. Tom struck the first guard on the temple with a hard fist, putting him out of action. The other man was still holding his gut with one hand but was crawling toward his pistol, which lay just inches from his outstretched arm. Tom had already spotted his target. He grabbed a leg, pulled and twisted, turning the surprised guard over, then dropped on top of him and punched him hard in the middle of his face. Tom, Hellen and Cloutard all heard the unmistakable crunch of the man's nose breaking. The pain from the blow seared through the guard, sending him into unconsciousness— the two security men were no longer a threat. Everything had happened so fast that neither Hellen nor Cloutard had had a chance to help Tom, although Cloutard had managed to screw up his face in disgust at the sound of the breaking nose.

"*Bien fait,*" Cloutard said. He stepped over the two men and headed in the direction of the northwest emergency exit, where they would be able to escape the Egyptian Museum unseen.

26

KHAN EL-KHALILI SOUK, CAIRO

The rental car, an old Mitsubishi Lancer, parked in a dark side street, away from all the noise of the city. Cloutard was at the wheel, with Tom beside him and Hellen in the back seat. She stared out the window, still in shock. Her fingers clenched the disk she had discovered among the remnants of the amphora.

Tom took out the flip phone he'd got from Ossana and called the only number on it. After a few moments, Ossana picked up.

"You're certainly fast," she said. "You must really miss your crippled friend. Don't you trust me to take care of him?"

"Where do we make the handover?" Tom asked, never one for niceties.

"Well, well. All business. I can appreciate that. Be at Bab al-Ghuri, by Khan el-Khalili bazaar, in one hour. Come alone," Ossana said and immediately hung up.

"She certainly picked a nice public spot for it. Ideal for disappearing," Cloutard said, when Tom had told him where the handover was to take place.

"What are you talking about?" Hellen asked quietly. "What are you even doing here in Cairo?" Tom and Cloutard looked around to her.

"Noah's been kidnapped. The amphoras are the ransom," said Tom bluntly.

Hellen sat up straighten. "What? Noah's been kidnapped? By whom?" Hellen was slowly coming back to life. "What's going on here?" she demanded.

Tom took out his phone and played Noah's message for her to hear.

"I didn't recognize the number, so I only heard it the next day. An hour later, Ossana dropped by my hotel for a visit. She told me she had Noah and what I had to do to get him back. And here we are."

"Ossana? What does that bitch want with the Library of Alexandria?"

"What do you mean, the Library of Alexandria?" Cloutard said, eyebrows raised. "That was destroyed centuries ago."

"I found those amphorae in the Anfushi Necropolis in Alexandria two days ago," Hellen began, and she told Tom and Cloutard the whole story. She ended with: "Arno bribed the night watchman and . . ." The thought of Arno was like a hand clenched around her throat, cutting off her words.

". . . and then we came along," Cloutard finished Hellen's sentence.

Tom looked at the time. "I have to be at that souk in less than fifty minutes to hand these scrolls over to Ossana. It's that, or we never see Noah again."

Hellen wanted to protest the loss of the scrolls, but then she recalled the disk hidden in her pocket. Could she risk keeping it a secret from Tom and Cloutard? Would she be risking Noah's life? No, impossible—no one could possibly know what was inside the amphorae. She decided to keep the disk to herself, at least for now.

"Time to go," Tom said, and Cloutard started the engine.

27

MIDAN HUSSEIN, CAIRO

A few minutes later they arrived at Midan Hussein, where two huge mosques faced each other across a plaza. The smaller and more modern of the two, the Sayyidna el-Hussein Mosque, perched directly beside the entrance to the bazaar. On the opposite side of the plaza stood the Alexandria-Azhar Mosque, over a thousand years old. It was the second mosque ever built in Cairo, and ever since its construction the city had been nicknamed "city of a thousand minarets." Today, it is recognized as the second-oldest continuously operated university in the world.

Cloutard pulled over to the right to let Tom out. It was late in the evening, but many people were still out and about in the area around the mosques. Tourists strolled, admiring the old buildings. The mosque looked radiant in the glow of white and yellow flood-lights that showed the impressive architecture in its best light. Tom trotted across the square to the eastern entrance to the bazaar, beside the tallest of the el-

Hussein mosque's minarets. He only had a few minutes left until Ossana's deadline.

"Check. Check," said Tom, testing the earpiece he'd planted in his ear before getting out of the car. He was grateful that his brief return to his old job gave him access to high-grade equipment like this, at least temporarily. Once he'd returned Chancellor Lang to the embassy safely, he had made a quick detour down to the equipment room.

"Coming in loud and clear," Cloutard replied.

Tom was picking his way through the narrow street known as Sekat al Badstan. It was lined with small shops and open stands offering spices, artfully contrived lanterns, pots and jewelry, the wares shimmering in the golden light of the gas lamps. Tourists bought souvenirs, trinkets and T-shirts for friends and family at home, while Egyptian men sat at outdoor tables drinking tea or coffee and smoking their aromatic shisha pipes.

Tom saw Ossana coming from quite a distance. Six feet tall and drop-dead gorgeous, she was hard to miss. She wore a long gown and a magnificent headscarf and strolled easily toward their meeting place beneath the elaborate arched entrance to the souk.

"Where's Noah?" Tom growled at her through gritted teeth.

"Easy, Mr. Wagner. One step at a time. Do you have what I want?" she asked, eyeing Tom warily.

"That's not how my name is pronounced, but whatever. The amphoras were too clunky. These were inside." He popped the cap off the cardboard tube and showed her the scrolls.

"Mr. Wagner, are you telling me you destroyed 2000-year-old amphorae just so you wouldn't have as much to carry?" She shook her head, a malicious smile playing on her lips.

"Where's Noah?" Tom repeated, growing angrier.

Ossana produced a cell phone from beneath her gown and held it out to Tom. On the display he saw a live video feed that showed Noah inside a van. "Give me the documents and my men will let him go."

"Where? Where will they release him?"

"Oh, we do home delivery," Ossana said. "We've had our eyes on you and your friends since you left the museum. Give me the tube, and my men will hand Noah over to your friends."

Tom hesitated a moment longer, but finally handed the scrolls to Ossana. She murmured a command in Afrikaans into her phone and cut the connection.

Then she leaned forward and whispered into the ear where Tom wore his earpiece: "I would just like to say hello to my ex-darling François. I will never forget those wonderful months we had together. Such a pity our little idyll back then was so rudely interrupted." She smiled at Tom, then gave him a peck on the cheek, turned away and was quickly swallowed up in the crowd.

"*Pute stupide*," Cloutard muttered when he heard Ossana's message on the radio. He had parked the Lancer beneath trees on Hasan El-Adawy, opposite the entrance to the bazaar. A van suddenly appeared next to them, and two black men pushed Noah in his wheelchair out of the back of the still-moving vehicle.

Noah toppled forward onto the road and the van raced away, tires squealing. Hellen and Cloutard jumped out and got Noah upright again—he was a little disoriented and clearly injured—just as Tom came running. He threw his arms around his old friend's neck, perhaps a little too warmly.

Noah groaned, but returned Tom's hug. "Thanks," he said, "You saved my life, all of you."

Tom lifted his friend into the car, and Cloutard folded the wheelchair and stowed it in the trunk. Then they set off together for the Austrian Embassy.

At the western entrance to the bazaar, Ossana joined her men in the van. She took out her cell phone and watched a small red dot on the display move slowly across a map of Cairo. She smiled. No one had spotted the small GPS tracker her men had hidden on the underside of Noah's wheelchair.

28

AUSTRIAN EMBASSY, CAIRO

"You're sure you don't want to go to the hospital?" Tom asked. He was sitting opposite Noah on a small swivel stool while an embassy staffer who used to work as a nurse patched his friend up.

"Yeah. Really. It's not as bad as it looks," Noah said. He inhaled with a hiss as the woman swabbed a cut over his eye with alcohol.

"I'm not so sure," the nurse said. "He could have a broken rib, or worse. They really worked him over."

"I'd know if I had a broken rib." He gave her a wink above a pained smile.

When all of Noah's visible wounds had been disinfected and bandaged, and the deep cut over his eye closed with tissue adhesive from the first-aid kit, the woman left the treatment room.

"Really, I'm all right," Noah assured Tom.

"You're sure?"

"Yes. You got me back before they got serious," Noah said, and waved a hand dismissively. "Let's find the others. I've got a lot to tell you."

Tom pushed his friend down a hallway, and they met Hellen and Cloutard in the embassy conference room. Situated beside the Nile and just behind the renowned Orman Garden, the embassy building offered a sumptuous view over the longest river in the world. Hellen stood and stared out of the window, indifferent to everything.

Noah told them in a few words about how Ossana's people had ambushed him a few days earlier in Tel Aviv, dragging him into a van on a public street in broad daylight. Hours or days later, he'd woken up in a basement—in Egypt, as he had discovered only today.

"One of the guards left his mobile lying around. That's when I tried to reach you. But the connection was terrible; I wasn't getting my hopes up. After that, they decided to teach me a little lesson." He prodded gently at the wound over his eye. "What did you have to do to set me free? And by the way: thank you all. I am so glad to be out of there."

Even Hellen gave him a momentary smile, but then turned back to the window.

"All Ossana wanted was two old vases," said Tom with a shrug.

"Two *amphorae*," Cloutard corrected him.

"And what was in them?" Noah asked.

"A few papyrus scrolls. One of the amphoras got broken and the other one was empty, so all we had were the scrolls. That seemed to satisfy her because—surprise, surprise—she kept her word," said Tom.

"Yes . . . frankly, it was all a little too simple, if you ask me," Cloutard added. "She could have found an easier way to get her hands on the scrolls than to kidnap Noah and to 'hire' Tom to steal them for her."

"Well, it wasn't quite as simple as you say," Hellen said bitterly.

"What do you mean?" Noah could see that she was hurt.

"It's not something I want to talk about. Not now. It won't change anything, will it? I found the two amphorae because of an anonymous tip," Hellen said. She was gazing out the window again. "In the Anfushi Necropolis in Alexandria. But they were taken away from me. Long story. There were three scrolls inside. That's all. All I can say with certainty is that the two amphorae came from the Library of Alexandria, or the Library of the Kings, as it's also known. They carried the mark of the library."

"Ah, and that's the connection. Now something I over-heard yesterday makes sense," Noah said. "Ossana called someone and said something about the Library of Alexandria. I only picked up scraps of the conversation."

As wide-eyed as children listening to an exciting story, Tom and Cloutard sat at the conference table and leaned closer to Noah.

"Her last words before she hung up were: 'We're one step closer to our goal,'" Noah said.

"I always thought the library was a myth, but if Ossana is also looking for it, then maybe there is something to it," Cloutard said thoughtfully. "Whatever's in the library would be priceless."

"The question is: where do we go from here?" said Tom.

Hellen turned away from the window, but did not look at Tom, her eyes shifting between Noah and Cloutard. "My father might be able to help with that," she said.

"I thought your father disappeared," Tom said.

Hellen continued not looking at him. "Okay, the *papers in my father's house* might be able to help us," Hellen said with irritation.

"Where is your father's house?" Noah asked.

"Belgium," Tom and Hellen said together. Their eyes met and Tom smiled sheepishly, but Hellen's expression did not change.

"Then we should get to Belgium, the sooner the better," Noah said enthusiastically.

"François and I can take care of that. Doesn't Rambo here have to fly the chancellor back to Vienna or something?" Hellen said quickly. She grasped Cloutard by the hand and pulled him along with her out of the conference room.

"What the hell's going on with you two?" Noah asked, rolling closer to Tom.

"Nothing. When we were in Rome back then, I asked her if she wanted to go to the States with me, but she had other plans. Her own plans. I haven't seen her since. And today of all days, I run into her in the Egyptian Museum ... her and her boyfriend, as it turns out."

"So?"

"So what?"

"So why is she so mad at you? She's literally flying to another country to get away from you."

"I shot Hellen's boyfriend. In the museum. He's dead," said Tom meekly.

"You ... what?!"

"He shot at me first. If I hadn't reacted, I'd be the one lying dead in the museum."

"Still, you killed her boyfriend. I think you can forget having any kind of relationship with her."

Tom said nothing but nodded imperceptibly, his mind elsewhere.

———

When they left the conference room, Hellen excused herself for a moment and went to the ladies' room. She checked first that nobody else was inside, then sat down on a closed toilet seat and burst into tears. All the pent-up feelings from the last few hours came pouring out. Arno was dead. And her ex had killed him. Nothing made any sense. She knew Tom. She knew him well. He was high-spirited, thoughtless, sometimes reckless, an adrenaline junkie—but he was also a professional. He wasn't afraid of a gunfight, and he would not have made a mistake like that. She was confused, and her emotions were in an uproar. Tom would never have shot blindly, not without a reason. But in God's name, what reason could there have been? Tom claimed that Arno had fired first, but that just didn't make sense. Why would he?

She was jolted abruptly out of her thoughts when someone suddenly knocked on the door of the cubicle.

"Hellen? Are you all right? Can I help in any way?"

"Yes. You can bring my boyfriend back to life."

"Tom had no choice. Aaron—"

"ARNO!" Hellen corrected. "And Tom always has that excuse, doesn't he? That he had no choice . . . of course he had a choice. He just thinks with his fists or with his gun, every time."

She wiped her eyes with toilet tissue, then stood up and threw the wad of tear-stained paper into the bowl and flushed it away. Grief, anger and despair were at war in her head, and there no sign of a clear winner yet. She found it unbelievably difficult, but she had to focus on the task at hand. Losing her nerve now would help no one. The rational scientist in her managed to gain the upper hand: she washed her hands and face and turned to Cloutard with new strength.

"Whatever the truth is, I don't want to be anywhere near Tom right now. You and I will fly to Belgium by ourselves and see what we can find in my father's papers."

29

ARCHAEOLOGICAL INSTITUTE, VIENNA

The American and his contact, Steinberg, had spent almost the entire day combing through the archives of the Archaeological Institute. Steinberg had tapped his connections and the head of the library had been exceptionally cooperative, but they had turned up nothing of any value—and nothing at all about an Italian questioned by the Nazis about the whereabouts of occult artifacts. The two men finally left the magnificent palace, which had housed the University of World Trade until its redesignation as the headquarters of the Archaeological Institute in 1975.

"Maybe we'll have better luck at the Documentation Centre," said Steinberg.

The American looked at his watch. "It's almost eight. Will they still be open?"

Steinberg took a bunch of keys out of his pocket and held them up for the American to see. "For me, they're always open."

Steinberg flagged down a taxi, they climbed in, and Steinberg barked: "The old City Hall, Wipplingerstrasse." The taxi driver pulled away.

The Documentation Centre of the Austrian Resistance had dedicated itself to the collection of documents and other materials pertaining to resistance, persecution and exile during the National Socialist regime in Austria. It also concerned itself with Nazi war crimes, postwar justice, right-wing extremism in Austria and Germany since 1945, and restitution and reparation for Nazi injustices. It was already late in the evening when the two men reached the foundation's archive, which was housed in Vienna's old City Hall.

"Our best bet will be the O5 documents," said Steinberg as he unlocked the door and they stepped inside. Steinberg punched a few digits into the alarm system, and they made their way downstairs.

"O5?" the American asked.

"O5 was an Austrian anti-Nazi resistance group. It first appeared officially in 1944, although it was probably around much earlier than that. O5 was a kind of trademark for an umbrella organization that brought together various resistance groups, all dedicated to the struggle for a free Austria, beyond party lines and ideologies. O5 is an abbreviation: the fifth letter in the alphabet is 'E', and if you put an 'O' and an 'E' together, you get 'Ö' for Österreich—Austria. Even today, there's an 'O5' carved into a wall of St. Stephen's Cathedral, just down the street."

Steinberg logged into the computer system and typed a few keywords into the search engine. For the next fifteen minutes he mumbled away to himself, grumbling and cursing. The American stood quietly by and did not interfere in the process. It was clear that research work was not one of Steinberg's favorite pastimes.

Steinberg's exclamation was so sudden that it made the American jump. "Finally!" Steinberg cried, and his high voice resounded in the empty archive. "Follow me," he said, scribbling a file number on a scrap of paper. "We have to go down to the basement."

Lined up down below were hundreds of yards of ceiling-high shelves, packed with file folders and cardboard boxes. Steinberg quickly found the shelf and the folder he needed. The folder contained handwritten notes and reports from various O5 members, records of their countless contacts with numerous resistance groups throughout Europe. One of those reports was the key.

"Here, look!" Steinberg tapped his finger on a name. "A man made contact with O5 and said he had an important package for the Americans, one that had to be kept safe from the Nazis. According to this, O5 made contact with the Americans and the package was duly handed over. After that, the man was captured by the Nazis, interrogated and shipped off to a concentration camp in Poland. His name—"

Steinberg broke off. He seemed surprised.

"Well, isn't that interesting. His name was Angelo Negozi." Steinberg frowned, thinking hard. "Negozi?

Negozi? Of course. He was the brother of Giuseppe Negozi, prefect of the Vatican Archive from 1925 to 1955."

The American raised his eyebrows. That made sense.

30

HELLEN'S PARENTS' HOUSE, ANTWERP, BELGIUM

Hellen hesitantly pressed the doorbell and stood waiting, shifting nervously from one leg to the other—she dreaded the thought of facing her mother now, especially so soon after Arno's tragic death. She had no desire to quarrel with her mother, but conversations with her unfortunately tended to culminate in differences of opinion at best, if not in outright arguments. Cloutard, who had shown himself to be a true friend in the last day, placed his hand gently on her shoulder. A sense of calm spread through her. Hellen and Cloutard had grown a great deal closer on the flight together. The art thief and the curator . . . an odd couple, to be sure, but they did share common interests. Of course, they would remain friends; Cloutard was old enough to be Hellen's father. But that was exactly what Hellen liked— she really did see him as a kind of father figure.

"Hello, Mother."

It had happened again. Hellen's voice had switched to being excessively correct and respectful as soon as her mother opened the front door. Hellen stepped past her into the house.

"Bonjour, Madame," Cloutard said in his unmistakable accent. He raised his hat and kissed Hellen's mother's hand. She gave him a disconcerted smile, taken by surprise by the charming gentleman accompanying her daughter.

"Uh, hello. Please come in. I have to say, you seem somehow familiar."

"Mother, you must know Monsieur François Cloutard."

"François Cloutard. The . . . the art smuggler?" Blindsided, Theresia de Mey's serious face returned the instant she turned to Hellen.

"Do not tell me that you're here because of your father's fantasies." She grasped Hellen by the arm and pulled her to one side. "And why would you bring a criminal wanted internationally into my house?"

"Mother, really, you of all people ought to give him a little credit," Hellen said, freeing herself angrily from her mother's grip. "You know what he did for Blue Shield, and that without him—"

"Yes, I know. Still . . ." She swallowed whatever else she was about to say. "Well, what's this all about . . . daughter?"

Hellen hesitated. "Well, it's—"

"I knew it! Why are you still chasing after your father's absurd fairy tales? Do you want to share the same fate as

—" She fell silent when Hellen suddenly held a clay disk about six inches in diameter under her nose. Mrs. de Mey reached for it as if hypnotized.

"That's the symbol of . . ."

"Yes." Hellen smiled. Her mother was spellbound.

"And these markings . . ." Hellen's mother turned the disk in her hands, examining the small holes arranged on it in no discernible order.

Suddenly, an athletic-looking and very attractive young woman emerged from the living room.

"Mrs. de Mey, I'm sorry to interrupt, but I have the director of UNESCO on the line. She wants to arrange a time for the budget talks," she said, a cordless phone in her hand. She acknowledged the two guests with a nod and waited for an answer from her new boss.

"Not now, Vittoria. Tell her I'll call her back in a little while," she said, and her assistant, vanished back into the living room.

Cloutard was also intrigued. He came up beside Hellen and looked on as Theresia de Mey examined the artifact. He nudged Hellen's shoulder and whispered: "It looks to me as if you have been keeping a rather important detail to yourself."

"Just be happy Ossana didn't get her hands on it," Hellen replied quietly enough that her mother did not hear.

She took the disk from her mother. "We're here because of these markings. When I was a child, if I remember right, papa showed me some scrolls that also had the symbol of the library. At the time he couldn't do anything with them. Whatever they contained led him nowhere, so he hid them away somewhere. Then he disappeared."

"Well, since I'm here, we can look for them together," her mother said, as if she were doing Hellen a huge favor.

Hellen just grinned, shook her head and led the way down to her father's basement office. It was not really a basement. The house was built on a hillside with the main entrance at street level, one floor above the garden level, and the "basement" opened directly onto the back garden. The house was more like an old villa, with three floors and a converted attic. That was where most of her father's documents were stored, but Hellen decided to start down in his office. The walnut-paneled room had bookshelves from floor to ceiling on three walls; the fourth was taken up by two huge glass display cases containing artifacts and *objets d'art* collected from different places and eras: African masks, Egyptian statues, a miniature of Michelangelo's David. More artifacts, large and small, were scattered around the room. In one corner, a few medieval swords and lances protruded from an umbrella stand; a huge, threadbare Persian carpet covered the middle of the room. The old desk was littered with documents, open books, and maps. The room had not changed since Hellen's father had disappeared.

In the midst of all the chaos, Hellen found a photograph of her and her father at the pyramids of Giza. She had been eight years old at the time. Her eyes filled with tears as she held the framed photo in her hands for a moment, recalling the trip they had taken together just before he vanished. But she quickly pulled herself together and replaced the picture on his desk.

"I haven't touched a thing," said Hellen's mother. "Everything is still just as it was the day he disappeared." She was obviously struggling with her own emotions as she moved slowly around the room. Hellen poked half-heartedly through the documents on the desk, but quickly gave up.

"They won't just be lying around somewhere among all this other stuff. It was the most significant find of his life. He would have treated it accordingly and put it somewhere safe."

Cloutard was fascinated by the collection of old writings and books filling the shelves and stacked in piles on the floor.

"All this . . . it's worth a fortune," he mused. But Hellen's mother had heard him.

"No doubt. Museums and collectors have approached me a number of times over the years, trying to get their hands on his collection. But until now I haven't been able to bring myself to part with any of it."

She looked at Cloutard with a certain wariness as he stroked the spines of the books almost tenderly.

"He did not have a safe?" Cloutard asked.

Hellen's mother shook her head. "He never wanted one."

Lost in her own thoughts, Hellen sat down in her father's huge old leather armchair. She turned her head slowly, scanning every inch of the office. *Where did you hide it, Papa? Tell me, where?*

Then, like an epiphany, she knew the answer. The scrolls were not in that room at all. They were on his nightstand.

"Is the Proust still in the bedroom?" Hellen asked, looking eagerly at her mother.

"You mean those old hardcovers your father read over and over?"

"Yes! *Remembrance of Things Past.*"

Hellen ran back up the stairs. Seconds later, she was looking at the German first edition of Proust's monumental work. Her father had had an elegant wooden slipcase specially built to house the seven volumes. Hellen removed the books and turned her attention to the slipcase itself, which was open on one side. *Déjà-vu,* she thought: like the amphora in the Egyptian Museum, it had a false back.

Carrying the empty slipcase, she ran back to her father's study; with the help of a letter opener she was able to pry the back wall forward. On the other side, four sheets of papyrus came to light, which Hellen carefully removed and laid on the desk. Even now that she had the disk, she did not really know what she was supposed to do with it. These papyruses were special: they were four pages of a letter containing both hieroglyphics and a text passage in Latin. They had been written and signed by someone named Ganymedes, but why this Ganymedes had written the letter, or who the intended recipient had been, even her father had never been able to discover.

"My great-grandfather unearthed these papyruses," Hellen explained. "Papa was vague about their true origin, and to tell the truth I think his grandfather may have stolen them."

She tilted the neatly handwritten sheets left and right and held them up to the light. Nothing. Cloutard and Hellen's mother each took one of the pages and did the same, but saw nothing that stood out. They shrugged uncertainly.

Then Hellen noticed something. She took the other pages and peered at them closely.

"Do you have a photocopier?" Hellen asked excitedly, turning to her mother.

"Of course. Up in my office."

Hellen jumped to her feet and ran off with the scrolls, returning two minutes later with copies of the ancient pages. She put the originals aside and worked with the copies as she explained: "On each of the pages, in different places in the text, you can see one quarter of the disk with the symbol. It's very small, see?"

She folded each of the four photocopies so that each quarter of the symbol formed a corner. Then she put the four corners together and, lo and behold, they fit perfectly, forming a miniature disk with the ankh symbol. Hellen quickly taped them together, then took the clay disk and placed it over the document so that the hole in the center was positioned exactly over the ankh.

She turned the disc slowly until the ankh was in the correct position. Like this, one letter appeared in each of the holes in the disk.

Hellen paused. "It truly is the key," she whispered as all three gazed at the holes in the disk. Hellen looked up excitedly at her mother and Cloutard. "And I know where we have to go next!"

31

HOTEL GRAN MELIÁ, NEAR THE VATICAN, ROME, ITALY

"How did we get a papal audience so quickly? How is that even possible?" Cloutard asked Tom. He bit into his biscotti and brushed away a few crumbs caught in the fluff of his bathrobe.

Noah and Hellen were also sitting out on the terrace of the suite and enjoying a lavish breakfast, by Italian standards.

"And why did the Vatican instantly give us this suite?" Noah asked, sweeping his arm wide to take in the breakfast table and the rooftop terrace with its stunning view of the city.

"The Pope likes me, that's all," said Tom. "I messaged him after we dropped the chancellor back in Vienna. He called me back pretty much right away, which was unfortunate, because I was, uh, preoccupied." He cleared his throat. "I was . . . using the bathroom," he said more quietly, but quickly added, "But we worked it out in the end, as you can see," said Tom, as if was the most natural thing in the world.

Cloutard looked at Noah. Noah looked at Hellen. Hellen looked back at Cloutard. And then all three of them looked at Tom in disbelief.

"You cannot be serious," Cloutard said. "Can you?" He was actually a little afraid of what Tom would say, and Tom certainly took his time, letting the suspense build. He fished out his mobile phone and put it on the table so that all of them could see it. He opened the list of recent calls and the display said "Pope Sixtus VI."

"Holy shit! You've got the Pope's private number?" Noah had just choked on a slice of prosciutto. "Not even Mossad has that. How did you even get it?"

"The Pope has a cell phone?" Cloutard mused.

Tom grinned. "When we were down in the catacombs the last time, after Barcelona, and you guys were busy talking shop"—he glanced at Cloutard and Hellen—"the Pope took me aside. He thanked me personally and said I should call him anytime, for anything. If I was in a tight spot or needed spiritual guidance, you know. Since then, we've chatted occasionally on WhatsApp."

Noah, apparently the bravest among them, summoned up the courage to ask: "And . . . uh, you were really on the throne when the Pope called you back?"

Tom was about to reply when all three of them cut him off with waving hands and shaking heads. "Spare us the details, please," Hellen said, speaking for everyone. Silence settled for a second, then they all burst out laughing. For a few moments, they didn't have a care in the world, despite all that had happened in the past few days. Cloutard raised his glass of champagne. "To us! And to Tom, the man the Pope calls in the bathroom."

They took their champagne glasses in their hands and shared a toast. Hellen's smile and her good mood were only feigned, but nobody seemed to notice. She was more on edge than ever, her thoughts first with Arno and then with her father—and the secrets she suspected lay hidden in the library.

An hour later, the disgruntled Camerlengo led them into the Pope's chambers. He looked at Tom reprovingly—his close relationship with the Holy Father clearly rubbed the Camerlengo the wrong way. None of them had expected ever to be here again, and certainly not together. The Pope greeted them warmly.

"May the Lord be with you. I am very glad to see you all again, although I must say the circumstances are still something of a mystery to me." The Pope asked them to sit at the small meeting table, around which five simple chairs were arranged. Seeing that there was no seat left for him, the Camerlengo, still piqued, remained standing. The Holy Father turned inquiringly to Tom. "What is so important that we must speak face to face?"

As if in a team presentation, Hellen and Tom took turns describing to the Pope everything that had happened in the last few days. Noah and Cloutard added what they could, and the Pope's head swung back and forth as if he were watching a tennis match.

"We think AF might be looking for the Library of Alexandria," Tom said. "And the trail has led us here, to you."

The Pope raised his eyebrows and his brow furrowed.

Hellen said, "My father spent his whole life searching for the library. With the disk I found in Egypt, we deciphered a code I found among his papers. The result was the word 'Pontifex Maximus.'"

The Pope nodded. "Pontifex Maximus, yes. It is a title that applies to the head of the Catholic Church, true, but not always. The Roman emperors used to call themselves by the same title," he said.

Hellen nodded. "Either way, the trail leads here," she said.

"And these are the same people who were responsible for the attack last year in Barcelona? They are now looking for the Library of Alexandria?" the Pope asked with a trace of fear in his eyes. He looked intently at Tom, recalling the horror that had taken place just six months earlier.

Tom nodded.

"These people are dangerous. Their power runs very deep." The Pope lowered his eyes.

Tom nodded again.

"We can only guess how far their influence goes," Noah said.

For a while, the Pope said nothing. He stood and went to the window, gazing out at St. Peter's Square below. For a long moment, the room was completely silent. Then, in barely a murmur, the Pope said, "It is here."

No one moved. They all believed they had misheard. Hellen was the first to break the silence. She joined the Holy Father at the window, wanting to be certain that she had understood him correctly.

"You Holiness, what do you mean, 'it is here'?"

The Pope returned to the small table and sat down again.

"Most of the treasures of the Library of Alexandria are here, in the secret archives of the Vatican."

Everyone, including the Camerlengo, drew a sharp breath and their eyes widened. Hellen opened her mouth to say something but could not get a word out. She reached instead for a glass of water and took a large gulp. Her hands were trembling. The Pope waited for a moment before he spoke again.

"When I say the secret archives, I mean the *truly* secret archives. Not the archives you find in films or books, not the ones the researchers can visit any time they want. I am talking about a section of the Vatican archives to which only two people in the world have access: the archivist and the incumbent Pope."

Hellen had recovered her voice. "Your Holiness, the Library of Alexandria is actually here? In the Vatican?"

The Pope nodded. "I don't need to tell you that you have just learned one of the Vatican's greatest secrets, one that we have kept to this day. But I believe it is necessary for you to know this. We have a danger to avert, a threat to the entire world. And I trust that you will preserve this secret of the Church."

Incomprehension marked the faces around him.

"A threat to the entire world?" Cloutard asked. "So AF is not only trying to steal the treasures in the library? They must be worth millions."

"The value of the scrolls is beyond almost anything in this world," the Pope said and Cloutard, almost imperceptibly, raised an eyebrow. When the Pope spoke again, his voice was a whisper: "But I am afraid it is not a question of money. I am afraid they are after the holiest relic of all."

"The holiest relic of all?" Hellen stammered. "What is it?"

"That is something I would like to show you personally." The Pope rose and went to the door. "Let us pay a visit to the Library of Alexandria."

32

47 B.C., ALEXANDRIA HARBOR, EGYPT

Gaius Julius Caesar gazed solemnly at the ships ablaze below. His experience as commander told him that he had won this battle, but the war against the Alexandrians was far from over.

"I bring tidings, Pontifex Maximus."

Caesar turned his attention from the destroyed Alexandrian fleet to the messenger who had just arrived.

"The books, scrolls and papyruses have all been brought to safety. Half our army was engaged in moving the hundreds of thousands of documents onto our ships, as ordered. The library itself now lies in ruins."

Caesar nodded, satisfied.

The messenger continued: "Unfortunately, we have lost many men. The eunuch Ganymedes gave orders for the underground passages that lead to our quarter to be flooded. Many have drowned, and the water supply has been contaminated. It is undrinkable, and some are already suffering from thirst.

Caesar was unmoved. "Have them dig new wells on the edge of the city. We'll find enough drinking water there." He turned to one of the generals standing with him. "Part of the fleet will bring the treasures of the library to safety. They are to set sail for Rome with the tide. The rest of the fleet will assault the Pharos lighthouse and the Heptasta-dion causeway. They are strategically vital to us."

The general hesitated. "Caesar, won't our fleet be severely weakened if half our ships begin the retreat to Rome?"

Without warning, Caesar struck the man across the face with the back of his hand. "This is not a retreat. With the documents from Alexandria, we secure the future of the Roman Empire. All the knowledge of the world was collected here. Now stop wasting time standing around. Go to the men. Launch the attack on the Pharos of Alexandria."

33

ST. PETER'S SQUARE, ROME

Farid had been waiting more than two hours in St. Peter's Square. He had watched Cloutard together with another man, a woman and a man in a wheelchair pass the Swiss Guards and enter the Vatican through the Arco delle Campane, the gate to the left side of St. Peter's Square. Farid had now settled in. He would wait as long as he needed to. He used the time to do a little research, and was surprised at how good Google's image search had become. It wasn't long before Farid knew a little more about at least one of Cloutard's companions: the woman was an archaeologist named Hellen de Mey. He had not been able to find out anything about either of the men, but it was clear to him that this was not just a friendly visit, nor had they come to marvel at the Vatican gardens. Cloutard was here for something big, Farid was sure of it. And he, Farid, would get a piece of it for himself. He would not let Cloutard get away.

Tom was rarely at a loss for words, but when he stepped into the true secret archives of the Vatican, even he was rendered speechless. From the moment the Pope instructed the archivist to take them to the secret archives, no one had spoken a word. Awe mingled with surprise, wonder with disbelief. The archivist had led them to an unremarkable old elevator that plunged into the depths, for what felt like forever. At the bottom, a completely new picture awaited them. Tom was reminded of "Mission Impossible" and similar films as they passed through the security measures, which included retinal and palm scanners, voice recognition, laser sensors and more.

"Impressive," said Noah, eyeing the equipment with respect. It was like running a high-tech gauntlet, until finally a large vault-like titanium door swung open to reveal a white corridor. Hellen inhaled sharply as she realized that she was about to enter the very place her father had spent decades searching for. At first glance, all they could see was a gleaming white corridor, unusually wide and seemingly endless. It looked like the entrance to heaven.

"What is this 'holiest relic'?" Cloutard asked impatiently. He had elbowed his way past the Camerlengo and was now walking directly beside the Holy Father. The archivist led the small group onward, followed by Pope Sixtus VI and Cloutard, then Tom and Hellen with the Camerlengo, with Noah rolling behind them.

The Pope stopped and stepped closer to one section of the wall. It looked seamless, but he swept his hand, Jedi-like, over a particular point, and a display appeared on the wall. He pressed a button and a section of the wall suddenly disappeared, revealing a room filled with high shelves made of some kind of transparent material. The shelves were stacked with thousands of scrolls.

Hellen stepped closer to the wall in a daze, and Noah could not resist the urge to take a few photos with his phone, though he knew he could never show them to anyone.

"The documents in these rooms are perfectly safe," the archivist said, although more to himself. "They are protected against temperature fluctuations, moisture, light, air. Anything that could possibly damage them has to stay outside." He was still surprised to find himself playing museum guide to this motley assortment of unexpected visitors. When they moved on, the wall turned white again, and the display switched off.

Cloutard was smiling. Tom, seeing Cloutard's covetous look, said, "No, François, you can't take any of it with you."

"*Merde*," Cloutard mumbled, looking as if he'd bitten into a lemon. The archivist looked at him with disapproval. He knew this Frenchman's face from somewhere, but he could not pinpoint where.

"Is there an index of the documents?" Hellen asked. "Does the Vatican have an overview of what it has and what they contain?"

"We've had several teams working on them for decades," the Pope replied. "Unaware, of course, that they are examining documents from the Library of Alexandria. Each conservator only works on a single scroll at a time, and does not know its origin. We try to reveal as little as we can. The documents are dated, scanned and digitally stored. Because of their age, however, even unrolling the scrolls is an extremely time-consuming process. Only then do others begin to explore the content."

"But we are far from finished," the archivist added. "So far, we have only managed to record about twelve percent of the collection. It is practically inexhaustible," he concluded proudly.

They had reached the end of the corridor. The archivist now swept his hand over the wall, deactivating the smart glass. This time, however, it was not a room that appeared, but a niche in the wall. Inside it stood a wooden casket about twice the size of an attaché case. The antique piece seemed to exude a strange radiation in this otherwise sterile environment. The Pope nodded to the archivist, who pressed a button on the display. The protective glass slid upward and the base on which the casket was standing glided toward them.

The Pope and the archivist crossed themselves, and the Camerlengo followed suit a moment later. The team stood alongside, breathless with anticipation.

"You all know the story of the Tablets of the Covenant that Moses brought down from Mount Sinai, don't you?" the Pope asked.

"The Ten Commandments, stored in the Ark of the Covenant?" Tom asked.

"Someone's watched *Raiders of the Lost Ark* too many times," Hellen said drily.

"The stone tablets are here?" Cloutard's voice trembled.

The Pope looked at the archivist and smiled.

"No, they are not. They are somewhere else."

Tom was about to say something, but Hellen cut him off: "And no, Tom. They're not in the Ark of the Covenant in a warehouse at Area 51."

Noah and Cloutard shared a smile—Tom and Hellen couldn't resist taking an occasional swipe at one another.

"This casket has never been opened, but it contains the third stone tablet God gave to Moses," the Pope said.

Apart from those of the Pope and the archivist, every eyebrow rose.

"The . . . the *third* stone tablet?" Hellen shook her head in disbelief. She wondered if her father had known about this, and if that was why he had become so obsessed. Cloutard held his breath—he seemed to be calculating the market value of a third tablet.

"Does this mean there are five more commandments that no one knows about?" Tom asked, stifling a grin.

"No. But everyone has heard of the third stone tablet," the Pope said. "Everyone knows it."

Hellen's face paled. She looked at the pope in shock, for she had suddenly realized what the third stone tablet must be.

"Hellen, I think you know what it is, don't you?" the Pope said. "Tell your friends what they are about to see."

All eyes turned to Hellen.

"I am fairly sure that when you say the third stone tablet, you mean the Philosopher's Stone."

Cloutard's eyes narrowed. "The Philosopher's Stone? The one that turns everything to gold?"

"That's the most widespread story about it, certainly, although it isn't strictly true," the archivist quickly said, his face stern. "The function of the Philosopher's Stone is more to *perfect* everything, but—" He stopped short and his expression darkened.

"But . . . ?" Noah pressed.

"It is no accident that the existence of the stone has been kept secret for millennia," the Pope said. "Because perfecting is only one side of the coin."

The archivist, meanwhile, had opened the lock on the wooden casket. He looked one last time at the Holy Father, who nodded. The archivist reverently lifted the lid. Surprise registered on all of their faces. The casket wasn't empty, to be sure, but its contents were not quite what they had expected.

34

A SUITE AT THE HILTON VIENNA PLAZA, VIENNA

The American rolled from side to side, unable to sleep. His mind was churning. Over and over again, he went through the information he had gathered in the last few days. He had to get to Rome as quickly as possible. His flight left in the morning, and he would only discover the name of his Roman contact then.

For now, though, he lay on his back and stared at the ceiling of his sparsely furnished five-star hotel room. Over the years, he had stayed at several Hilton hotels in different parts of the world. This one, however, had a special flair. The furnishings were Art Deco and reminded him of the golden age of the imperial city. Hundreds of genuine masterpieces adorned the walls throughout the hotel, and the Carrara marble floor in the lobby never failed to impress. Immersed in his thoughts, he almost missed the quiet "click" from the living area. A split second later, the American was on the alert— someone had come into his room.

The next moment he mentally cursed himself.

Fuck. My gun's out there, the American thought. It had been a long time since his days as a field agent. He'd grown careless, or maybe he was just getting old. He slid out of bed and tiptoed to the door to the living area, but first arranged two pillows end to end in the bed and covered them with a sheet. A closer look would reveal them for what they were, but the American did not expect the intruder to be equipped with night vision.

The door opened slowly and a pistol with a silencer appeared, pointing at the bed. Five shots punched through the bed, then the gunman changed his aim and fired two more. The American was holding his breath just behind the door. Everything seemed to be moving in slow motion.

If the assassin simply left now, the American would do nothing—and he secretly hoped it would go that way. Close combat was no longer his forte; he wasn't as young as he used to be. But his hopes were disappointed when he heard the assassin's hand groping for the light switch. The American did not hesitate. He slammed the door shut before the man could turn on the light. The door struck the assassin's forearm and the Glock fell to the floor. The American grabbed the intruder's arm and dragged him into the room. He swung a punch at the man's head, but his younger opponent's reflexes were lightning-quick. His fist missed the man's chin. The action and reaction caused them both to lose their balance, and they crashed together through the doorway and onto the floor of the living area.

Both men were quickly back on their feet. The assassin grabbed a heavy candlestick from the table in the living area, while the American armed himself with an unopened complimentary bottle of champagne from the ice bucket on the table. The younger man lunged, brandishing the candlestick like a short sword, and stabbed the older man in his left shoulder. The American cried out as an old shoulder injury, a souvenir of Operation Desert Storm, flared. He gritted his teeth against the pain.

The candlestick came at him a second time, but this time he was ready for it. He parried with the champagne bottle, which shattered the instant it collided with the candlestick. The American had been prepared for this and had closed his eyes, but the assassin got the full charge. Shards of glass and icy champagne sprayed his face. The American moved fast. The bottleneck that the American still held in his hand had become a lethal weapon. His hand shot forward and the broken bottle plunged into the assassin's neck. Both men knew that the fight was over—the glass had severed the assassin's artery. The man fell to the ground, gurgling and holding the wound at his neck. The American got to his feet, took a deep breath and turned on the light, only to recoil at the sight before him. The younger man's despair at his rapidly vanishing life was inscribed on his face. There was a plea in his eyes. The American knew the man, and even now wished that he could help him. But a few moments later the young man's body went limp. He was dead.

They had met not so long ago, but there was no time to think about that now. He reached for his cell phone, entered his authentication code and requested a cleanup. The fact that the Agency kept a crew in Vienna that would clean crime scenes within a few hours was both amazing and fortunate. The American took off his blood-stained clothes, stuffed them into a garbage bag and went to take a shower. After that he packed the rest of his things and left the hotel room, hanging the "Do Not Disturb" sign on the doorknob as he went. He headed for the airport. His flight was leaving in a few hours anyway.

35

THE PAPAL CHAMBERS AT THE VATICAN

"*Madonna mia!*"

The archivist crossed himself. He looked in shock at the Pope, who was struggling to recover from his own surprise. The casket in which the Philosopher's Stone had been stored for centuries contained only part of the original stone. The emerald tablet had been broken. More than half of the recess in which it had lain was empty: two thirds of the stone were gone.

Back at the table in the Pope's chambers, Tom was the first to speak up. "I know the stone is probably worth a fortune, and I don't want to downplay its historical value, but what is the point of the thing? Your Holiness, you said that the whole world might be in danger," he said.

"The myth of the Philosopher's Stone first appeared during the Middle Ages," the Pope said. "But it does not tell the whole story."

Now Hellen spoke up: "My father used to tell me about it. It always seemed to me that the research into the

Philosopher's Stone was just make-believe and delusions."

"That was the intention," said the Pope. "Alchemy was supposed to become the realm of crackpots, so that people would stop looking for the stone."

"I always thought the Philosopher's Stone was a kind of recipe for manufacturing gold," Cloutard said.

"The stone is an emerald tablet on which the formula is written," the Pope explained. "But as I said earlier, the stone does not make gold. It perfects things. It makes worthless things valuable. It makes the sick healthy. It turns old people young again. At its most fundamental, it represents the transformation of the lowly into the exalted, the crude into the refined. In whatever form that might take."

"So the danger is that the stone will make you young, rich and healthy?" Tom said, his words laced with irony.

"I'm afraid not. The stone, like all things in this world, follows the principle of dualism. As with everything else in life, the truth of the stone also has two sides."

Hellen nodded. "Like my father said: The stone heals and destroys, both at the same time. It makes you both poor and rich."

The pope buried his face in his hands. He was clearly shaken. "There is no telling what evil people are capable of if they use the stone."

"If they *use* the stone?" Cloutard asked. "What does that mean?" The Frenchman looked at the pope, genuinely curious.

"Exactly *how* the stone is used is a closely guarded secret. It is not something you need to know," the Holy Father said reverently.

Tom looked doubtfully at the pope. "With all due respect, Your Holiness, this is a little too much hocus-pocus for me. I managed to get my head around that thing with the Sword of Peter last year, but this? The Philosopher's Stone that can make gold and destroy the world?"

He looked from the Pope to his friend Noah, the most rational man he knew. The Mossad-agent-turned-IT-wizard had no time for the supernatural or the occult.

"Sorry to disappoint you, Tom," Noah said. "I used to write off all the conspiracy junk and crazy stuff swirling around the internet as ridiculous, too—the web is full of it, and most of it is just outrageous or stupid. But some of it really is credible. A lot of sources connect the stone to the great catastrophes, diseases, storms and epidemics of history, and much more."

"Noah is right. The stone has been misused often in the past. It has been stolen from the Vatican several times, but has always been returned."

"If Ossana and company are looking for it, then there's probably something to it," Noah went on. "The biblical plagues and the Black Death are just some of the disasters attributed to the Philosopher's Stone."

The Pope nodded his agreement.

"There were also reports about the stone in Count Palffy's secret papers, which were probably Ossana's source," Hellen said now. "Famous people throughout history have tried to decipher the formula: Sir Isaac Newton and Franz Stephan of Lorraine, the husband of Empress Maria Theresa, to name just two. But there was one who was said to have actually used the Philosopher's Stone to attain immortality—the French writer Nicolas Flamel. He was born in 1330, although the stories connecting him to the stone and immortality didn't appear until well after he is supposed to have died. Most people probably don't even associate his name with a real person—at least, not since J. K. Rowling used him in the first Harry Potter book."

Tom was amazed. He was about to raise an objection, but the door opened and a nun came in, pushing a trolley with tea and coffee. Tom recognized Sister Lucrezia immediately.

"*Dio mio*, Signor Tom! What a pleasure to see you again!" The nun embraced Tom for a moment but released him immediately when she saw the Holy Father's reproving look. "What are you doing here? Oh, before you say anything, I must call the others. Sisters Alfonsina, Renata and Bartolomea are also here." She bustled out again before anyone could say a word.

Tom looked at the Pope, who explained: "After the episode in Barcelona, I wanted to express my gratitude to the sisters, to grant them a wish if I could. And I must say I was overjoyed when they all decided that they would like to serve with me here in the Vatican." He smiled, but his face quickly grew serious again. "But let us return to our problem. Wherever the rest of the stone is, AF must not be allowed to get their hands on it." He looked around the group, his somber gaze moving from

Hellen to Noah and Cloutard, before coming to rest on Tom.

"You have to get the missing part of the stone back. It needs to be returned here, to be stored securely. The Vatican and I will be forever in your debt."

"May I be allowed then to explore the library more closely?" Hellen suddenly blurted, realizing as she spoke how out of place her interjection was. Cloutard, too, seemed eager when the Pope promised to put the full support and all the resources of the Holy See at their disposal. Noah, however, looked doubtfully at Tom, and Tom confirmed his doubts.

"We wouldn't know where to begin," said Tom, looking around the rest of the team. "We stumbled into this by pure chance. We have no clue where the stone could be."

"Maybe we can help with that." Sister Lucrezia had just re-entered the Pope's chambers, this time with the other sisters in tow.

The Pope narrowed his eyes at the nuns. "You haven't been eavesdropping at my door again, have you?"

Sister Lucrezia reddened a little, but quickly gathered herself. "I hope, Your Holiness, that you might forgive my moment of weakness, but there is someone who might know more about the whereabouts of the stone."

36

ST. PETER'S SQUARE, ROME

Farid had paced up and down St. Peter's Square countless times in the past few hours. A few minutes earlier, he had spoken on the phone with Armeen. She had sounded more desperate than ever; Shamira's condition had worsened, and the doctors gave her only a few days to live if surgery wasn't performed as soon as possible—an operation for which they had no money. Farid's eyes had filled with tears as he lied to his wife.

"Don't worry. I will have the money we need before long. Everything will be work out. Soon Shamira will be well again."

Armeen knew that Farid was lying, but she also knew he was doing his best, so she said nothing more. Farid's hands were shaking when he hung up. His despair grew, and with it his rage. He had to get the money from Cloutard, whatever the cost. Farid was also anxious to know what the Welshman would ask of him in return for his help in finding Cloutard. Nothing was ever free in these circles. He hadn't yet told Armeen about that, and he would be careful not to. Impatiently, he looked at his watch.

"Where is that damn Frenchman," he grumbled aloud. He looked around immediately, but he was standing far enough away from the tourist groups for anyone to have heard him. His eyes scanned the large square nervously, and then he saw the little group. He was a hundred yards away, but they were unmistakable: the man in the wheelchair, another man, a woman—and Cloutard. Now three nuns had also joined the group. He saw them stop in front of the Arco delle Campane and talk. Farid turned away to avoid Cloutard's eye, but kept glancing back over his shoulder.

The group split up. The nuns and the man in the wheelchair steered in his direction, the man and the woman turned into the Via delle Fornaci, and Cloutard remained where he was, alone and looking a little lost. Farid saw his chance. He fingered the gun in his jacket pocket. His hands were still trembling, and his mouth was dry. He had always hated guns. He had never wanted to become one of those people who achieved their goals by force. His heart was pounding, but he was more determined than ever before in his life. This was for Shamira.

He went after Cloutard, who strolled away toward the road running along the south side of the Vatican, the Via della Stazione Vaticana.

37

A SUITE AT THE ST. REGIS HOTEL,
WASHINGTON D.C.

Ossana Ibori seldom had time for herself, but she didn't attach much importance to it. Her life ran on danger, action, excitement, and adrenaline. She could not understand people who needed time to relax, who were looking for equilibrium in their lives, who wanted to switch off. She loved life at the limit, and she loved having to prove herself every single day. And yes, she also loved the power she had over life and death. She believed firmly in the survival of the fittest, the natural law of eat or be eaten—and she had no intention of being eaten. So moments like this were rare. She lay in the oversized tub in the bathroom of her suite, drinking champagne and listening to music: Georg Philipp Telemann's "Tafelmusik."

She didn't know where the idea had come from, but she had suddenly remembered the piece of music that Jacinto Guerra had always listened to. *Pity about him*, she thought. He had been a good soldier. He had fought valiantly for the cause, and had almost seen their mutual plan through to success in Barcelona. If only that cop, Tom Wagner, hadn't blundered in. Ossana was a stranger to banal feelings like revenge. But one day Tom Wagner would have to pay for Guerra's death. Maybe one day soon: this time she had done the planning, and her plan was fiendishly good. She knew that Wagner would never expect what was coming his way. She smiled, closed her eyes and tipped her head back. She breathed in the scent of the essential oils in the bath salts, and understood for the first time why Guerra had loved this music so much.

The buzz of her cell phone broke the silence. She snatched at the phone, but when she looked at the display her face brightened.

"Isaac!" she called.

A moment later a naked man appeared at the bathroom door and smiled at her.

"Again? Really? You can't get enough, can you."

"Shut up, idiot." She held the phone out for him and he read the message she had just received. "Book a flight, now. I'll take care of the rest. You'll get all the details later."

Isaac Hagen nodded. A few minutes later he reappeared in the bathroom.

"My plane leaves in two hours."

Ossana grinned lecherously. "Looks like we have time for another round after all."

38

1904, EPHESUS, GREECE

Louis de Mey was thrilled. He'd made it: he was part of the Austrian Archaeological Institute's team, taking part in the Ephesus excavation. It didn't matter to him that he was just there to dig and would probably never find anything of any real value. He was going to witness first-hand the reawakening of ancient history. Only a few years had passed since the British archaeologist John Turtle Wood had discovered the Temple of Artemis in Ephesus, and the first remains of the city had already been excavated. Now, the Austrians had been hard at work for several years and had recently been tasked with excavating other parts of the city, including public buildings and private residences. And Louis was there with them. He had been issued his tools the day before and had already made a few friends among the other workers. He was so excited that he couldn't sleep, though he knew he had an early start the next day. But maybe the other workers had a hand in his sleeplessness, too—almost everyone else in his tent was snoring loud enough to wake the dead. Either way, for Louis, sleep was out of the question.

Instead, he went for a walk through the excavation site. The moonlight bathed the dusty mounds, the boulders and pits, in a milky, almost romantic light. Louis felt that he had arrived at the destination of his dreams. Even as a child he had been fascinated by the ancient Greeks, and now he had the opportunity to experience them for himself, up close. He was wandering aimlessly through the camp when he suddenly heard voices. In the largest tent, a light still burned. That was most likely the tent housing the excavation leaders, he thought. He didn't really want to eavesdrop, but his curiosity got the better of him. He crept closer to the tent, crouched by one of the walls and listened.

"Can that really be possible? It seems highly unlikely to me," Louis heard a voice say.

"I know it is difficult to believe, my dear colleague, but let us recapitulate the sequence: Arsinoe was sent into exile by her sister Cleopatra and fled to Ephesus. And perhaps, in the Octagon, we have indeed found her grave," a second voice replied.

"And her eunuch, Ganymedes, was a thorn in Caesar's side during the Alexandrian war. It is certainly possible that Ganymedes was able to spirit parts of the library to safety, and that these then found their way to Ephesus with Arsinoe," added a third.

"Can you imagine what that would mean?" the second voice said. "Can you imagine what would happen if we could tell His Imperial Highness Franz Joseph that we had found the Library of Alexandria far from Egypt, here in the heart of Greece?"

Louis's eyes widened and he almost squealed with excitement, but managed to pull himself together before he actually made a sound. He pressed his hand over his mouth and kept listening.

"It would be a sensation, no doubt about it. But we have to be absolutely certain before we reveal any of this to the public."

"I could not agree more," the second voice said. "So what would you suggest?"

"We keep this between us. It's for the best. We work night shifts, retrieve the documents from the site ourselves, pack them in plain boxes and ship them to Austria as quickly as possible. We can analyze everything there at our leisure and consider our next steps."

Louis could hardly believe his ears. Had they really found documents from the Library of Alexandria here? He needed to know more. Gone from his mind was the excavation. He didn't know how he would accomplish it, but he had to get to Vienna and find out more about this discovery.

39

CLOSE TO ST. PETER'S SQUARE, ROME

"Hellen, give me a minute to explain what happened in Cairo. Please."

After they had left the Vatican, Tom had managed to persuade Hellen to talk in private.

Hellen looked at Tom in a way he could not put into words; rejection and disillusionment were etched on her face. She sighed. She had heard Tom explain his way out of things too many times. She was starting to tire of his justifications.

"I don't know what it's supposed to change, but go ahead. Explain to me why you killed my boyfriend. Explain to me why you solved yet another problem with a gun and not like a normal, civilized human being."

Hellen's voice was icy. The hot wind that swept the streets of Rome did nothing to lessen the chill that had settled over Tom and Hellen, colder than ever before. They had never been as distant from each other as they were now; not even when she had told him in Vienna, after the

Florentine diamond affair, that she was going to take the job she'd been offered at UNESCO—and in doing so, deprived their relationship of any hope of a future. Tom decided not to try to match her cynicism. That was a game he could only lose. For the first time, he found himself speaking to Hellen with a clear mind, instead of launching himself headfirst into an argument. Instead, he focused on the facts.

"We searched the museum for the room where the amphoras were being kept. We had no idea you or your friend would be there."

He knew he was not telling the complete truth; he and Cloutard had actually seen them enter the museum. But, erring on the side of caution, Tom decided to leave that detail out for now.

"And?" Hellen said, annoyed. She had turned away, and was looking absently into the display windows outside the Teatro Ghione. She wouldn't, or couldn't, look him in the eye.

"We came around a corner and ran practically head first into that guy. Arno, I mean. He had a gun in his hand and he shot at me without warning. Cloutard just managed to push me clear of the line of fire. Then we were both facing each other with guns drawn, but he didn't listen to my warnings. I pulled the trigger before he fired a second time."

Hellen suddenly stopped. For the first time since Arno's death, one thing suddenly stood out: she had completely ignored the question of where Arno had gotten the gun. Everything had happened so fast, and emotions and events had been tumbling over each other: Noah's liberation, the library in the Vatican, the memories of her father.

"Arno really did fire first?"

"Yes. I've been trying to tell you that the whole time."

Normally, Tom would have had more to say at this point. *You never listen to me*, for instance. But he bit his tongue and swallowed the words. He knew exactly what Hellen looked like when she was thinking. And right now, her gray cells were definitely working overtime.

"This is too much right now. I have to think it all through. Let's forget about it for now."

Tom was amazed. He was just starting to think "that was easy" when Hellen's index finger shot up. "That doesn't mean we're done with this," she snapped. "I loved that man. But, clearly, there are still questions to be answered."

Tom's phone pinged. He looked at the display and raised his eyebrows in surprise.

"Let me guess," said Hellen. "Noah's organized a flight for us to Salzburg."

"Yes and no. The Pope has given us one of the Vatican's private jets."

40

CLOSE TO THE VATICAN, ROME

Cloutard had already walked some distance along the Via della Stazione Vaticana, following the walls of the Vatican. He loved the Eternal City. Business had often brought him here in the past, and he had even negotiated a very lucrative deal or two with the Vatican itself. He smiled bitterly when he thought back to those times, but after the dry spell of the last few months, he was starting to feel strong again. If he did not manage to turn the present situation to his own advantage somehow, he thought, then he must truly be dealing with the devil.

"*Vous n'êtes pas un idiot, bon sang!*" he murmured to himself. "You're not an idiot, damn it!"

He paused. He had reached the dead end and now turned left onto the steps that led down to Via Aurelia. He had only descended a short way when he heard footsteps behind him, and a second later, felt the barrel of a pistol at his neck.

"François, the clock is ticking. I have heard nothing from you for 48 hours. I don't want to wait for my money any longer."

Farid surprised even himself. He actually sounded angry and threatening. He circled Cloutard until they were standing face to face, but he kept the pistol pointed at Cloutard's head.

"Farid, I need a little more time. A few more days. But it really will be worth your while," Cloutard said, trying to pacify him.

"We . . . I don't have a few more days," Farid bellowed, suddenly beside himself. His voice echoed threateningly from the walls of the stairway.

"We?" Cloutard asked in surprise. "Who is 'we'?"

"This isn't about me. My daughter is . . . is dying, and we need the money for her surgery. But that is none of your business. You were at the Vatican just now. I want to know what you were doing there. Whatever your business was, I hope it will bring you enough money, because I want *my* money not in a few days, not one day, but tomorrow, as agreed. Tomorrow!"

Farid took a step toward Cloutard and pressed the gun beneath his chin.

"*Calme-toi!* I'll tell you everything," Cloutard said breathlessly. Farid stepped back again, but kept Cloutard in his sights. An old woman, walking with her grandchildren and scolding them loudly in Italian, came down the stairs just then. She looked at the two men and the pistol and kept walking past as if it were the most day-to-day sight in the world. The two children made finger-pistols and shouted "bang, bang!" play-shooting at each other as they ran down the stairs. Seconds later, Farid and Cloutard were alone again, still staring at each other.

"I suspect you won't believe a word of what I'm about to tell you," Cloutard said.

"Try me. Speak!" Farid snarled.

Cloutard straightened up, adjusted his hat, took a breath and tried to sound as credible as he could.

"We went to see the Pope, because the Library of Alexandria is hidden in the Vatican. One part of this library contains the Philosopher's Stone. You know, that thing that can turn anything into gold. The problem is that part of the stone is missing and now the Pope has given us the task of retrieving it."

Cloutard, abashed, cleared his throat and looked at Farid, whose expression hadn't changed.

"Oh, well, if that's all it is. Why didn't you say so right away?" Farid said calmly.

Cloutard raised in eyebrows in surprise. A heartbeat later, Farid jumped at him and pressed the gun even harder between his eyes.

"Are you fucking kidding me, you ridiculous frog? You think I'm stupid enough to swallow a story like that?"

Cloutard threw his hands in the air, his eyes clenched shut in fright as he cried, "Wait! Wait! I can prove it!"

Farid seemed unimpressed. The barrel of the pistol still bored into Cloutard's forehead. "I'm curious to know how you're going to do that," he said. His voice had turned merciless.

"My phone is in my left jacket pocket. Take it out."

Farid removed Cloutard's phone from his pocket and handed it to him. "Show me your proof."

"I knew that no one would believe me. No one really believes in this hocus-pocus. Except for the Pope, he obviously does."

Cloutard opened his phone and found the video he was looking for.

"Look at the video. I took this a few minutes ago in the Pope's chambers. I promise you that you will get your share, more money than you ever dared to dream of."

Cloutard pressed the play button and held the phone for Farid to see, but it only made him angrier.

"You can't see a damn thing here. Is this really supposed to change my mind? All the Catholic Church has ever done is lie, cheat and kill." Farid was spitting with anger. "I'm giving you one extra day, no more. If you don't have my money 48 hours from now, you're a dead man. Don't underestimate me."

41

NONNBERG ABBEY, SALZBURG, AUSTRIA

Nonnberg Abbey was the oldest continuously used Christian convent in the world. It had been built atop the Nonnberg, a small hill situated just below and to the northeast of the larger hill known as the Festungsberg, close to the heart of Salzburg.

"The entire Nonnberg Abbey complex, including all its walls and archaeological finds, is a listed as a UNESCO World Heritage Site, along with everything else in the historical center of the city," said Hellen as they followed the winding path upward.

The four nuns led the way in single file, as they marched up the hill. Sister Lucrezia, the Mother Superior, led the way. Behind her, like organ pipes arranged in order of size, came Sister Alfonsina, Sister Renata and Sister Bartolomea. They were an odd-looking quartet, with Sister Alfonsina, at six foot three, looming over the others and Sister Bartolomea not even five feet tall. Sister Renata, like the Mother Superior, was somewhere in between.

"The convent also houses an important collection of medieval manuscripts, Gothic sculpture and paintings. The late-Gothic winged altarpieces are particularly impressive," said the Mother Superior.

"The ivory pastoral, the staff used by the abbess from 1242, is also extremely valuable," Hellen added.

"Then it's probably good that François didn't come. He probably could have put it to good use," Tom quipped.

The four nuns, appalled at the very idea, frowned at Tom, but nodded. All four had already had a taste of terror and violence during their last adventure with Tom, but theft—to say nothing of murder—still seemed preposterous to them.

"Let us drop that topic for now, Signor Tom," said Sister Lucrezia sternly. "We are on holy ground."

"And how do we find this sister who's supposed to be able to help us?" Tom asked as a group of ten nuns passed by in the other direction.

Sister Lucrezia said nothing, and Tom could tell that she was avoiding something. The other three nuns began to whisper. Tom stopped and looked ahead at Lucrezia.

"Is there a problem?" he asked.

Sister Lucrezia stopped but still said nothing, so Alfonsina, the tallest of the nuns, screwed up her courage and said, "The abbess, Sister Agnes, is not very fond of Sister Lucrezia."

Sister Lucrezia frowned. Tom looked at Hellen in surprise and she shrugged. Finally, Sister Lucrezia took a deep breath and hesitantly said, "Sister Agnes is the worst cook in the world."

Tom had to swallow hard to stop himself from laughing out loud. "Excuse me?" he managed to say.

"Many years ago, we worked together in the kitchen. From time to time we had . . . differences of opinion."

Bartolomea could no longer contain herself. "Differences of opinion? You threw pots of spaghetti at each other!"

Now Tom and Hellen could not hold back their laughter. The three younger nuns joined in, and a smile slowly appeared even on Sister Lucrezia's face. "Maybe she's forgotten about it," she said meekly, but no one was willing to believe her.

"Another thing," Tom said. "Just to make sure I've understood everything correctly. How exactly can this Sister Simonetta help us?"

"Sister Simonetta worked for the archivists of the Vatican for decades," Sister Lucrezia said. "She had, I think, just turned eighteen when she began her service there. Among us women of the cloth, she is known for one thing: she always knew every little thing that went on in the Holy City."

"To put it another way, she's an incurable gossip," Renata said, saying aloud what the others were thinking.

"She used to tell us all about all kinds of things—about the treasures down in the secret archives, stuff like that. It was always a mystery to us how she knew so much. She must have been very close to the archivists," said Alfonsina, her face a study in innocence.

Tom grinned crookedly and raised his eyebrows. "How close, exactly?" he asked, earning himself an irate glare from Sister Lucrezia, while Hellen elbowed him in the ribs. A nun approached their group, interrupting the conversation. After exchanging a few pleasantries, the newcomer led the way to the abbess. The door to Sister Agnes's small office opened and the abbess's welcoming smile froze to ice when she saw Lucrezia.

"We are here in the service of the Holy Father," said Sister Lucrezia. She stepped forward to the abbess and handed her the Pope's letter.

Sister Agnes crossed herself when she saw the seal of the Holy See. She began to read, but kept looking up at Lucrezia with disapproval.

"This is highly unorthodox," she said dourly. "Our abbey is not open to the public. One cannot simply walk in and start interrogating our nuns, especially not someone as special as Sister Simonetta. She is about to celebrate her 99th birthday and it is our duty to protect her from any kind of excitement. Her heart is very weak. Besides, someone from the Vatican is already here to visit her."

Tom's eyes narrowed. Hellen and the nuns shared a look of surprise.

"Who?" Tom asked.

"We received a call came this morning from the Vatican to say that we were to expect a certain Tom Wagner, coming on behalf of the Pope. When he arrived, we took him to see Sister Simonetta right away."

"I'm Tom Wagner," said Tom. The nuns nodded diligently behind him.

The abbess looked at Tom in confusion. "Then who is in St. John's Chapel with Sister Simonetta?"

42

W.A. MOZART AIRPORT, SALZBURG,
GERMANY

"*Très bien.*"

Cloutard swirled the fine glass he held and gazed at the amber liquid inside.

"It's not Louis XIII, but it's not bad. These church leaders know how to live." He recalled his old life, when he was still travelling the world aboard his luxury private jet. The leather armchair he sat in was as big as a couch, and the mini-bar—hardly mini at all—was stocked with top-shelf liquor. He took another sip and turned to Noah.

"You are such a snob!" Noah said and smiled at him.

"I really can't pour you a glass?"

"No thank you. I need to keep my head clear."

"Come on, Noah. Loosen up a little. You just survived a kidnapping and have now discovered that ancient, absurd myths, things that no one in their right mind would believe, are actually true. Tom and Hellen will be gone for a few hours, and while I am sure they have no time for sightseeing in Salzburg, they will certainly find enough to relax just a little."

Cloutard refilled his own glass and then poured some more cognac into a second, which he handed to Noah. "Here. No arguments." Noah tentatively took the glass. "To us! And to the success of our holy mission." Cloutard raised his glass, prompting Noah to do the same.

"So what is it actually like to lose all your power overnight?" Noah asked, a touch too directly.

Puzzled by the tone of the question, Cloutard replied, "I admit it hasn't been easy, but I get by. I still have my father's estate in Tuscany, and my foster mother still lives there. And it is true, I don't have my millions anymore and even less power, but I am much more relaxed than I used to be. I sleep much better," he lied. He flashed a smile and took another sip of cognac. "How have things been for you since the last time we met?"

"When Tom left the Cobras I went back to Mossad, but I didn't exactly get the warm welcome I'd hoped for. In my situation"—he indicated the wheelchair, and for a brief moment his bitterness shone through—"things were not as easy in Israel as they had been in Vienna. A few months later, I got an offer I couldn't refuse. I was contacted by—" Noah stopped speaking when Cloutard's cell phone rang.

Cloutard's face clouded over as he looked at the display. "Excuse me for a moment," he said. He stood up and stepped out of the plane, waiting till he was outside to accept the call. Noah looked out the window of the luxury jet and saw him pacing back and forth out on the tarmac. Something was wrong.

"What do you want now? I thought I had 48 hours," Cloutard hissed into his phone.

"You do. I just wanted to remind you how serious I am about this, so I've come up with another incentive for you. It should not be only my daughter's life at stake. I will call you again." The line went dead. Cloutard stared at his phone in confusion.

Noah, watching through a window of the plane, wondered: *What's going on with Cloutard?*

43

NONNBERG ABBEY, SALZBURG

Tom raced outside. The moment he charged into St. John's Chapel, he saw him: Hagen had his hands wrapped around the old nun's throat, but he released her when he saw Tom. A second later, he had pulled his gun and was firing at Tom, who threw himself behind a pew for cover. Hagen took advantage of the moment and ran, sprinting out of the chapel to the west exit of the courtyard.

Tom did not hesitate for a second, but took off in pursuit. Hagen took a left and ran down a narrow alley. Tom could already see where he was going, and saw instantly that if he didn't come up with something fast, Hagen would slip through his fingers: he was racing for a motorcycle parked in the alley near the monastery wall.

Hagen swung himself onto the seat of the black MV Agusta Brutale 800 and Tom pulled out all the stops, hoping to reach him before he got the motorcycle started. But Hagen pressed the start button, and the engine sprang to life. He kicked it into gear and accelerated away, Tom no more than a step behind, but not close enough to grab him. The rear tire smoked as Hagen opened the throttle and roared down Nonnberggasse, on the south side of the monastery—but Tom wasn't about to give up. He kept after him. A car was driving up the hill just then, and the roadway was so narrow that even Hagen had to brake and squeeze the motorcycle past the car. Tom was catching up. His lungs and thighs were burning and he realized that he was a little out of shape. *Damn, all that grunt work with Cobra had a point after all*, he thought, as he gained ground on Hagen. Then Hagen was past the car and speeding away again.

Suddenly, farther down, another vehicle appeared, and Tom smiled: now he had a real chance. Hagen was just riding past another motorcycle coming up the hill. He'd practiced the move a hundred times with Cobra: how to get a man off a motorcycle without harming either yourself or the rider. Tom stepped into the path of the rider, who braked hard. Tom jumped to the side, grabbed the handlebars and used his momentum to shove the surprised rider off the saddle. The man fell to the ground, swearing but unhurt. Tom swung himself onto the bike and opened the throttle. With the rear wheel spinning and the front brake clenched, he spun the machine 180 degrees. When he let go of the brake, the tire found its grip, and the bike took off with the front wheel rising. Tom was back in the game. He took up the chase, remembering all too clearly that he'd been on this guy's heels once before, in Amsterdam. This time around, he had to do better.

44

OFFICE OF THE PREFECT OF THE CONGREGATION FOR THE DOCTRINE OF THE FAITH, VATICAN

For many years, he had known that the arms of the CIA reached very far indeed. With each mission he'd been assigned over the decades, it had become increasingly clear to him. But he was still amazed to discover that their influence reached deep inside the Vatican, and that several CIA agents were embedded there. Cardinal Edmondo Baresi, the militant Jesuit and Cardinal Prefect of the Congregation for the Doctrine of the Faith was one of them. When the American discovered this, he had to laugh: as an organization, the Congregation for the Doctrine of the Faith had succeeded the Holy Inquisition. It was the same Catholic organization that had ordered witches, heretics and traitors to the faith to be burned at the stake—and today it was headed by a CIA agent.

Divine providence, the American thought to himself as he waited in the cardinal's anteroom.

"The cardinal will see you now," said the nun in a timid whisper. Baresi was already waiting at the threshold and hastily closed the door behind him.

"What on earth has happened to make you contact me directly?" Cardinal Baresi sounded almost frantic. "I've been with the Agency for almost forty years, and no one's ever contacted me so—"

"It's about the stone," the American said, cutting the cardinal off harshly.

Baresi looked at him in amazement. "*The* stone?"

"Yes, *the* stone. It is in danger. A terrorist organization largely unknown to us is after it, and they seem to be making headway."

"What kind of terrorist organization? I thought you had ISIS and company under control."

"It's not the Islamists. They call themselves Absolute Freedom. We don't know much, but we do know that whoever's behind them is from the West. Remember last year? The stolen Crown of Thorns? The Holy Lance? The burning of Notre Dame? That was them. But let's not waste time. The president himself has ordered me to get the stone to safety."

"It's in the secret archives. There isn't a safer place in the world. It is out of the question that we would let the stone be taken from here. His Holiness would never allow it."

"His Holiness doesn't need to know anything about it. This is how it's going to work: you get me into the archive as quickly as possible. I take the stone for safekeeping and get it back to the States. We have places to keep such things, as you know. It wouldn't be the first time." The American looked the cardinal in the eye, leaving no doubt about how serious he was. The gaunt cardinal paled, looking even sicklier and more emaciated than usual.

"That is absolutely impossible. I wouldn't even know where to begin." His voice trembled with indignation.

The American brought the flat of his hand down hard on the table, and the cardinal, startled, sprang to his feet.

"Then I suggest you figure out where to begin, fast!" the American snarled. "I don't think I need to point out to Your Eminence what the agency has on you. The two affairs and the children you have from them are the least of your problems."

Baresi snorted, his nostrils twitching. No one had dared to talk to him like that, not for decades. But he knew he was beaten.

"All right," he said. "We'll pay a visit to the archivist. He owes me a favor, but I can't promise it will be enough."

The American smiled. "If it isn't, we have a file on him, too. I'm always happy to help."

The two men were about to leave the cardinal's office and go to the Vatican Apostolic Archive when the door swung open. Two Swiss guardsmen rushed in.

"Your Eminence, we are here for your protection. Terrorists just broke into the archive. We don't yet know how many there were, how they managed to get in, or what they were after. For your own safety, we must insist that you do not leave your office until we have the situation under control."

The American glared at the cardinal. "So there isn't a safer place in the world than the secret archive?"

45

OLD SALZBURG

Tom pursued Hagen at a hellish pace down the narrow Festungsgasse, the ancient cobblestones rattling the motorcycles. On Tom's left were the houses on the northern slope of the Hohensalzburg Fortress, on the right the wall from which one could look down into the winding streets of the old city. Right now, thankfully, only a few people were walking, and they jumped clear as the two men roared down the narrow, twisting street. Hagen steered toward the historic city center.

Tom knew Salzburg well, and knew that every season hordes of tourists thronged the city. He imagined the worst and tried to go faster, but the machine was already at its limit, the throttle wide open. Hagen crossed the spacious Kapitelplatz diagonally, flying past the famous golden ball at the center of the courtyard, and headed for the narrow street known as Kapitelgasse. Tom was able to cut the corner, and gained some ground. Hagen turned back for a moment, pulling a pistol from his jacket pocket, and fired two shots back at Tom as they raced toward the busy Mozartplatz. Tom swung his motorcycle to the right, onto the sidewalk. He swerved around a sidewalk café with parasols, managing to dodge the waiter just then serving sweet *Salzburger Nockerl* souffleés to a curious group of Japanese tourists.

"*Guten Appetit!*" Tom called in passing, waving an apology for the disturbance.

Hagen was facing front again. The crowds filling the Residenzplatz demanded his full attention. People scattered in all directions as he roared through. So far, no one had come to harm: the center of Salzburg was a pedestrian zone, and the howl of their engines could be heard from several streets away—which also meant that the Salzburg police were soon alerted. Tom raced past a patrolman in the direction of Salzburg's city hall. They had entered the luxury quarter now, where high-end jewelers vied with designer stores and expensive restaurants to draw the attention of moneyed tourists.

"I need backup!" Tom shouted at the cop as he sped past the legendary Café Tomaselli, his slipstream knocking over the umbrellas in front of the door. "I'm a Cobra officer!"

That was no longer true, of course, but it would definitely get the cop's attention. In the meantime, Hagen had turned off into the narrow Getreidegasse, and had to slow again. The pedestrian zone was packed with tourists heading for the house where Mozart had been born. Hagen took out his pistol again and fired twice in the air. Tom was keeping count—he had to know how many shots Hagen still had.

The crowds scattered in fear as Hagen sped through the tight passageway heading for Wiener-Philharmoniker-Gasse. In the narrow alley, they had to cut their speed considerably. Tom had caught up and they now rode side by side, inches apart. Without warning, Hagen nudged his motorcycle a fraction to the left and sent Tom scraping along the wall, forcing him to brake to avoid hitting anything attached to the wall—that could prove fatal. But try as he might, Tom was unable to hold his course. The motorcycle slewed and slipped from under him. He skidded along the ground with it, and was lucky to stop before he crashed into the crowd at the end of the alley.

He jumped to his feet, hauled the bike upright and looked ahead at the disappearing Hagen. He smiled. Hagen had clearly never spent much time in Salzburg, because he had no idea where he was going. In that direction he would never be able to pick up speed: the streets were too narrow, there were too many people and there was no room to accelerate properly. This was Tom's chance. He turned right in front of the Collegiate Church and shot across University Square. He would catch up with Hagen again at the next intersection. Hagen was headed for the Great Festival Hall, and from there he could only go one way: toward Sigmundstor, the tunnel that cut through the Mönchsberg, one of Salzburg's five mountains. Tom's route was shorter. He would be able to intercept Hagen when he turned toward Herbert-von-Karajan-Platz.

46

ST. JOHN'S CHAPEL, NONNBERG ABBEY

Hellen held the dying woman in her arms and called desperately for help. Seconds later, the first nuns appeared in the chapel. They threw their hands up in mortification, but two tended immediately to Sister Simonetta while the others went for help.

"My . . . my . . ." whispered the old woman. Her voice was no more than a breath. Hellen leaned close to hear her final words.

". . . diary . . . May twenty-fourth, 1942."

The abbess entered the chapel, and two nuns with medical training knelt by Sister Simonetta to administer first aid. After a few moments, though, one of them shook her head and crossed herself. They were too late. A deathly silence suddenly filled the chapel, and the nuns gazed at their deceased sister. Almost in unison, each of them took her rosary, crossed herself and began to pray. "Hail Mary, full of grace . . ."

Hellen knew there was nothing more she could do. If

Sister Simonetta's diary contained important information, she at least had to make sure it was safe. What if Hagen had not come alone? She had to find the diary. It was her only chance to learn where the stone had been taken. Sister Simonetta must have revealed something important to Hagen, or he would have had no reason to kill her. Hellen hoped she would find the same clue in Sister Simonetta's diary. She jumped up, laid her hand on the praying abbess's shoulder and softly asked where she could find Sister Simonetta's room. Seconds later, Hellen was running to the nuns' quarters. Sister Simonetta's chamber was on the ground floor near the entrance, so she did not have far to go. Hellen found the room and opened the door.

47

OLD SALZBURG

Hagen shot past the Felsenreitschule theater. He had lost sight of Tom, and briefly slowed down to get his bearings. There was only one way out. He gunned the motor again and headed for the intersection, but at the last moment he saw Tom racing at him from the right. He braked hard, swinging the bike around, and opened the throttle, plunging back into the line of traffic passing through Sigmundstor tunnel. It was a two-way tunnel, but its ends were barely wide enough for two cars to pass each other, so oncoming traffic was constantly forced to stop. Hagen had to risk it: he slalomed between the cars on his side of the road and the oncoming traffic. Tom did not hesitate at all, but stayed hard on Hagen's tail. They scraped car doors and clipped side mirrors, but were out of the tunnel again seconds later.

"Fuck!" Tom swore. That had been his best chance to catch Hagen, and he'd blown it. The crazy Englishman had really gone for the zigzag course, and Tom's shortcut had done him no good.

Things were harder now that they had left the old town. The streets were wider, and there were fewer pedestrians and more opportunities to accelerate. That's where Hagen's powerful MV Agusta had the edge, as Tom had already noticed at the start of the chase. He had to hold on and hope that Hagen got lost again. Suddenly, he heard police sirens. *About damn time*, he thought.

Hagen roared north and Tom knew he would soon reach the Salzach River, where the traffic would be heavier again. Hagen made another wrong decision. Instead of turning left at the river and heading out of the city, he turned right and rode along Kaipromenade, the riverside esplanade. But Tom rejoiced too soon: Hagen had the pistol in his hand again. He turned and squeezed off another shot at Tom, and Tom was again forced to slow down and take evasive action. He swerved onto the grassy embankment, running the risk of going straight down it into the river. At the same time, he was doing his best not to run down the pedestrians strolling in along the promenade. Hagen had fired his last bullet. He threw the pistol away and reached into his jacket again and, although he could not see exactly what Hagen was up to, Tom was already reckoning with a second weapon. Hagen made another risky move, swinging left onto the Müllner Steg, a pedestrian bridge over the Salzach River, where a few pedestrians had to jump the rail into the river to avoid getting run down. In front of them now lay the Mirabell Palace, its park full of visitors. Hagen plowed straight across the gardens, and Tom, who had made up some ground, followed, though not without a guilty conscience. The artfully designed flower beds, hedges trimmed to the millimeter and lawns as neat as an

English golf course were transformed into something like a turnip field as they tore through.

Police sirens were wailing from all sides now; it was only a matter of time before they would intercept Hagen. He had no escape. Tom saw that a roadblock had already been set up on Franz-Josef-Kai, the boulevard along the far bank of the Salzach. All Tom had to do was force Hagen back over Salzburg's second pedestrian bridge, the Makartsteg, to the other side. Tom dug in, squeezing every last ounce of horsepower out of his machine, and cut Hagen off at Herbert von Karajan's birthplace, driving him onto the bridge. Hagen was trapped. With a squeal of smoking tires, Hagen skidded to a halt in the middle of the bridge. Tom, thinking that Hagen might have another gun, pulled to a stop on his end of the bridge. But Hagen calmly put down the kickstand of the MV Agusta and dismounted. He stepped over to the side, and Tom—too late—realized what was happening. Hagen was over the railing in a second and jumped into the river, just as a boat passed by beneath. In seconds, Hagen was pulled on board. Police cars now sealed both ends of the bridge, but it wasn't Hagen who was trapped. It was Tom.

By the time he explained everything to the cops, Hagen was long gone.

48

SISTER SIMONETTA'S CHAMBER, NONNBERG ABBEY

Hellen could see at once that the room had not been touched. No one had been there, and it clearly hadn't been ransacked. Hellen quickly found what she was looking for in the modestly furnished room: a large pile of diaries in the bedside cabinet. She flipped through them as quickly as she could, but it took some time before she found the date the dying nun had whispered in her ear.

May 24th, 1942

I have been in the Holy City for one month and I am getting used to everything now. At the moment, I mostly help in the kitchen. The big city still scares me, but with God's help I will pass this test. I miss my Val Gardena, my mountains and all the animals. Of course, I am eternally grateful to Reverend Matteo in Santa Cristina for giving me the opportunity to serve in Rome and to dedicate my life to the Savior here.

Today after Holy Mass, there was an accident in the kitchen.

Sister Angelica cut her hand with a knife and had to be treated, but it happened right when it was time for the prefect to take his tea. The prefect is a strict man and we are all scared to death of him, even Sister Angelica, who takes him his tea every day. Because of her injury, I offered to take the tea to him in her place, and I picked up the tray and carried it upstairs to the prefect. Outside his office, I put the tray on a low cupboard next to the door. I knocked, waited a few seconds and then opened the door.

The prefect recognized me and waved me in to serve the tea. There were two other men in the room, and they all looked a little alike. I think the other two were probably the prefect's brothers. The three men kept on talking, but they changed from Italian to Latin because they thought I would not understand a word of it. As children back at home, however, Father Matteo had taught us a little Latin every week in Sunday school. He wanted us to understand what the priests said at Mass, so I understood some of what the men were talking about. There is one thing especially that I recall. The prefect instructed the other two men to bring their stones to safety. Where the one man was to take his stone, I forget. He used a strange word that was unknown to me. But with the second man, I am certain there was talk of a large museum in America, something with "Smith." One man said he knew the director of the museum from his student days in Florence and that the stone would be safe there. I have no idea what they were talking about, but I could tell it was something very important, because they all three watched me so suspiciously.

Hellen skimmed over the rest of the diary entry but found nothing else of interest. So the stone had been broken into three pieces. It made sense, of course. And she knew now where they had to go from here. A second later she caught herself worrying about Tom. She wondered if he was all right, if he had caught Hagen. When she left the nuns' quarters and returned to the convent garden, she saw Tom climbing out of a police car. The look on his face spoke volumes. Hagen had gotten away again.

49

W.A. MOZART AIRPORT, SALZBURG

"I'm sick to death of that guy. Who does he think he is, Valentino Rossi?"

Tom was beside himself as he climbed the few steps up into the luxurious cabin of the private jet. Noah and Cloutard, engrossed in a game of chess, only looked up as he entered. They had heard him coming long before he actually boarded the plane.

"Let me guess: someone gave him the slip," Noah said, regretting it the moment he saw Hellen appear behind Tom, shaking her head and waving her hands.

"What happened? Tell us," Noah said.

"We were almost too late," Hellen explained because Tom was too worked up to talk sensibly. "Isaac Hagen got there before us and we caught him strangling Sister Simonetta. Tom went after Hagen. We did what we could for the sister, but it wasn't enough. Her heart gave out. But with her dying breath the poor woman gave me a clue. We're headed for Washington D.C."

"Hagen? *Mon Dieu*," said Cloutard. Tom prowled back and forth through the cabin. He was furious.

"Yes, Hagen! How did AF even know about the nun? Is there a leak in the Vatican? Is that it? Maybe the Camerlengo? He looked like he was pissed off the whole time we were there, right? Or maybe the old archivist?"

Tom looked around but saw only surprised, incredulous faces. Had he really just charged the upper echelons of the Catholic Church with having connections to AF?

"I would not go so far," Cloutard said.

"Anything's possible," said Noah.

"Tom, please, calm down," Hellen soothed. "Let me have a look at you first."

She wanted to check him over, see if he needed patching up—he'd taken a fall with the motorcycle, after all, and he would at least have some scrapes and bruises. Tom pushed her away.

"I'm fine. Thanks."

Hellen lifted her hands and turned away. "Okay, okay, okay! But I'm wouldn't accuse the Camerlengo of being an AF sleeper agent," she said, shaking her head.

"Come and sit, *mon ami*. Have a drink." Cloutard quickly filled a glass handed it to Tom. Cognac was Cloutard's panacea, and he had just taken a dose to dull his own concerns, at least for a little while.

Tom sat, picked up the glass without thinking and lifted it to his lips. He paused only when he sniffed the contents.

"Not now, François. I need a clear head," he said, and put the glass down again.

"I for one could certainly believe it," said Noah. "About the Camerlengo, I mean." He moved one of his chess pieces. "At Mossad we saw plenty of evidence that the Vatican had leaks, pointing in every direction."

Tom was back on his feet. He stalked over to the bar and poured whiskey into a tumbler, then drained it in one gulp. He put the glass aside and went back to his restless pacing.

"Very consistent," Cloutard murmured with a smirk.

"But it's weird, right?" Tom said. "We show up at the Vatican and Sister Lucrezia, in the presence of the Pope and the Camerlengo, tells us about an old nun. And a day later Hagen shows up right here. That's strange, isn't it?"

The others nodded thoughtfully.

"There is much that I would believe of the Catholics, Tom, but even I would not go that far," said Cloutard, deep in thought, gazing at the chessboard. His queen was in danger.

"But if the leak isn't in the Vatican, then they've bugged us," said Noah, looking around.

Tom took out his iPhone. He held it up with two fingers and spoke in its general direction. "Calling Ossana. Come in, Ossana," he said, and everyone laughed.

"It's not the phones," Noah said. "That was the first thing I did when we flew to Rome. Your phones are all bug-proof."

"I know, I know," Tom said, and he clapped Noah on the shoulder as he returned to the bar. A silence settled over the small assembly. Cloutard sipped his cognac and looked out the window, lost in thought. Noah glanced at him with a look of slight distrust. Hellen, sitting in one of the large leather chairs, pulled her legs up and clasped both arms around them, her head resting on her knees. Tom had refilled his whiskey. For a minute or two, no one said a word. Abruptly, Hellen, Cloutard and Tom all looked at each other, then all three turned to Noah—all had had the same alarming thought.

"Checkmate!" Noah cried, happy to beat Cloutard for once. He looked up from the chessboard, only to see three deadly serious faces looking back at him. "What?"

All three went to Noah at the same time. Hellen knelt in front of the wheelchair and checked the footrests. Tom reached beneath the seat. Cloutard checked the back.

"What the hell?" Noah complained. A moment later, Tom came up with the bug.

"Fuck, I'm getting rusty," Tom said angrily. "I should have thought of this as soon as we got you back."

"Blame me for this one," said Noah. "I'm supposed to be the tech guy. I should have thought of it."

"You're the least to blame," Hellen said. "I know what it's like to be kidnapped. When you rescued me that time . . ." Hellen looked first to Tom, then Noah, ". . . you

211

wouldn't believe the things that were going through my head. It makes sense that you wouldn't think of something like that."

Cloutard had fallen silent. Noah looked at him and was about to say something, but changed his mind and stayed silent.

"The fact is that, because of this, AF accessed crucial information." Tom slumped into an armchair with his whiskey. "And an old nun paid the price. We can't make a mistake like this again."

The others all nodded.

50

A FEW HOURS LATER, WASHINGTON D.C.

Leg jiggling nervously up and down, Tom sat in the lobby of FBI headquarters in the J. Edgar Hoover Building in Washington, waiting for Special Agent Jennifer Baker. The conversation he was about to have definitely did not count among his favorite activities. Walking out without a word while your partner is in the shower after a night of torrid lovemaking leaves you with a lot of explaining to do. And that was exactly what Tom would have to do.

He jumped up when he saw Jennifer storm out of the elevator and walked quickly in her direction. She just shook her head, grabbed his arm and dragged him outside.

"You've got a nerve," she hissed at him. "Showing your face around here. It's a little late for breakfast, buddy. Now here you are, days later, asking for my help! After the stunt you pulled!"

"You've got every reason to be pissed at me, I know, but give me five minutes and I'll explain everything that's happened since that morning."

"Why should I do that?" she said and turned away.

"Please, Jennifer. Maybe I can even help you find the people behind the Smithsonian raid."

Jennifer thought it over for a moment and finally agreed to listen.

Tom started with Noah's phone message and how it had led him to Egypt. He told her about the break-in at the museum, Arno's death, the clue in Belgium, the audience with the Pope, the mission he'd given them, the old nun and the chase in Salzburg, and the bug they found in Noah's wheelchair.

"The bitch actually bugged him, and we didn't even spot it," Tom said, bringing his story to a close.

"Are you kidding me?" Jennifer asked. "You just confessed a museum break-in and probably a murder to an FBI agent?"

"It was self-defense. Besides, isn't Egypt a little outside your jurisdiction?" Tom said, and gave her his best wide-eyed, innocent look. "And we have to get into the Smithsonian archive again," he went on, once again serious. "I'm one hundred percent certain the break-in here is tied in with everything else that's happened. We have to know if they found anything, or took anything with them."

Jennifer paced back and forth in front of Tom, thinking it all through. "Damn it, Tom. My job's on the line here."

He looked at her pleadingly.

"All right. Give me one hour. We'll meet at the Castle, the main entrance." She was still a little hesitant. Tom thanked her and crossed the street quickly to where his friends were waiting. "One hour," she called after him.

As agreed, one hour later, Hellen, Noah, Cloutard and Tom found themselves standing in front of the destroyed glass vault in the underground archive of the Smithsonian Institute.

"I see you were hard at work again," said Noah, swinging his wheelchair full circle and admiring the havoc that Tom and his uncle had wreaked. Forensics and FBI agents were still busy with the crime scene. Hundreds of numbered yellow cones marked spent bullets, bloodstains and ruined artifacts, each meticulously photographed and recorded.

Hellen was thrilled. She did not see the chaos at all. She saw the treasures hidden from the outside world, tucked away there in the archive. Cloutard was also starting to realize where he was, and what this could mean for him.

"Don't touch anything, please," said a passing FBI agent, and Cloutard flinched. The agent had noticed Hellen and Cloutard's unusual curiosity.

"All right. What do you hope to find?" Jennifer asked.

"A clue. Something that will tell us if Hagen found what he was looking for," Tom said without thinking. "Do you know yet if anything is missing?"

"Hagen? Who's Hagen?" Jennifer narrowed her eyes and planted herself in front of Tom, her arms crossed over her chest.

My God, she's sexy in her FBI gear, Tom thought, and cleared his throat. He'd opened a can of worms now. "Isaac Hagen was the eighth man," he admitted, looking her in the eye.

"What 'eighth man' is this? I thought we had everyone involved in the break-in, either in custody or in the morgue, thanks to you and the admiral."

Tom smiled apologetically. Noah, Hellen and Tom retreated a little, extracting themselves from Jennifer's and Tom's firing line.

"Tom never misses a chance, does he? What do you think he sees in Scully here?" Hellen shook her head and turned away.

"You really think so?" Noah asked.

"*Oui, bien sûr*," said Cloutard. "A blind man could see there is something between them."

"I remember perfectly well," Jennifer said. She kept her voice low, not wanting to attract undue attention. "There were *seven*. Both you and your uncle assured us that was all of them." She paced furiously back and forth. "Anything else I ought to know?" She had her hands pressed into her hips now and shook her head in disbelief. "Not only have you confessed to murder and burglary, you stone-cold lied to my face when we questioned you," she growled. "And that, buddy, is well within my jurisdiction.

It's called making a false statement to a federal agent, and in this country it can cost you five years of your life."

"Are you finished?" Tom asked. He took her by the shoulders and peered at her intently. "Look, Hagen is a dangerous man who works for an even more dangerous organization, with its fingers in more pies than I like to think about. Maybe even inside the FBI. Hagen has already slipped through my fingers more than once. I wanted to get him myself, and I'm sorry for that. But I'll tell you everything I know about AF and Hagen. Promise."

"Maybe I can add a little something of my own," a familiar voice suddenly said.

Admiral Scott Wagner appeared from behind a rack of shelves and joined Tom, Jennifer and the others. Tom looked at him in astonishment.

"Uncle Scott," Hellen said, greeting Tom's uncle with a kiss on the cheek. "It's good to see you again."

"*Ravi de vous rencontrer*," said Cloutard, shaking Scott's hand.

"Noah," said Scott with a nod to Noah.

"What do you mean, add a little something of your own? What are you even doing here?" Tom said, unable to get over his surprise even as he embraced his uncle.

Scott took him by the arm, led him aside a short way and whispered: "You won't find what you're looking for here. It's been somewhere else for fifty years."

51

ADMIRAL SCOTT WAGNER'S HOUSE,
WASHINGTON D.C.

"Say that again. You work for . . .?" Tom looked at his uncle in disbelief.

"The CIA. I report to the president personally. When you and I got tangled up in this break-in, it was clear to me that something big was at stake. The president confirmed my suspicions and told me the incredible story of the stone. Since then, I've flown halfway round the world trying to track it down. But what amazes me is that you found your way into the same story, from a completely different direction."

Tom was speechless. His uncle, a CIA agent? Secretly, Tom was pleasantly surprised—but he was still a little put out that Scott had never told him.

"And were you successful?" Hellen asked.

"I'm afraid not. And the stone stored in the Vatican was stolen yesterday."

"What? We were just at the Vatican. We saw that part of the stone!" said Tom in shock.

The others listened with no less astonishment. Tom's uncle had their full attention.

"It's true. A team like the one that broke in here forced its way into the archive and got away with the stone. They must have gotten inside information from somewhere."

The faces surrounding Scott fell. "They got it from us," Tom said meekly.

Scott looked at him, not understanding, and Tom told him about the bug.

"I know I should have guessed that AF would plant a bug. AF is the organization that—"

"Thank you, Tom. We know what AF is," his uncle interrupted him.

Tom nodded. "Okay, that's something the CIA actually ought to know."

"Not only do we know what AF is, but we also know that one of your former colleagues worked for them." Scott looked grimly at Tom. Tom returned his gaze with a mixture of surprise and doubt. "That young Cobra officer who showed up at the bar in Washington and took you off to see your chancellor."

Tom's eyes widened. "Leitner?"

Scott nodded. "He tried to kill me in Vienna. It looks like he saw me and reported my location to AF. I can't imagine why else he would show up in my hotel room in the middle of the night and unload a clip into the mattress of my bed."

"He did *what*?" Tom could not disguise his shock. He was about to ask something, but Scott spoke first.

"If you're wondering what happened to him, well, I'm here and still alive. I'm afraid I can't say the same for him."

Tom shook his head. He had to tell the chancellor that the Cobras actually had an infiltrator in their midst. AF seemed to be everywhere.

"Scott, you said you knew where part of the stone was," Noah said, turning the discussion back to their reason for being there. "How safe is it?"

"We have to get the stone," Tom said adamantly. "Wherever it is, it's no longer safe. If AF managed to get into the Vatican, then the stone here is in danger."

"Where is it?" asked Hellen, beating Noah to the question.

"If you know about the Vatican's secret archives, then you also know we're dealing with parts of the ancient Library of Alexandria," Scott said.

Tom, Hellen, Cloutard and Noah looked uncertainly at Scott. Hellen was the first to gather herself.

"Parts? We thought . . ." Hellen let her sentence unspoken. She wanted to hear what Scott had to say.

"What neither the Pope nor anyone else knows is that more material from the Library of Alexandria exists than what is in the Vatican. Here in the States, we have an archive similar to the Vatican's, and it also contains a small part of the library. And to tell the truth, it's not that far from here."

"Now I'm confused," said Hellen. "How did part of the Library of Alexandria find its way to the USA?"

52

1945, A SALT MINE IN ALTAUSSEE, AUSTRIA

Most of his comrades were sleeping soundly. Tents had been pitched around the entrance to the mine, but there were far from enough, because they had had to bring in reinforcements: a virtual mountain of treasure needed to be packed and taken away. The mine contained literally thousands of works of art stolen by the Nazis after they came to power in the 1930s. For the last three days, he and his people had been removing them from the mine. The hoarded treasures were being trucked as quickly as possible to the coast, where a U.S. warship was waiting to carry them to America.

Captain Jack Gordon led the so-called "Monuments Men," the special U.S. Army unit responsible for recovering Nazi-plundered treasure. Gordon was not only a soldier, but also an art historian, as were some of the others in his unit. But he was not an expert in modern, baroque or renaissance art—he was a professor of Egyptology at Harvard University. And Captain Gordon had a secret. In one of the side tunnels, he had made a discovery that held little more than passing interest for his colleagues. With all the paintings, sculptures, tapestries, antique furniture, Persian carpets, gold and jewels in the mine, no one cared much about a pile of boxes filled with old scrolls.

No one apart from Captain Gordon, at least. When he first saw the crates bearing the inscription "Austrian Archaeological Institute – Ephesus – Arsinoe," he had been surprised, and the following night he had entered the mine alone and pried open the crates. Although the mercury had dropped below freezing again—he and his team had been chilled to the bone for weeks—Captain Gordon suddenly felt a wave of heat run through him. He could not believe what he was holding in his hands.

The next day he informed the director of the Smithsonian Museum in Washington, who in turn contacted President Harry S. Truman personally. Truman was neither an aesthete nor an art lover, far from it, and God knew he had enough other things to keep him busy these days, but he was no idiot. The importance of the discovery was clear to him immediately. Captain Gordon was ordered not to let the crates out of his sight until a special unit of Marines arrived in Altaussee to take them into safekeeping. That night had now arrived. Gordon led the Marines into the tunnel, and they did their job quickly and quietly. While everyone else slept, they loaded a pair of trucks with the crates. Two hours later, they were gone.

Gordon's heart bled to see them go. He would have loved to explore the contents of the crates himself. Later, he tried his best to do so: back in the States, after the war

223

was over, he tried to retrace the route the crates had taken. He contacted the Smithsonian, worked his way up the chain of command in the Marines, even wrote to President Truman himself. But there was no trace of the crates, which Captain Gordon was convinced contained parts of the ancient Library of Alexandria.

53

ADMIRAL SCOTT WAGNER'S HOUSE, WASHINGTON D.C.

"I see," said Hellen, when Scott had told them the story of the Monuments Men.

"Come on. We don't have time to sit around. We're all after the same thing. Where is this stuff these days?" Tom said, and Hellen gave him her most scathing stare.

"It's in Alexandria. Where else?" Scott smiled.

"*Pardonez-moi.* I thought *la bibliothèque* was here in the United States," Cloutard said, puzzled.

"It is. We have a town called Alexandria here, too. It's just a stone's throw to the south of here, in Virginia."

"Isn't that where the George Washington Masonic National Memorial is?" Hellen asked.

"Correct," said Scott. "More precisely, the library is deep below the George Washington Memorial."

Hellen could hardly believe it. Things were getting more incredible by the minute. Her father would never have dreamed of this.

"Then call your boss and tell him we have to get the stone someplace safer," Tom said.

"The president would never permit it. As far as he's concerned, it's already safe where it is," Scott said. "And besides, it really *is* safe in there. One hundred percent." He paused as he realized that the CIA cardinal in the Vatican had surely thought the same thing.

"Then we'll have to just have to go and break into the Library of Alexandria ourselves."

The room fell quiet for a moment. Everyone first had to digest what Tom had just thrown out. Then everyone started talking over each other.

Scott listened to the chaos for about two seconds before he bellowed: "Enough!"

The team fell silent.

"Tom's right. We have to do something." Scott could hardly believe it, but he too had just switched to the dark side. Tom was right—they *did* have to get the stone to safety. His own mission, in fact, called for just that. They had to get in there as soon as possible, if not today then tomorrow.

Hellen, who had been studying her phone, now spoke up: "There's a charity concert and dinner taking place there tomorrow night; a super-rich hotel heiress is hosting her annual cancer charity gala. They're expecting all kinds of celebrities, influencers and business leaders."

She had wasted no time in accessing the memorial website. "There'll be a concert in the memorial theater and dinner afterward with a celebrity chef."

"How do we get in?" Tom asked.

"That's easy," said Noah. "We make a donation. A big one."

"I don't really need to be there, you know. Americans simply don't know how to cook. Whatever that 'celebrity chef' serves we would not feed to the street dogs in Paris. I will pass," said Cloutard, reminding everyone once again why the whole world thought the French were pretentious snobs.

"Phew!" Hellen said, when she looked at the ticket prices. "If you want to be there, you've got to dig deep. One seat will set you back ten thousand dollars," she said.

Cloutard whistled in surprise. "And no doubt it will be impossible to buy a normal ticket so close to the event. To get a seat now, I'm afraid we will have to dig a little deeper," he said.

Noah, who had been tapping away quietly on his laptop the whole time, said, "I think I might be able to help with that."

All eyes turned to Noah.

"How, exactly?" Cloutard asked, curious about how Noah could conjure up that kind of money at short notice.

"Easy. I still have access to one of Mossad's under-the-radar accounts. They use it to finance ops that are not exactly legit. With the money stashed in this account, I don't think they'll begrudge us a hundred grand or so."

He turned the laptop around to show Scott and the others, and they all gaped dutifully at the balance on display: close to fifty million dollars.

"Cool!" said Tom. "Mossad is taking us to a party." He gave his old friend a congratulatory clap on the shoulder. "Nice work."

"Putting it through as we speak," said Noah.

Cloutard's mobile phone suddenly buzzed. "Excuse me for a moment," he said.

Noah looked over his shoulder at Cloutard as the Frenchman stood up. He could tell by his expression that it had to be the same caller who had already gotten him worked up back in Salzburg.

"What's up with him?" Tom asked.

"I'm not sure," Noah said somewhat absently, and his eyes followed Cloutard thoughtfully.

Cloutard took the call in the backyard. This time it was a video call, and after a moment Farid's face filled Cloutard's screen.

"So you are calling by video now to back up your threats with your nasty face? I have a plan, and we have a deal. I still have time," Cloutard muttered. He kept his voice low and had his back turned to the house. He could feel eyes on his back.

"I'm not so sure you'll come through. And since I can't hold a gun to your head around the clock, you could say I've found a substitute."

Farid disappeared from the screen and after some jiggling and blurring, the image once again settled down. Cloutard inhaled sharply when he realized where Farid was and what he had done.

"Giuseppina? Mamma?"

Things had suddenly turned very, very personal, and not just for Cloutard. Farid had no idea of the wasps' nest he had just stirred up. Cloutard had to sort out this mess once and for all.

54

"Morning," said Tom as he stumbled drowsily into the living room to find Hellen, Scott and Noah sitting stone-faced at the dining table.

"Sit down, Tom," his uncle said, and pushed a chair out for him.

Tom yawned. "What's up?"

"Cloutard's gone," Hellen said.

"What do you mean, gone?"

"He got into my laptop during the night. He shifted everything left in the Mossad account to a Swiss account number. Now he's disappeared."

"Fifty million bucks?"

Noah nodded, his face both earnest and sad. He turned the laptop around to Tom and started a video.

"This is one of my temporary security systems," Noah said. "I don't have my own laptop here, so I had to improvise. If someone, in this case Cloutard, logs in with my password . . ." He paused, "I obviously have to be more careful about who's looking over my shoulder," he mused, then continued his previous line of thought: "If they don't deactivate the secondary security measures, the webcam is automatically activated."

Tom stared incredulously at the monitor and saw Cloutard wildly navigating the laptop, looking behind him repeatedly in the dark room. Just before he closed the laptop, Tom saw him pick up his cell phone to call someone. Tom, deeply troubled by what he was seeing, leaned back in his chair.

Noah went on: "I first noticed that something was going on with him in Salzburg, but I didn't want to say anything until I was sure. And then that mysterious call last night . . . I hacked into his phone records afterward."

"You hacked Cloutard's phone and didn't tell me?" Tom looked at Noah a little reproachfully.

"I just wanted to be sure before I said anything."

Tom nodded. He could see Noah's point.

"He's back in touch with people from his old life. Some-one's after him for money. Cloutard was being black-mailed and he decided to help himself," said Noah. "Once a thief, always a thief. Who knows? Maybe AF got to him and he's done more than just stolen the money. God knows he's got enough information. Now that we found their bug, maybe they needed a new source."

Tom rubbed both hands roughly over his face and through his hair. It all felt like a bad dream: first the bug, and now this.

"No way. Cloutard isn't with AF." Tom didn't know what else to say.

"Cloutard was a career criminal who lost his assets and his status overnight. It would make sense for him to exploit an opportunity like this. And we know for sure that his ex is AF. Maybe it's she who's blackmailing him," Hellen speculated.

Tom's brain was working at full speed. Had he really been naive enough to let a man he considered one of his closest friends and confidantes pull the wool over his eyes? A man with whom he'd already survived more than one potentially deadly situation? Cloutard had saved his life in Cairo, and without him he would never have been able to rescue Noah so quickly.

"Fuck! If Cloutard's really working for AF, we can sure as hell expect company tonight." Tom jumped to his feet. "Uncle Scott, you and Noah sort out our tickets. Send a picture of Cloutard to security on site—I don't want any surprises there. Hellen and I are going to get the right clothes and a car fit for this kind of bash," Tom said, switching to military-command mode. Everyone nodded and went to work.

55

SOMEWHERE IN THE UNITED STATES

Ossana Ibori's laptop trilled: an incoming video call. She clicked the green button and both sides activated their cams. The first thing she saw was a chunk of emerald-green stone, filling the center of the screen.

"Mission accomplished," said Hagen, whose face replaced the stone onscreen a moment later.

"Good. Finally, something goes as planned."

"When you and I call the shots, things always go as planned," Hagen said with a trace of pride that Ossana ignored.

"Are you on your way to the airport?" she asked.

"Of course."

"Slight change of plans. You'll pass the stone to one of our couriers at the airport. He's a pilot with Egypt Air. He'll take the stone to Hurgahda, and we can get it to the yacht quickly from there. Daddy's already getting restless."

"You really want me to hand over the stone? I'd feel a lot better taking it to Hurgahda myself."

"No. You've got a new job to do. You might get a kick out of this one, too."

Hagen raised his eyebrows with interest.

"Really? I'm all ears."

"You need to eliminate someone—someone who knows too much and who's always sticking his nose where it doesn't belong. He could be dangerous to us in the final stage. I'd do it myself, but Daddy insists that I lead the next phase personally."

Hagen listened closely as she told him the details.

"You're right. This one's going to be a real pleasure."

"And do a better job of it than Leitner did in Vienna. He was supposed to take care of Admiral Wagner. But no, he let a broken-down old man on the verge of retirement get the better of him. You can't trust beginners," Ossana said.

56

CLOUTARD'S HOUSE, TUSCANY, ITALY

Cloutard had never thought he'd be back so soon.

This was where he'd spent his youth. As an orphaned boy, Cloutard had made his way from France to Italy, but once there, he had quickly run afoul of the powers that were. He had been only ten years old when he first robbed a man. What little François didn't know at the time was that the man he had robbed was Innocento Baldacci, the local mafia boss. Innocento had taken an instant liking to the proud little French boy; he had taken him off the streets, and he and his wife, Giuseppina, had raised him. They had treated him as if he were their own flesh and blood.

It soon became clear to Innocento and Giuseppina that François would never become a mafioso. Even at that tender age, he had a sense for the good things in life. He was interested in art, culture and good food. When he was old enough, he had left Italy and devoted himself entirely to art, and within a few years he was already running the largest art smuggling and grave-robbing operation in the Mediterranean. That is, until that cursed day when the work of many years had collapsed around him like a house of cards. AF—and Ossana Ibori personally, who also had Farid's father on her conscience—were to blame. Things had spiraled out of control, and Cloutard was left overnight with nothing but the tattered remnants of his criminal empire. Faced with this seemingly insurmountable disaster, he had returned to his parental home, where he promised Giuseppina that he would get it all back.

But now things looked even worse than they had then. He hadn't managed to rebuild his organization, and now his actions had put his foster mother in danger. But Farid did not know that Cloutard still had allies among the northern Italian mafia, and messing with Giuseppina meant messing with them. On his way to Italy, Cloutard had made a few phone calls, and the Capi had sent their soldiers. Farid was in for an unpleasant surprise.

Cloutard stopped some distance away from the house. Like many Tuscan country homes, it was situated on a hill overlooking the vineyards and gently rolling hills of the Italian countryside. A winding gravel road led to the house but Cloutard had no intention of taking it. He parked his car beneath a small cluster of pines and walked up a hill, along a narrow forest path. He had not gone far when he saw them: three men, the sons of old friends of his father, all prepared for the job ahead. Giuseppina had not been killed, it was true, but nobody threatened the wife of a mafioso. These men did not take such things lightly. To get inside the house, Cloutard planned to use a tunnel that was actually meant to serve as an emergency escape route. Of course, he could have just sent the men in without him, but if he were to do that his mother would never speak a word to him again. He had to do this himself.

The men nodded a greeting to Cloutard. In a few words, they discussed the plan, then parted ways. Minutes later, the three mafiosi burst through the front door of the house and confronted Farid, their guns leveled.

"What the hell is this? Who are these guys?" Farid asked nervously as he held the gun to Giuseppina's temple. She did answer his questions, but started to insult him angrily. Sweat beaded on Farid's scalp and his hands were suddenly clammy.

"You down-and-out little drifter! You have no idea who you're dealing with. You have signed your own death warrant. Your mother did not put you over her knee often enough. She did not teach you to think. She did not teach you to find out who you are dealing with before you break into the houses of strangers and point guns at them!"

Giuseppina scolded Farid as if he were a wayward child who had broken his grandmother's expensive vase. Cloutard, meanwhile, had entered the house unnoticed through the secret passage, and now stood calmly behind Farid. He and the other men were struggling hard not to burst into laughter at Giuseppina's tirade. And Farid was slowly but surely beginning to realize how big a mistake he'd made.

"Are they Maf—"

He did not get to finish saying the word because Cloutard hit him over the head with his walking stick, and Farid

237

fell to the ground like a sack of cement. The men disarmed Farid, tied him up and carried him down to the basement, Giuseppina following close behind.

"Who is this amateur?" Giuseppina asked when she returned with the men from the basement.

"The son of Karim," Cloutard said. "He lost everything after his father was murdered and has been living hand-to-mouth ever since. He can hardly feed his family, and in his desperation he thought he could help himself through me."

"Dilettante," said Giuseppina. The men laughed, but were happy when the old woman, a moment later, brought out a silver tray with a bottle of grappa and five schnapps glasses. She poured the grappa and handed the glasses to the men.

"Salute e grazie tante."

Giuseppina raised her glass and tipped back the spirit. The men followed suit. They had to drink fast—she was already waiting to refill the glasses. Then they all took seats on the terrace and began to talk, Italian-style: exaggerated old stories, told loudly and as much with their hands and feet as with their mouths. Lots of laughter. Cloutard hadn't felt this good for a long time, and he knew it. He missed this. When the three men finally said goodbye, he brought the conversation back to his captive.

"Farid is a beginner, I admit, but I can understand how he feels. He did all of this for his family, that's all. His daughter is very ill. She is dying, apparently."

Giuseppina listened attentively as Cloutard explained all that had happened, and her eyes grew sad. She was the widow of a mafia boss and had seen more than her share of death and violence, but her heart was still in the right place. She went to Cloutard and embraced him, longer than she usually did.

"Then we will help the little girl, won't we, Francesco?" Giuseppina rarely used the Italian version of Cloutard's first name, and only when she was serious.

"We will find a way, Mamma," he said, and hugged her back.

It was late, and Cloutard and his foster mother were preparing for bed when the old telephone in the kitchen rang.

"Who would be calling at this hour?" Cloutard asked.

Giuseppina picked up the receiver, nodded earnestly, and quickly hung up again.

Cloutard looked at her curiously.

"Your old mother makes no mistake twice. I have a few men outside, guarding the house. I don't want to have any more uninvited guests. Fredo has just seen a man come out of the woods on the north side of the mountain. He is watching the house from there. Do you have any idea who that could be?"

"*Je ne sais pas du tout,*" said Cloutard.

"*Non è importante.* We are prepared!"

57

GEORGE WASHINGTON MASONIC NATIONAL MEMORIAL, ALEXANDRIA, VIRGINIA, USA

A long line of limousines crawled up the winding access road. Glimpses of the stately tower were visible now and then through the trees of the estate, before it finally revealed itself in all its glory. The glamorous stretch limos pulled up one after the other at the foot of the monumental staircase fronting the George Washington Masonic National Memorial. A red carpet led up the torch-lined staircase to the portico. Two tuxedoed young men greeted the arriving vehicles, opening doors and welcoming guests dressed in the most elegant evening wear. A flurry of flashes from the press photographers lined up at the foot of the stairs announced each new arrival.

The portico that formed the entrance to the memorial borrowed heavily from the design of Greek and Roman temples. Spotlights illuminated the impressive 333-foot-high tower, itself modelled after the ancient lighthouse of Alexandria. A handful of security guards patrolled the area. *Just a few ex-cops, probably*, Tom thought. No doubt there would be more inside.

The limousine carrying Tom, Hellen, Scott and Noah did not stop at the stairway like the others, but drove around to the side of the building. Because of Noah's wheelchair, Scott had arranged for them to enter the building through the higher side entrance.

Noah's role was that of a generous benefactor who had made a substantial last-minute donation. Undercover work was nothing new for the former Mossad agent; he slipped easily into his new character. Once he found his way into a part, he could be very convincing.

The monumental Memorial Hall, with its eight gigantic polished-granite columns soaring more than forty feet overhead, was an awe-inspiring sight. At the end of the large hall was a domed alcove containing a bronze statue of George Washington over fifteen feet high, unveiled in 1950 by President Truman, who had been a Masonic Grand Master himself.

"I'll give you Americans this: you do know how to throw a party," Hellen said to Scott as she soaked in the ambience and the people. The champagne reception, a prelude to the concert, was in full swing, with well-heeled Washingtonians brushing shoulders with business moguls and a scattering of celebrity faces. Waitresses moved among the guests, plying them with champagne.

A young woman with a clipboard in her hand and wearing a plain cocktail dress and a headset approached the team.

"Professor Asher? Welcome," she said, and she held out her hand to Scott. Not wanting to attract unnecessary attention, Scott was not wearing the dress uniform belonging to his military rank, but a tuxedo like Tom and Noah.

"Sorry to disappoint you, ma'am," Scott smiled, shaking her hand. "I'm Scott Wagner. But allow me to introduce my nephew, Thomas Maria Wagner and his charming companion, Dr. Hellen de Mey."

Tom in his tuxedo with Hellen at his side in a stunning scarlet evening gown made an elegant couple. Tom rolled his eyes when Scott mentioned his middle name, and Hellen could not believe that Scott had introduced her as Tom's "companion." Then Scott turned to Noah.

"And last but not least, our public-spirited benefactor, Professor Benjamin Asher."

Tom and Hellen stepped aside, and Noah rolled toward the young woman and extended his hand.

"Welcome to the George Washington Masonic National Memorial," the hostess greeted him, smiling and shaking his hand. "Mrs. Holten was very pleased to receive your generous donation. She would like to express her thanks to you personally after the presentation in the theater. I will meet you after the concert and accompany you to dinner, which will take place downstairs in the Grand Masonic Hall. But if you like, I'd be happy to offer you a brief tour of this unique building first."

"Gladly. And I am looking forward very much to meeting Mrs. Holten. She seems a most fascinating and admirable woman," said Noah, playing up his role as the suave Israeli philanthropist.

"Wonderful. If you would follow me, please?" The young hostess led them behind the massive green granite columns framing the Memorial Hall, stopping at an expansive mural.

"Construction of the building began in 1922. Here we have one of the two impressive murals painted by Allyn Cox, this one depicting George Washington laying the foundation stone of the Capitol on September 18, 1793. Cox painted it in the 1950s. Now if you'll come with me to the other side . . ."

The tour dragged on, and Tom began to lose patience. "We can't spend hours touring this place," he whispered, leaning close to Hellen. "If Cloutard really passed information to Ossana, she could show up at any moment."

But Hellen was deep in thought and did not hear a word Tom said. She was listening to the young woman's lecture about the building, about George Washington and the Freemasons. As she listened, something suddenly became clear to her—something she had already known, but had not yet seen in the right context.

She turned to Tom, wanting to share her thought with him, although she knew it sounded like the wildest speculation. "So, here we are in a Masonic temple," she whispered. "Whoever had enough influence to have the secret archive built must have also been a Freemason. Harry S. Truman became president the same year the stone came to America, and *he* was a Freemason. This building was not officially finished until 1970, more than enough time to hide a clue to the third part of the stone here. But where?"

Their hostess continued: "Please follow me this way to the elevator. On the upper levels we have our observatory, below that the Templar chapel, and on the seventh floor is a replica of Solomon's Temple".

At the mention of Solomon's Temple, a light switched on inside Hellen's brain.

58

A dark shadow flitted silently across the grounds. Clad completely in black, the soldier wore state-of-the-art night-vision goggles over a balaclava and held a silenced G36K Heckler & Koch assault rifle at the ready. On his thigh was a holstered pistol, also silenced. He took up his position, target in sight. But he was not alone. He and nine comrades-in-arms had the memorial surrounded and awaited their orders.

A massive, black eighteen-wheeler rumbled northwest along King Street, past the memorial. About a quarter of a mile beyond the museum complex was a small road, Carlisle Drive, that became an access road serving the memorial complex: this would give them far better cover. Ossana sat in the cab next to the driver. As they turned left onto Carlisle, she spoke into her radio.

"I hope you're all in position. Wait for my command," she said, her voice stone cold.

The semi rolled up Carlisle and continued straight onto the access road. Only one security guard was posted at the back entrance to the memorial, and the semi pulled to a stop. The guard came up to the cab.

"This way's closed," he said. "You're gonna have to turn this thing around."

"I'm terribly sorry, sir," said Ossana from the passenger seat in her sweetest voice. Then, like a striking snake, she leaned across the driver and shot the guard between the eyes.

"Now!" she barked into her radio. Perfectly synchronized, ten silenced rifles fired and ten security men went down. Ossana activated the jamming transmitter, which blocked all cell phone networks and radio frequencies in the area—except her own, of course. The truck pulled into the parking lot behind the memorial, and Ossana climbed down from the cab, wearing a stunning white evening gown slit up to the hip. She made her way toward the side entrance while her soldiers advanced quickly toward the main stairway.

59

SOLOMON'S TEMPLE, SEVENTH FLOOR, GEORGE WASHINGTON MASONIC NATIONAL MEMORIAL

The tour should have continued directly to the observatory, but at Hellen's request Noah had insisted that they stop on the 7th floor of the tower, at the replica of the Temple of Solomon.

"What does Solomon have to do with the Freemasons?" Tom asked, earning a withering look from Hellen.

"The Freemasons trace their origins to the earliest stonemasons," their guide explained. "The biblical King Solomon is considered the greatest master builder in the stonemasons' tradition, and the Freemasons see Solomon's Temple as a symbol of punitive and executive justice—a sort of spiritual temple for humanity. They believe that every time a Freemason works for humanity, they're building Solomon's Temple."

Tom was impressed. "She's pretty sharp," he said.

"I could have told you that," said Hellen, a little piqued.

"Solomon is also non-sectarian; he's an equally important figure to Jews, Muslims and Christians."

"For Christians, too?" Noah asked. "I hadn't heard that before."

"Only one branch, actually," the young woman said. "Solomon had an affair with the Queen of Sheba, and the son born of that liaison was Menelik, the first of the Ethiopian emperors. The Ethiopian Orthodox Church still has a strong connection to Solomon to this day."

"Also because of that." Hellen smiled knowingly and pointed toward a drawn curtain visible through a narrow archway.

Tom was confused. "What's behind the curtain?" Hellen didn't reply, but her eyes widened when she noticed the subtle pattern of crosses along the bottom of the curtain. She took a few steps toward it and examined the pattern more closely to confirm her suspicion.

Returning to the others, she whispered, "I know where the third stone is now."

Noah, Tom and Scott looked at her with surprise.

"It all fits," Hellen said, and she pointed to the curtain.

"What's behind it?" Tom asked again.

"It doesn't matter what's behind it. The curtain itself is what matters."

"You're talking in riddles, Hellen," Scott said.

"Along the bottom edge of the curtain is a cross pattern, but it's got nothing to do with the Freemasons. It's a Lalibela cross. A medieval Christian orthodox cross in a Masonic temple makes no sense; the pattern must have been put here on purpose—as a reference to the rock churches of Lalibela. The third part of the stone must be there. It would be the perfect place. One part of the stone stayed in Rome; the second sailed across the Atlantic to the largest museum in the world, in America—and they hid the third one in Ethiopia, in a rock church 8000 feet above sea level," Hellen said.

"Sounds plausible," said Noah.

"Well, looks like we're off to Lala . . . Luli . . ." Tom said struggling with the name.

"Lalibela. La-li-be-la," Hellen corrected him.

"Okay. Then go get the stone downstairs," Scott said. He turned to Tom and handed him a small package that Tom immediately slipped into a pocket inside his tuxedo. "Remember: bring it straight to me. I'll get it to a safe place."

"But we're supposed to get all three of the stones back to the Vatican, where they came from!" Hellen said.

"No discussion; we're doing this my way. It's bad enough that I'm helping you steal the stone from here at all. That alone could get me hauled in front of a military tribunal."

"Okay, agreed," said Tom.

"The main thing is to make sure it's safe," said Noah. Hellen nodded.

"We'll meet back in the Memorial Hall," said Scott, and Tom and Hellen headed for the elevator.

"Mr. Asher, we should be getting back downstairs now. The concert will be starting in a few minutes and I'm sure you don't want to miss it," the young lady said to Noah. "I'm terribly sorry. I seem to have lost track of the time. There's still so much I would like to have shown you."

"No problem at all. It's all been very enlightening," said Noah reassuringly. He secretly shared a look with Scott and sighed with relief. The three of them headed for the elevator. When they reached the bottom, their hostess offered to show Noah and Scott to their seats.

"Thank you, that's very kind, but we'll find them ourselves." A little surprised at Noah's tone, the young woman smiled then left him and Scott alone and disappeared into the theater. A large crowd was now gathered at the entrance, the guests wanting to get to their seats as quickly as possible.

Noah suddenly started. Was it really possible? He pulled Scott down to him and nodded toward the mass of guests.

"She's here!"

"Who's here?"

"Ossana. Back of the crowd, white dress."

As unobtrusively as he could, Scott turned to look.

"Go find security, fast. Before it's too late," Noah said.

Scott didn't need to be told twice. A minute later, he returned with two security guards.

60

GEORGE WASHINGTON MASONIC
NATIONAL MEMORIAL, LOWER LEVEL

The elevator doors opened and Tom and Hellen stepped out at the level of the Masonic Hall, but quickly realized they had gone one floor too far. This was the level where the dinner would take place later, but for now it looked as if the entire floor had been abandoned. They turned to get back into the elevator, but it was already on its way back up. Tom jabbed at the button impatiently.

"Oh, that's going to make it come faster," said Hellen, pulling his hand back.

"I've got a bad feeling about this," said Tom, looking around, puzzled.

"Because of Cloutard?"

"No. I mean, this, here, now. Where is everyone? Where's all the staff? They're supposed to be doing dinner for four hundred people in one hour. This place should be crawling."

Now Hellen was getting nervous herself. Tom was right. A security guard suddenly appeared from around a corner.

"Hey, what are you doing here? You're not supposed to be down here." He strode toward them. He was wearing a black suit and as he walked he raised his radio to his mouth. The sleeve of his jacket slipped down a little as he lifted his hand, and Tom saw it.

Hellen's not going to like this, he thought, and in the same breath he had already overwhelmed the man. A blow to the throat to shut him up, a boot to the family jewels, and when the man dropped to his knees, a chokehold silently sent him to dreamland.

"What are you doing? Are you out of your mind?"

"Take his legs," said Tom, and they dragged the man into a small closet. Tom searched him, found a pistol and took it.

"Ossana's here. We have to hurry."

Tom grabbed Hellen by the hand and pulled her with him up the stairs to the level above. Not wanting to run into another "security guard," they stopped just before they rounded next corner, and Tom peeped around cautiously.

"What makes you think Ossana is here?" Hellen asked in a whisper.

"I'm guessing you didn't see that guy's tattoo. I'd know that pattern anywhere, even if only a corner of it is visible."

"You mean THE tattoo? The one you saw when you recognized Guerra after all those years?"

"Yes. The AF special."

"We have to warn the others!" Hellen took out her cell phone to call Scott.

"That won't work. They'll be blocking everything."

Tom was right. The mobile network was dead.

"Uncle Scott's going to have look after himself. Our job is to find the stone as fast as we can and get it away from here."

"But—"

"We knew all along that something like this could happen. Uncle Scott and Noah are capable guys. They'll work it out," he said, trying to calm Hellen down.

He took her by the hand again, and when the coast seemed clear, they dashed down the hallway and into the Memorial Hall, now deserted. They ran to the alcove where the statue of Washington stood.

The bronze sculpture stood on a stone plinth about six feet high. A narrow space led around the base, inside the alcove. They climbed over the red cord that blocked access and slipped behind the statue. Hellen was surprised. Was there a door back there? But no, once they were in the narrow space behind the pedestal, she saw nothing at all in the seamless block of stone.

Before she could say a word, Tom took out the small package Scott had given him upstairs. He unfolded the paper to reveal a metal card with irregularly arranged holes. It was the size of a credit card and hung from the kind of ball-link chain soldiers usually used for their dog tags. He handed the paper to Hellen and looked at the card for a moment. It reminded him of an ancient computer punch card.

"What are you going to do?" Hellen whispered as she watched Tom's fingers glide over the massive stone block. He paused. He'd found it: a slot as thin as his thumbnail. Scott had explained precisely how and where he would find it. He took the card and slipped it carefully into the opening. A moment later, a section of the plinth moved inward with a grating noise. At the same time, two rows of base plates slid downward, forming the first step of a staircase.

Hellen and Tom looked at each with a mixture of amazement and delight. Tom removed the key, took out his cell phone, activated the flashlight and led the way down the dark stairs, with Hellen close behind.

At the bottom of the short stairway, they reached an old elevator. On the wall next to it was a keypad.

"Read me the code," Tom said, and Hellen recited the string of twelve numbers printed on the piece of paper that had been wrapped around the key. Tom tapped the numbers into the keypad, a little red light on the console switched to green, and a moment later the elevator door opened and they stepped inside. The tiny cabin, just large enough for two people, dropped instantly into the depths.

"Who would ever be in such a hurry?" Hellen said, already feeling a little nauseous as the elevator came to an abrupt stop. A light flickered on. In front of them a narrow, seemingly endless corridor disappeared into the darkness. Hesitant, they stepped out of the elevator. With every step they took, another light came on and the one behind them switched off again.

"According to Uncle Scott, we're now about 250 feet below the Memorial Hall. This corridor is aligned east to west and leads right under the huge Masonic symbol displayed out the front."

Moving quickly, they covered the length of the corridor. Tom estimated they covered about 130 yards. At the end was a steel door; as before, Tom inserted the punch card into a slot. Below an old monitor, a keyboard slid out of the wall.

"Old-school security," Tom said, surprised. "Kind of a steampunk vibe."

"Budget cuts, probably. This whole place is funded by donations from the Masonic community."

"What's the text under the code?"

Hellen handed him the piece of paper and he typed the first phrase into the computer. The door opened to reveal an airlock, and a light came on automatically. They stepped inside. The airlock clearly doubled as an additional level of security: for a moment, they were trapped between the two steel doors. A second terminal secured the door at the other end of the room. Tom typed the second phrase from the piece of paper into it, and pressed the "Enter" key.

Hellen's excitement grew—she was about to see the second part of the Library of the Kings, just days after her visit to Rome. The door hissed and swung slowly on its hinges. The space beyond it was quite a bit smaller than the Vatican archive, but for Hellen it was no less fascinating. The lights blinked on with the familiar *pop-pop* of neon lamps, illuminating a room about forty yards long. The left wall consisted of at least sixty vertical columns of small doors, six to a column, with hundreds of transparent viewing windows set one above the other. Behind the small windows lay thousands upon thousands of scrolls. *Climate-controlled vaults*, thought Hellen. Small control panels could be used to individually regulate the atmosphere inside each one. The right wall looked the same, with the exception of two large doors set into the middle of the wall. Behind the doors were two laboratories in which the scrolls could be studied under controlled conditions.

A pity, thought Hellen. Despite her excitement, the situation made her a little sad. Would she ever have the opportunity to enter this room again, or to take a closer look at what it contained?

Tom noticed Hellen's despondency as she walked, mesmerized, past the climate-controlled chambers, no doubt tempted to take out every single scroll and study it more closely. "We don't have the time for what you want, Hellen. But I'm sure Scott can try to arrange a longer visit for you," he said, hoping to cheer her up.

Hellen smiled radiantly at the notion, and her focus returned. The wall opposite the entrance, at the far end of the room, consisted almost entirely of safe-deposit boxes, the kind usually found in a bank vault. On one side was another small card terminal, but this time only the card was needed. Tom slid it into its slot, and a single safe-deposit box in the center of the wall popped out a short distance. Excited, cautious, they eased the drawer out a little farther and lifted the lid. And there it was. Before them, embedded in ordinary foam rubber, lay the second fragment of the emerald-green Philosopher's Stone.

61

MEMORIAL HALL

"I'm sorry, Tom," were the first words Tom heard when he stepped out from behind the stone plinth and back into the Memorial Hall. Momentarily startled, he reassessed quickly and took cover with Hellen behind the base of the Washington statue. It was a no-win situation. In the center of the empty hall, Ossana held a gun to Scott's head. Noah sat in his wheelchair next to Scott, his hands raised. Three of the mercenaries had assault rifles aimed in Tom's direction. On the left, by the entrance, lay two dead security guards.

"Mr. Wagner, I believe you have something that belongs to me," said Ossana.

"How do I know you'll let us go if we give it to you?"

"You don't, of course. Nevertheless, I give you my word. Give me the stone and your uncle doesn't have to die."

Tom thought it over for a moment. Hellen nodded. They were crouched together at the stop of the narrow stairway.

"All right. I'm coming out."

Tom held the stone over his head in both hands. He moved slowly out of the niche and stepped over the barrier cord.

"The stone. Now!"

Ossana kicked the backrest of Noah's wheelchair and Noah hesitantly rolled toward Tom. Tom nodded almost imperceptibly at Noah and looked intently at Scott, a signal that something was about to happen. Everything happened fast. Tom tossed the stone to Noah in a high arc. Scott exploited the distraction: he turned and ducked, knocked Ossana's weapon clear and slammed his shoulder into her, sending her flying. She went down hard, and her gun clattered onto the floor and slid across the smooth marble. Scott, moving quickly, turned and snatched it up as he jumped behind one of the green marble pillars. Bullets ricocheted off the column next to his head. At the same time, Tom drew the pistol tucked into the back of his pants and, aiming fast and accurately, took out two of the soldiers as he sprinted to the opposite side of the hall and took cover behind another column.

Hellen, who had followed close behind Tom when the mayhem broke out, grabbed the handles of Noah's wheelchair; he had rolled quickly in her direction after catching the stone. Tom and Scott took turns firing at the last soldier, keeping him pinned down and covering Noah and Hellen's escape from the Memorial Hall. With Tom and Scott both barricaded behind the columns, the tables had turned.

The third soldier gave Ossana cover, firing alternately at

Tom and Scott. Furious, she ducked behind a column on Tom's side of the hall, and kicked off her high heels.

Only now did Tom see that Scott had been hit. His face twisted in pain, Scott crouched at the foot of a column and examined the gunshot wound in his stomach. He looked over at Tom and, with more of a grimace than a grin, raised his thumb to signal that he was okay.

Tom had to get the situation under control, fast. He signaled to his uncle that he would come to him, but Scott signaled back *No.* Tom was to stay where he was. In severe pain, Scott struggled to his feet, pushing himself up the column with the last of his strength. He checked his pistol. Then he saluted Tom and broke cover.

"Hey, asshole," Scott shouted, and he fired his last three shots at the column where the soldier had taken cover. Then he threw the empty pistol in the same direction. When the soldier realized Scott was unarmed, he peeked out from behind the column. Far enough—Tom took the opportunity and put a bullet through the soldier's head.

Tom sprinted to his uncle, who had collapsed at the bottom of the three steps that ran the length of the colonnade.

"Hurry, or she'll get away," Scott croaked and pointed at the opposite side, where Ossana had just run off.

"Stop! Hands behind your head!" Tom shouted, and Ossana froze.

"Go help your friends. I'm okay. I'll survive."

Scott was sitting on the steps. He pressed one hand onto his wound, and signaled again with the other to Tom to go. Tom glanced back at his uncle and gave him a nod, then he went to Ossana, who was standing where she'd stopped with her fingers laced at the back of her head. Along the way, he picked up one of the soldiers' assault rifles and tossed the pistol aside.

"Mine was empty, too," he said.

Tom pressed the rifle to the back of Ossana's head and they started to move outside. Tom looked back one last time at his uncle, who waved him on.

"How do you see this playing out?" Ossana asked.

"An exchange of prisoners," Tom replied confidently. They were headed toward the side exit, which led to the rear parking area. But when they stepped outside, Tom was struck speechless. An enormous black eighteen-wheeler stood in the parking lot. The canvas walls of the trailer had been folded back to reveal a Black Hawk helicopter perched on the flatbed. Six guns rose instantly as the side door of the memorial opened. And in the middle of it all stood Hellen, her hands in the air, with Noah beside her.

But more than anything else, Tom's brain was failing to process the sight of Noah with a gun in his hand, aimed straight at Hellen.

62

OUTSIDE CLOUTARD'S HOUSE, NEAR
SIENA, TUSCANY

Peering at the house through the thermal imaging
camera, Hagen could make out two figures in separate
rooms. Both seemed to be asleep. Ossana's instructions
had been clear: "Eliminate Cloutard. He knows too
much. More importantly, he has our money."

Thankfully, Ossana also knew exactly where to find
Cloutard. In retrospect, Hagen found himself a little
upset at her promise that he "might get a kick out of it."
Not this. This was going to be the least exciting kill he'd
taken on in years. They were out in the Italian boon-
docks, in the middle of nowhere. A lonely house, no
neighbors close by, an open access road, the nearest
police station miles away, and a completely unsuspecting
victim—for him, no challenge at all. He checked his
watch.

In, kill, out, he thought. Like taking candy from a baby.

Hagen checked his thermal imaging a final time. The
two bodies did not move. Both appeared to be sound

asleep. He covered the distance from the top of the hill to the house in ten minutes. He checked the windows and doors on the ground floor but found no sign of an alarm system, which only annoyed him more: nothing, not even the smallest obstacle. Still, there was one small decision to make: one bedroom was on the ground floor, the other on the floor above. Where to go first? According to his information, Cloutard's aging mother lived in the house, so no danger there. He decided to flip a coin. With barely a sound, he opened the front door and crept through the hallway to the foot of the staircase. The house was totally silent. He felt in his pocket for his lucky penny, took it out and looked at it through his night-vision goggles.

Heads, first floor. Tails, second floor, he thought. He tossed the coin and caught it: heads. *First floor first.*

Suddenly, every light in the house came on, blinding Hagen. He tore the night-vision goggles from his head and found himself staring into the eyes of an old woman, not even five feet tall, wearing a friendly smile. Then everything went black again, as the blow to the back of his head knocked him out. Hagen slumped to the floor.

———

"*Evviva il mattarello!*" said Giuseppina and she grinned at Hagen, who had just come to. Someone had poured a bucket of ice-cold water over his head. "And because you English can't speak Italian, that means 'hooray for the rolling pin.'" He had to be hallucinating. He was tied to a chair, and in front of him stood an eighty-year-old woman with a rolling pin in her hand. Cloutard was sitting a few feet away in a rocking chair, a glass of cognac in his hand; he stood and sidled toward Hagen.

"I can already imagine who sent you. Our dear mutual friend, Ossana Ibori, *n'est-ce pas*?"

Hagen's face revealed nothing. He strained at his bonds, but he was secured with several well-placed cable ties. Nothing he could do about that.

"You don't need to answer. I know Ossana well enough."

Giuseppina came to him now. She pulled up a chair in front of him and calmly sat down, looking at him with eyes like chips of ice. Cloutard knew that look. He also knew no one in the world who could look so deeply into your soul and scare the living shit out of you quite as well as Giuseppina. She had never gotten her hands dirty personally, not while Innocento was still alive. That was what soldiers were for. But she had learned psychological warfare from her husband, the art of manipulating people. For years, she had seen how one look from her husband could make an adversary, or even a friend, break into a cold sweat. She had learned that people yield to a strong leader, and that it all comes down to who had the power. Or who pretended to. It was the gestures, the face, the voice and the body language that made people compliant—there was no need to threaten someone with torture, let alone to actually do it. Nor was there any need to set an example. Giuseppina was pulling out all the stops, and Cloutard watched as Hagen's facade began, slowly but surely, to crumble. And she hadn't even asked him a question yet.

When she spoke, however, her words astonished Cloutard as much as they did Hagen.

"You work for AF," Giuseppina said. "And we are part of a very big family, if you know what I mean. We would be well within our rights to take revenge—you were trying to kill us, after all. But we like to think ahead."

Giuseppina looked up at Cloutard; he already knew where she was going. The aging mafia *donna* had spent decades learning from the best. Never act out of emotion; always have a long-term plan. Always look for an advantage, even if none seems obvious at first glance.

Giuseppina's tone softened a little, and Hagen's face relaxed.

"We could be of great benefit to one another," she said, standing up and moving slowly around the room. From Giuseppina's first sentence, Cloutard knew that Hagen would accept whatever she was offering. It was an offer he couldn't refuse.

63

BEHIND THE GEORGE WASHINGTON MASONIC NATIONAL MEMORIAL

Tom stared at Noah, but he couldn't get a single word out.

"Wow. It's worth it just for the look on your face," Noah said. He lowered his gun. There were already enough weapons pointed at Tom and Hellen to blast them into next week if Tom made one false move. Tom let the assault rifle fall to the ground.

"That stupid, stunned look. That's what I wanted to see." Noah rolled toward Tom and handed his pistol to Ossana, who turned, stepped back and trained the gun on Tom. Tom raised his hands and crossed them behind his head. He was still not able to say a word.

"I've been waiting a long time for this moment, old friend," Noah said, spitting the last two words out savagely. "The moment when I finally get to throw your incompetence back in your face."

Slowly but surely, the truth was dawning on Tom. His expression changed.

"Finally! The wheels are starting to turn. It always takes a while with you."

Noah rolled very close to Tom and looked him in the eye. For a few seconds, nothing happened. Then the words practically exploded from Noah's mouth, with a level of vitriol that made Tom recoil. "I've been stuck in this thing for years because of your rookie mistake. We were on a mission, and you weren't at your post. You didn't secure your area as we'd agreed, and they were able to shoot me down because of it. Your stupidity left me a sitting duck, and I paid for it with a shredded spinal cord."

"But Noah—" Tom stammered.

"Shut your fucking mouth!" Noah bellowed, and the veins on his forehead swelled. "Because of you, I'm not a man anymore. I was Mossad's top agent. They came to me when they had nowhere else to go. They *needed* me. They needed my help. And then suddenly I couldn't even go to the shitter by myself."

Tom tried to say something, but he didn't get the chance.

"You don't know what it's like. You don't have the slightest idea how it feels when you lose everything you've ever lived for from one day to the next. This job was my life. And what can I do now? I've been downgraded to tech nerd. I get to mess around on computers and play the hacker for all the rest of you."

"You faked our friendship all this time?"

"'By way of deception, thou shalt wage war,'" said Noah, and he laughed loudly. Something maniacal had crept into his eyes. "I never thought the motto of good old Mossad would serve me so well."

"But why are you helping . . . her?" Tom nodded toward Ossana.

"A few months ago my doctor updated my prognosis. My condition's deteriorating. He read me my death sentence."

Tom was shaken. He did not understand what Noah was doing, or why he had switched to Ossana's side, but he certainly didn't want him to die. He looked into the hate-filled face of his best friend. Or rather, the person he'd thought was his best friend until a few minutes ago. No matter how absurd the situation had become, he could understand where Noah was coming from. True, he had no idea what it was like to suddenly be in a wheelchair, but he could imagine that it could break a man. And he knew that it was his fault. But what made Noah want to help AF?

"Why am I helping her, you ask? Once again, you weren't listening. The Pope already explained it to you. He told you about the power of the stone. How it can perfect things. How it can make you rich. How it can make you healthy. How it can heal. It's the stone that will heal me."

Tom could not remember the last time he'd wept, but he could feel tears filling his eyes now. Compassion was getting the better of him. Noah was grasping at every straw in his desperation to be well again, to escape death. Ossana and AF must have promised him heaven, and the broken man had bought it. Tom knew there was nothing he could do. Not here, not now. There was no point in arguing.

"Tom, Tom, Tom. I liked you. I really did. Your heart's in the right place. Even now, after I've threatened your little girlfriend, after your uncle's been shot, and with your back to the wall, you're still playing the hero, the man who wants justice for everyone. Look, now he's crying, too." Noah turned to Ossana, who giggled softly. "And if I know you, those are tears of pity. You pity me. But you know what?" Noah turned away from Tom and rolled back a short distance, then he turned and glared at him. "You can take your fucking pity and shove it. This is where it ends. You've lost. I've won. I'll be able to walk again. And then, my friend, you'll pay for all the years I've lost because of you."

Ossana signaled to her men that it was time to go. In the distance, Tom could hear sirens. The police and FBI were on the way. The helicopter's rotors began to turn.

"We have to go," Ossana called to Noah, who was still staring at Tom like a madman. Tom slowly lowered his hands. His legs gave way and he slumped onto the ground in shock. Stunned, he could only watch as the soldiers heaved Noah into the helicopter. Ossana was the last to board. She gave Tom a final, spiteful smile and closed the door. Hellen, almost knocked over by the downdraft from the departing chopper, ran to the help-less Tom and dragged him to his feet. Together, they ran back into the building.

Drawn by the deafening roar of the departing helicopter, the first confused guests came out of the theater. Some cried out, startled, when a blood-covered man suddenly stumbled across the Memorial Hall and collapsed.

Tom and Hellen ran to him in time to catch him. They could see immediately how seriously Tom's uncle was hurt.

"Is there a doctor here?" Hellen shouted, tears in her eyes. The sirens of the approaching police grew louder and louder, and several guests ran outside.

Scott, in his pain, could only stammer. "Maybe I was wrong, my boy. It's a bit more than a scratch." He coughed and grimaced in agony.

"You'll make it, Uncle. Hold on just a few more minutes." Tom's voice trembled and tears again welled in his eyes.

"You've got to finish this, Tom. You have to get the stone to safety. You have to . . ." His words gave out and he coughed again.

"Everything will work out. I'll take care of it. What matters now is that we get you patched up."

Tom did not believe a word he was saying. He'd seen people die in action. He knew what it looked like. Scott's coughing ended abruptly, and his body went limp in Tom's arms. The police stormed into the building, doctors and paramedics with them. They reached Scott seconds later, but it was too late. All their attempts at resuscitation failed. Hellen held Tom in her arms. All he could do was stare into space. The red and blue flashing lights of the emergency vehicles cast an eerie light over the tragic scene. Tom saw the world around him in slow motion. He felt utterly alone.

64

CLOUTARD'S HOUSE, NEAR SIENA, TUSCANY

Giuseppina and Cloutard sat on the terrace, satisfied with their work. Giuseppina had cooked, and the table was straining under the weight of enough delicacies to feed a small army: *bruschetta, crostini, insalata caprese, fiori di zucca, prosciutto e melone, pesce spada affumicato, cozze gratinate*, and much more. And those were just the starters. The pasta was still simmering in the kitchen. Cloutard was French and loved his haute cuisine, but when *la mamma* cooked, there was nothing to beat it. Besides, meals were the only times Giuseppina refrained from her usual scolding and remonstrations. Food made her happy.

Cloutard sprinkled a slice of bruschetta with a little olive oil, bit into it and washed it down with a sip of Villa Antinori Rosso. He was happy, too.

"We made a good deal with this Englishman, *o cosa ne pensi*?" said Giuseppina.

Cloutard smacked his lips and nodded. In his mind, he was running through the many new options that would soon be available to him. The sudden ring of his cell phone shattered the idyll and made both of them start. Giuseppina was instantly back in protest mode.

"*Madonna mia, il tuo fottuto telefono*," she snapped when Cloutard looked at the display. He recognized the caller.

The call lasted a few minutes, during which Cloutard only nodded and mumbled an occasional "*Oui, oui.*" He was on his feet and pacing nervously back and forth across the terrace. Giuseppina had turned to her food again. In the meantime, she had loaded mounds of *spaghetti aglio con olio e peperoncino* onto their two plates and begun to eat, her face the picture of bliss. Cloutard finished the call, but tapped at his cell phone nervously: he had another call to make.

"Francesco, *gli spaghetti si raffreddano*," she said reproachfully. "Don't let it get cold."

But Cloutard finished the second call before sitting down with his foster mother again.

"I have to go. There's something I have to take care of, something that will solve all my problems once and for all. And it fits in well with our new plan."

"How many times have you said that before, and how many times have you brought shame on our family? Innocento, God rest his soul, would be deeply disappointed in you."

"Please, Mamma. Spare me the old song. I know what papa would think and do, and I will do my best, I promise. But I am not him, and one day you will have to accept that."

His tone had become sharper and to Cloutard's surprise, Giuseppina did not reply immediately. She simply continued to eat.

"Do whatever you have to do," she said after a while, getting to her feet and kissing him on the forehead. "But take Marcello and Giuliano with you. Better safe than sorry."

Her tone was so adamant that Cloutard could not say no. It wouldn't make any difference if he did. He looked at his watch. "I have to hurry. My flight leaves in two hours."

65

1943, OFFICE OF THE PREFECT OF THE
VATICAN ARCHIVE, THE VATICAN

Monsignor Giuseppe Negozi, Prefect of the Vatican
Council, was worried as his brother Silvio left the office.
Silvio and their third brother, Angelo, had accepted an
important duty: to bring the Holy of Holies to safety. The
Vatican was no longer safe from Hitler's thugs.

The Nazis' interest in historical, mythical and occult artifacts had been general knowledge for years. Himmler,
and even Hitler himself, were intensively engaged in the
pursuit and had sent diverse teams around the world to
track down important relics and treasures. And there was
no doubt in the prefect's mind that the Philosopher's
Stone was high on their list. Worse still, there had been
contact between the top echelons of the Vatican and
Hitler's Germany, which meant that anything could
happen—including the Nazis getting their hands on the
fabled stone and using it to do irreparable damage. The
prefect was one of the few people who had actually
witnessed the power of the stone, who had seen the good

—and the evil—of which the stone was capable. And when the grasping fingers of the Nazis began to reach out toward the Holy See, he and his two brothers had decided to break the stone into three pieces, taking two of them far away from the Vatican for safekeeping. Angelo had made contact with members of the Austrian resistance, who in turn were in touch with the Americans, and the brothers had decided to send one of the pieces to the United States. He himself and his brother Silvio maintained good relations with the Coptic Church, and had therefore decided to take the third stone to Abyssinia and hand it over to Emperor Haile Selassie. Both journeys would be dangerous, and the monsignor's concern was etched deep into his face.

Silvio Negozi arrived in Civitavecchia the following day, and was horrified at the destruction he found. The city and port had been torn apart by air raids. The arsenal, the watchtowers, the old lighthouse and Bramante's fortress had all fallen victim to the bombing. But Silvio's luck was in. He found a captain who agreed to take him across the Mediterranean and through the Suez Canal to Abyssinia. Silvio had received substantial funds from his brother to finance the voyage, almost all of which went toward the captain's wages: the crossing was exceptionally dangerous, and correspondingly expensive. One week later, the ship docked in Assab, where Silvio was met by Tekle Haymanot, a friend of Giuseppe who was also a cleric of the Ethiopian Orthodox Church. Together, Silvio and Tekle set off on an even more arduous journey. In an old rattletrap that bore only the slightest resemblance to an actual car, and was apparently a remnant of Benito Mussolini's occupation, they drove far inland to Addis Ababa, the capital of the Empire of Abyssinia, and one day after Silvio's arrival in the city, he was received by Emperor Haile Selassie himself, the 225th successor of King Solomon. The King of Kings, as Haile Selassie was often known, was extraordinarily popular in his own country, where he enjoyed godlike status and where, with the help of the British, he had returned to power in 1941.

"My brother, Monsignor Negozi, has sent me. I bring with me a fragment of the holiest relic of all. The Philosopher's Stone must be kept safe. We hope that this piece of it will find a haven in your empire."

The Emperor nodded his thanks and accepted the package from Silvio. "My country has suffered greatly under the yoke of the fascists. We are glad that we have been able to free ourselves from their oppression. We give thanks to the Lord for that, and thanks also to know that our greatest treasure has not fallen into the hands of our enemies."

Silvio knew what the emperor was talking about. According to the tradition of the Ethiopian Church, the Ark of the Covenant had been stolen by minions of Menelik, the son of Solomon and the Queen of Sheba.

"You will accompany me with the package to our holy city," said Selassie.

Silvio, equally moved and thrilled at the invitation, bowed deeply before the emperor. Would the emperor take him to Aksum and show him the Ethiopian Church's greatest treasure? According to the Kebra Nagast, the country's thirteenth-century national epic, the Ethiopian emperors could be traced in a direct line back to Menelik . . . and the Kebra Nagast also told of a holy relic reportedly kept in a chapel beside the church of St. Mary of Zion.

66

RED SEA, OFF THE COAST OF ERITREA

The "Avalon," almost five hundred feet of mega-yacht, cut through the stormy sea. The weather had turned unseasonably rough in the last hours, and the spray whipped high against the hull of the ocean-going behemoth, which nevertheless glided with amazing serenity through the Red Sea.

The end is near, thought the man, as he stood at the stern window on the master deck and gazed out over the turbulent sea. In the distance, he saw Ossana's helicopter approaching at high speed across the foaming waters.

She had actually done it. In a few moments, he would be holding the second piece of the stone in his hands, and in a few hours they would have the third. He had waited a very long time for this, but today would bring him a huge step closer to his goal.

Superficially, the magnate's ship looked like a normal, if exceptionally large, luxury yacht, the kind any super-rich businessman might command. But in reality it was more like a warship. Equipped with computer systems and listening equipment equal to anything in the NSA's arsenal, with a missile defense system, two helicopter landing pads and laser-based anti-paparazzi shielding, the yacht was probably the most dangerous non-military vessel in the world. The anti-paparazzi shield prevented the yacht from being photographed; anyone trying to do so would get no more than a blank image. The ship housed four separate paramilitary units, one of which was on the foredeck preparing for its mission, loading another helicopter, a dark-gray Airbus H215, with all the equipment they would need. The ship could accommodate a second helicopter at the stern, where it could be stowed below deck with its rotors folded.

The rough seas and the high speed of the yacht caused Ossana's pilot some difficulty when he tried to land the helicopter, but she and Noah were soon making their way inside, out of the storm. Immediately, three of the crew refueled and loaded the helicopter, making it ready to join the Airbus on the upcoming mission. Ossana and Noah rode the elevator to the master deck.

"Well done, my dear," the man welcomed his adopted daughter, welcoming her with open arms and embracing her warmly. She kissed him lovingly on his cheek.

"Thank you, Daddy," she said, her voice almost girlish. She stood beside her father with one arm around his waist.

"Well, let's take a look, shall we?" the man said. He turned to Noah, who had a small, cloth-wrapped parcel on his lap. Noah handed the man the stone piece that

Hellen and Tom had retrieved from deep below the Masonic memorial.

Nervous with anticipation, as cautious as if it were made of glass, the man carried the stone fragment to put it with the one he already had. The fragment from the Vatican lay inside an open suitcase on a sideboard in the center of the suite. He peeled apart the wrappings and put the cloth aside and, after gently examining the shimmering green stone, he placed it in the suitcase beside its twin. When the two stones touched, he could have sworn he felt an electrical discharge. The hair on his forearms bristled.

"Thank you for your assistance," the man said, finally turning to Noah and extending his hand.

"Just remember our agreement," Noah replied with a trace of bitterness.

"Don't worry. I am a man of my word. You want to be able to walk again, and I promised you that," the man replied, and he smiled at Noah. He closed the lid of the suitcase and snapped the clasps shut, then turned and handed the case to Ossana.

"Finish it."

"Yes, Daddy." She took the suitcase, gave her father another kiss on the cheek and turned away. Noah nodded to the man and rolled after her. She was already waiting for him in the elevator.

When they stepped out onto the rear helideck, four fully-equipped soldiers jumped into the helicopter's cargo hold. Eight more boarded the chopper on the front helideck: twelve combat-ready soldiers in two choppers awaited Ossana's orders. Two men from the ship's crew hoisted Noah into the machine and secured the wheelchair in place. The rotors, already idling, began to turn faster.

Ossana, not yet on board, looked up one last time at her father, who watched her departure from the master deck. She waved at him, then made a circular movement with her left arm, signaling "GO" to the pilot. With catlike elegance, she sprang into the helicopter, took her place on the end of the bench seat and closed the door. Moments later, the two machines lifted off in perfect synchrony from their respective helidecks and turned toward the west.

67

LALIBELA, ETHIOPIA

Riding in the De Havilland DHC-8-200 turboprop was a bone-rattling affair. Unfortunately, they had been forced to leave the Pope's luxurious jet behind in Addis Ababa; machines like that could not land at airports as small as the one at Lalibela. To get to such a remote place, especially with a storm on their tail, took something of a spirit of adventure. Normally Tom would have been in his element, but the events of the last days had sucked all the joy out of the trip.

Tom stared out the window, lost in thought. Even in the worst patches of turbulence, his expression didn't change. Hellen sat beside him. She felt sorry for everything he had been through, but for the moment had pushed aside whatever other feelings she might have for him. She wanted and needed to be there for him, but there was too much at stake. Right now only one thing mattered, and that was getting through this flight in one piece. Eyes closed, she sat with her seatbelt cinched tight and her fingers digging into the armrests.

Tom's own emotions were stuck in a loop. He couldn't think. Anger, vengefulness, disgust, desolation, disappointment—the feelings cycled every second or two. Uncle Scott was dead, and Noah was working with Ossana. He still couldn't get his head around either fact. His best friend had switched allegiance, and was now working for the people who had killed not only Tom's parents, but his beloved uncle and friend. He could understand that Noah was angry with him, even that he hated him. He was the reason Noah was in the wheelchair in the first place. But to turn into a terrorist and put the world in danger? Tom could not stand by and let that happen. He had to stop Noah.

When the plane finally landed safely on the remote runway in the middle of the barren landscape of Lalibela, Hellen literally had to slap Tom out of his maudlin thoughts. He hadn't even realized they had landed. They took their few belongings from the overhead lockers and disembarked with the other passengers. The plane had come to a stop in a small service area directly in front of the terminal, beside the lone runway. Except for the air traffic control tower, the building looked more like a regional bus station than an airport terminal.

They left the building and were met immediately by their local contact, in an ancient vehicle reminiscent of a jeep. Abebe Abiye's dark-tanned, leathery skin made it almost impossible to estimate his age, but there was a welcoming smile behind his black beard. Like most of the men around them, he wore light, sand-colored pants beneath a knee-length caftan and the traditional white scarf. On his head he wore a plain white turban.

Next to him stood a young woman, also wearing a white scarf: Vittoria Arcano.

"Thanks for coming," Tom said as he greeted the athletic and attractive young woman. The former Interpol agent had literally bumped into Tom on her first day of work in Rome six months earlier, and he had turned her life upside down. A couple of hours later, she had saved his life. He could trust her.

"Nice to see you again," Hellen said, shaking Vittoria's hand and looking her up and down. She turned to a puzzled Tom and added, "We met at my parents' house in Antwerp."

"The pleasure's mine," Vittoria replied. She turned to Tom. "And thanks for calling. I really needed to get away." She jumped enthusiastically into their transport.

"Mr. Wagner, Ms. de Mey, welcome to Lalibela," said Abebe Abiye cheerfully. He held out his hand toward the car invitingly. Somewhat skeptically, Tom and Hellen took their seats in what Tom guessed was a mostly home-made car.

"You should put these on." Vittoria handed Tom and Hellen the same kind of scarf that she was wearing. "We'll blend into the crowds much better."

"Thanks," said Tom, accepting the scarf that all pilgrims wore when they visited the rock churches of Lalibela. "I hope we're not too late," he shouted as they roared away.

They had been driving for about twenty minutes through the harsh, hilly landscape when the small village appeared down below. Abebe Abiye stopped the car.

"Very strange," he said. "There are never storms in the dry season." He pointed away to the east, where dark clouds loomed. The massive thunderstorm was moving in their direction, and only minutes later the first fat drops began to fall. But rain was not all that the dark clouds brought with them. Two dark-gray helicopters rode in on the storm, thundering over the little village of Lalibela.

68

LALIBELA, ETHIOPIA

The dark helicopters swooped in to land over the small clearing between the northern and eastern groups of churches, scattering hundreds of the visiting faithful. The soldiers leaped clear of the helicopters the instant they touched the ground. Pilgrims on their way to the churches turned and ran in fear, back along the road that led to the valley. Mothers grabbed their children and fled. Within minutes most of the people in the area had moved to safety, leaving the area around the churches all but empty.

The noise abated when the helicopters shut down their engines.

"Bring me the priests," Ossana ordered. Followed by three soldiers, one of them pushing Noah's wheelchair over the uneven ground, she headed for the eastern complex of churches.

Nine soldiers fanned out to carry out Ossana's order.

Abiye's "jeep" bumped down the main road into the village. Once they had seen the approaching helicopters, they were forced to make their arrival as covert as possible. Abebe Abiye parked the car behind some trees below the eastern churches, and the four of them crept through the bushes and up the red boulders, concealing themselves in a rocky niche a little off the track with a clear view of the Bet Amanuel church and what Ossana and her men were up to.

———

The twelve churches of Lalibela were divided into a northern and an eastern group about five hundred yards apart over an area of forty acres. However, Bet Giyorgis— the church consecrated to St. George—lay a little farther away, up the hill a short distance to the west. The soldiers worked their way methodically through the twelve churches. Some were no more than small holes carved into the rock, one had formerly been used as a prison, and others were impressive sculptures in their own right. The soldiers dragged the peaceful priests, who normally spent their days at their desks reading from the ancient scriptures, away by force. They drove the priests in front of them, herding them together like cattle. Even now, some of the faithful were still trying to find their way to safety. Soon, all of the priests were crowded before Ossana beneath the artificial canopy that covered the church of Bet Amanuel and its surrounding chasm.

Abebe Abiye gasped when he saw the captive priests. "We have to help them," he said, his voice filled with desperation.

"No, stay here," Vittoria said, pulling him back. "There's nothing you can do right now."

From their hiding place they watched Noah, who seemed to be enjoying himself immensely. He forced the priests to kneel side by side in a single line. Then he rolled from one to the next. Behind them stood three soldiers, covering the priests with their automatic weapons.

"What is your name?" Noah asked the first priest.

One of the soldiers translated his words.

"Tesfaye," replied the fearful priest.

"Where is the Holy of Holies?" Noah said.

Tesfaye shrugged and shook his head. "Everything here is holy. It is a sacred site," he replied. Noah slapped the man, knocking the turban from his head, but Tesfaye ignored the humiliation. The other priests had their eyes closed and murmured prayers to themselves. Noah's impatience grew. He demanded a pistol from one of the soldiers, who hesitated and looked to Ossana. A small nod from her was enough: the man obeyed and handed Noah the gun. Noah cocked the weapon demonstratively in front of the second priest and pressed the pistol to his head. With fiery eyes, Noah glared at the man.

"Look at me. Open your goddamned eyes. Where is the Holy of Holies?" Noah bellowed, his question echoed instantly by the translator. The priest did not react. Like his brothers, he rocked back and forth, praying. The ear-splitting blast of the gun smashed through the monotonous drumming of the rain. Even Ossana flinched—she had not reckoned with this. The man's head jerked back and then rocked forward again, and his lifeless body slumped sideways to the ground. Tesfaye, his face and clothes covered in his brother's blood, looked at Noah in terror. For a moment Noah did not move. He gazed vacantly, maniacally, at nothing.

A silent scream escaped Hellen as she tried to process the horror of the crime committed by a man whom she had considered a friend until a few hours earlier. Fury coursed through Tom's veins. Noah had gone completely out of his mind. All four of them were soaked to the skin, and yet the tears of anger welling in Hellen's eyes were unmistakable.

"We have to do something," said Vittoria with an edge of desperation. Abebe Abiye crossed himself.

"Yes, we do. We can't let Noah shoot them one by one until he gets what he wants," Tom whispered.

"The priests won't say a word," Abiye said bitterly. "They've sworn to protect the stone, even if it means their own death."

"What do you suggest?" Hellen said to Tom.

"We have to get our hands on the third fragment. If we can destroy it, then all of this is over."

"We can't just destroy it! The Holy Father s—" Hellen protested, but Tom cut her off.

"No! What we can't do is let a dangerous artifact fall into the hands of psychopaths who want to unleash a catastrophe that will make the seven biblical plagues and climate change look like a Teletubbies picnic." Tom held his breath for a moment and looked Hellen in the eye. She knew he was right.

69

LALIBELA AIRPORT, ETHIOPIA

Cloutard passed through the arrivals hall at the small airport. The entire building was unadorned, and was painted a bland, ugly grayish-beige. Several tourists milled in the hall, there to visit the rock churches. Lalibela had not yet suffered the indignities of mass tourism, but even UNESCO was afraid that the internet and people's insatiable urge for ever more exotic destinations would one day reduce this holy place to yet another backdrop for obligatory Instagram selfies.

Cloutard's gaze wandered through the hall until he found something to admire: the artfully decorated ceiling. It was paneled in wood and depicted crosses in various shapes, calling to mind the rock churches of Lalibela. In the past, Cloutard had often been a frequent visitor to the village: the entire region had always been a lucrative site for a tomb raider and smuggler of historical relics. He deactivated the flight mode on his phone and a half-second later a message reached him: a picture of his contact. Cloutard memorized the face and eyes and scanned the none too spacious hall.

"Monsieur Cloutard?"

Cloutard turned to see the man whose picture he had just received.

Cloutard nodded. "*Oui, c'est moi.*"

"We have no time to lose. We have quite a bit to do, and the clock is ticking. Come, come."

The man hurried him to the exit and out to an old, dented van covered with stickers of Bob Marley, Rastafarian motifs, and portraits of the last Emperor of Abyssinia, Haile Selassie. Cloutard tossed his travel bag into the back seat and climbed in. Seconds later, the man was already stepping on the gas.

"We have to take a small detour to get to the entrance unseen."

They left the airport grounds and drove north along a gravel road.

"*Cela pourrait être une mauvaise tempête,*" Cloutard murmured and pointed to the dark clouds that starting to gather over Lalibela.

"Pardon?"

"Sorry. I just said that I was surprised at the storm," said Cloutard.

"Yes. So are we . . ." said the man, a trace of worry in his voice.

After about thirty minutes, they reached a hotel called

the Old Abyssinia Lodge. As soon as they had passed by, the driver made an abrupt left turn and drove cross-country. The bus bumped down the hill past the hotel. Cloutard held on tight, afraid that the bouncing, bumping vehicle might break apart at any moment, but it stayed in one piece. At the bottom of the hill, something resembling a roadway reappeared and the drive continued in a more civilized manner. After another five minutes, the man braked and the vehicle rolled gently to a stop. Cloutard could see no reason for him to do so—all around was barren land, dried up trees, rocks and withered, prickly bushes.

"Here we are," the man said, as if that must be obvious to anyone, and he climbed out of the van. Cloutard followed him, looking around in confusion.

70

THE ROCK CHURCHES OF LALIBELA, ETHIOPIA

The storm was gradually growing to biblical proportions. Muddy rivulets splashed down the hillside and washed the priest's blood away into the valley. The rain whipped mercilessly into Ossana's face, but it did not bother her. She was a soldier.

She stood at the edge of the rocky plateau and looked down on the church of Bet Amanuel. Along with the famous Bet Giyorgis, it was one of the two churches of Lalibela whose rooflines were flush with the ground. Here, the tuff had been excavated to a depth of more than thirty feet to create an impressive, monolithic house of God. The muddy rainwater, inexorably following the pull of gravity, washed around Ossana's military boots and plunged downward into the "churchyard"—a narrow, excavated area surrounding the structure and separating it from the rock face. The only entrance was on the upstream side, so the water had nowhere to run off. Instead it pooled there, filling it little by little. The water from the paths and the other churches higher up the hill joined it; the walkways, hand-cut ravines and church-yards carved into the volcanic rock were only equipped with rudimentary drains; they weren't made to handle such an unprecedented downpour.

Ossana gazed out from under the canopy at the surrounding landscape and wondered where Tom Wagner was. He would not have given up. Was he already here? Was he watching? Had he perhaps already found the stone? *I have to play this safe*, she told herself and she made a barbaric decision.

"Stop this! Noah, you won't get anywhere like this. They won't talk." Ossana went to Noah, who was about to send the priest Tesfaye to join his brother with a bullet. "I have a better idea." She turned to one of her soldiers and gave him an order in Afrikaans. He nodded.

"On your feet! Move!" the soldier barked cruelly, and they herded the priests down to the Bet Amanuel church. Ossana watched from a ledge above and Noah rolled to a stop beside her. They both looked down.

"This is your last chance," Ossana shouted down as loudly as she could. Even so, the storm all but drowned her out. "Where is the Holy of Holies?" The priests, already standing knee-deep in muddy water, continued to ignore her and went on muttering their prayers. A small wave of Ossana's hand was enough; the soldiers forced the distraught priests inside the church. One by one they were pushed through the narrow doorway, then the soldiers closed the rough wooden door and wedged it shut, leaving no way for the poor clergymen to escape.

The water was rising relentlessly. Soon it would swallow the church completely.

The voices of the priests, resigning themselves to their fate with prayer, could no longer be heard. The din of the rain drowned out everything.

"Find me the Holy of Holies," Ossana shouted at her men. She looked around, wondering if this would be enough to lure Tom out from wherever he was hiding.

———

"She's going too far," Tom growled. "When I get my hands on the stone, I'm going to find her and jam it somewhere the sun never, ever shines."

"I'll take care of the priests," Vittoria said. Tom nodded and she slipped away.

"Tell us, where exactly is the stone?" Hellen asked Abebe Abiye. He hesitated. Could he really trust these two? They had come to rescue the stone and with it the legacy of his people, not to enrich themselves with it. And in the broadest sense, they had been sent by God, after all.

"It is in Bet Giyorgis, about five hundred yards up the hill to the west. But there's a tunnel. We can get up there without being seen."

"Then show us the way," Tom said.

Cautiously, Tom, Hellen and Abiye left their hiding place and circled around the church complex, while Vittoria crept in the opposite direction. A short way to the west, beneath a small group of trees that gave the trio the cover they needed, they were able to slip into another of the hand-cut ravines. They moved slowly along the thirty-foot-high rock face, the deep water making it all but impossible to progress either quickly or silently.

Suddenly, at a corner, Tom's fist shot into the air: HALT! His arm swung back, pressing Hellen, close behind him, against the rock wall. He signaled to her and Abiye to be quiet. One of Ossana's soldiers was heading straight toward them. Tom motioned to Hellen and Abiye to retreat a few steps, while he waited for the mercenary. When the man's assault rifle appeared at the corner, Tom grabbed hold of the barrel, yanked it forward and was able to swing around and grab the surprised man from behind. The audible crack of the man's neck made Hellen recoil, and Abiye crossed himself again. The body slumped, lifeless. Tom quickly unstrapped the soldier's tactical vest and put it on, then strapped the man's holster and pistol to his own thigh. He checked the radio, but it was of no use: it was secured with a PIN code.

Next time I should make sure I get the code first, he thought. Then he checked the pockets of the vest and found something he could use.

"Let's go. No time to lose," he said, and looked back at two shocked faces.

They were only a few steps from the mouth of the tunnel. They slipped into the small hole in the ravine wall and began the climb to Bet Giyorgis. As they made their way along the passage, water shot out from openings on all sides, pouring through the extensive system of tunnels.

"Looks as if whatever gods are up there already know what Ossana and Noah are up to. I think they're giving us a little taste of what's ahead," Tom joked, jabbing a finger skyward.

Soaked to the skin and ducking low, Tom, Hellen and Abiye trudged through the low tunnel, heading west.

71

BET GIYORGIS, LALIBELA, ETHIOPIA

At first, the ascent through the narrow tunnel was hard going. But the higher they got, the less they had to fight against the water. Now it was down to ankle deep, and they made better progress.

"We are almost there," said Abiye.

And then there it was, the proverbial light at the end of the tunnel. Moments later they left the tunnel behind and clambered out into the open air again, to find found themselves face to face with the forty-foot stone wall of the monolithic church known as Bet Giyorgis.

"The Church of Saint George," Hellen whispered reverently.

"Really? *The* Saint George?" Tom asked.

"Yes," Hellen replied.

"The one from back then?"

"Yes!"

"... with the sword of—"

"Ye-ess!"

"... and the dragon ..."

"Of course!"

"Okay," said Tom. He'd got it.

Like the other churches of Lalibela, Bet Giyorgis had been carved like a sculpture directly into the red volcanic tuff: first the outer form, then the huge block had been hollowed out and decorated. The elaborately hewn church was unofficially known as the eighth wonder of the world, and was actually the newest of this complex of churches, which had been intended to recreate Jerusalem. The spread of Islam through northern Africa in the 7th century had literally cut Africa's Christians off from the original Jerusalem, so a second Jerusalem needed to be built.

"The first churches here were carved out about eight hundred years ago, during the reign of Emperor Gebre Meskel Lalibela, who gave his name to this place," Hellen explained. "Not much is known about their construction, though it's generally thought to have taken more than a century. According to legend, however, Emperor Lalibela, with the help of angels, carved the churches out of the solid rock by himself in just twenty-six years."

The church was certainly an impressive sight. The cruci-form building towered in the center of a forty-foot-deep hole that extended only a few yards beyond the walls of the church itself. Here, too, the water was running over the rock edges and pouring into the "churchyard." The numerous small waterfalls would have been quite a spectacle, had they not been caused by a terrible storm and threatened the lives of the dozen priests trapped inside the Bet Amanuel church, farther down the hill. The inky blackness of the sky and the unrelenting thunderstorm only added to the apocalyptic atmosphere.

They walked up the few steps and entered the dimly lit church. Located as it was at the top of the mountain, the water could still flow down the path. The interior of the church was elaborately decorated; the floor was completely covered with carpets, and as in mosques it was customary to remove one's shoes before entering. The rear section was covered by a heavy curtain. Tom stood in the center of the church and turned in a circle, intrigued by the unusual structure.

"It must be behind the curtain," Hellen said. Abiye let out a small audible gasp. In over a thousand years, no one except Coptic priests had ever stepped behind the curtain. But in this situation, an exception had to be made. Abiye crossed himself and followed Hellen behind the curtain, where they found more carpets, a candlestick, books, scrolls and, out of sight beneath a cloth, a shrine. On top of the shrine lay an elaborate cross.

Hellen went down on her knees, moved the cross aside and carefully lifted off the cloth. Beneath it was an acacia-wood chest, decorated with gold. She moved her hands tentatively toward the ornate object and just before she touched it, a small spark zapped her finger. She flinched, but smiled. She lifted the lid and there it lay, atop a bed of soft cloth: the last fragment of the Philosopher's Stone!

"Tom! I've got it!" Hellen cried, and Tom also stepped behind the curtain. Hellen lifted the stone carefully out of its box and held it out to him.

"Nobody move!" a voice suddenly barked. The command came from inside the church.

"Out! Now!" a second voice shouted.

Tom, Hellen and Abiye looked at one another. They'd been discovered. Tom was not particularly surprised. He'd suspected all along that he would have to face his enemies sooner or later and he had taken precautions. He winked at Hellen, opened a pocket on his vest, took out a small object and called to the soldiers outside: "I want to talk to Ossana, face to face!"

Tom stepped out from behind the curtain. In one hand he held the third piece of the Philosopher's Stone. In the other he held something that scared the hell out of the soldiers outside.

72

THE ROCK CHURCHES OF LALIBELA,
ETHIOPIA

The two helicopters stood in a clearing to the northwest of the lower church complex. Only the two pilots had remained with the machines, and both of them were dozing. Vittoria observed two patrolling soldiers who had stopped at the helicopters, and overheard a radio message informing them that Tom and Hellen had been captured. A sense of panic bubbled up inside her, but her training allowed her to keep her emotions under control. Her sensei had always told her: "Thoughts are like seeds: you will reap what you sow."

Tom and Hellen are okay, she decided, and shifted her focus back to her own task. Tom, at least, could look after himself.

Vittoria had last seen Tom four months earlier in Vienna. After the first time fate had thrown them together, he had recommended her for the job that had first been offered to him. Since then, she had been working as the first official special agent employed by the newly reorganized Blue Shield. Theresia de Mey, Hellen's mother and

Blue Shield's new boss, had spent the last six months trying to breathe new life into the organization—but she had met with little success so far, due to a lack of funding. Now here Vittoria was, on her first official field assignment for Blue Shield, coincidentally working with Tom Wagner again. What could possibly go wrong?

"Now that's a job I'd like to have," one of the soldiers said with a nod toward one of the dozing pilots.

"Yeah. Nice and safe. And dry," the second added. With every step he took, water squelched out of his boots.

The second man suddenly jerked open the door of the chopper, and the startled pilot fell out and landed face first in the mud. The raucous laughter of the soldiers woke the pilot of the second helicopter, and he left his comfortably dry cockpit and ran across to see what was going on.

This was Vittoria's chance. She crept cautiously out of her hiding place and over to the empty helicopter, keeping one eye on the soldiers and pilots. Silently, she slid back the door to the cargo hold and climbed inside. She needed a weapon, fast, and soon found what she was looking for. In a small case attached to the rear bulkhead was a Heckler & Koch pistol with a spare magazine. She took both. And then she found the jackpot. Just as she was about to exit the helicopter, she saw that the pilot was on his way back. She was trapped.

"These special forces guys are all kinds of fucked up," the pilot muttered to himself, shaking his head and chuckling as he climbed back into the cockpit. He leaned back in the pilot's seat and closed his eyes again.

Behind him, in the cargo bay, Vittoria lay flat on her stomach, petrified. She barely dared to breathe, let alone actually move. *Time's running out,* she thought. Every second counted if she was going to save the drowning priests. She had to do something. And she had to do it soon.

73

BET GIYORGIS, LALIBELA, ETHIOPIA

Ossana stepped into the gloomy church, followed a few moments later by two soldiers carrying Noah as if he were on a palanquin. Tom stood in the center, holding the stone fragment aloft, while Hellen and Abebe Abiye sat on a small bench a little to one side. The two soldiers who had radioed Ossana had their rifles trained on Tom.

"Looks like I was right," she said, applauding sarcastically and stepping toward Tom.

"Not so fast, Princess," Tom said. He turned the stone fragment around. On the back he had attached a small lump of C4 explosive, and in his other hand he held a remote detonator. He raised the detonator demonstratively in the air. "Here's how this is going to play out," he said. "We're all going to go back over to the church where you've got the priests locked up. You're then going to release them. When we're all nice and safe, I'll think about giving you the stone." He spoke with more bravado than real confidence. This time even he was scared shitless. He was far from certain that his plan would work.

"Mr. Wagner." Ossana moved around Tom, shaking her head. She took the pistol from the holster on his thigh and handed it to one of her soldiers. "You come here with a little lump of explosive and think that gives you any power to make demands? Well, you are mistaken. I have time. The priests, on the other hand, have thirty-five minutes. Maybe." She looked at her watch and rocked her head side to side in time with the passing seconds. "Then they drown. And I can't really see you blowing yourself up along with the rest of us. I know you're bluffing, and I call. Let's see what you've got."

She stopped directly in front of Tom and stared deep into his eyes. Tom swallowed.

"No," Ossana continued. "This is going to play out a little differently. You give us the stone and then you help us find the Holy of Holies. Ideally . . ." she glanced at her watch ". . . in the next twenty minutes. That will give you enough time to save the priests. I give you my word about that."

"The Holy of Holies?" Tom asked. "I thought the stone was—"

"She's after the Ark of the Covenant," said Hellen before Ossana could say another word. She stood up and saw Tom's confusion. "Yes, *the* Ark of the Covenant, the one with the Ten Commandments. 'Raiders of the Lost Ark'. Indiana Jones . . ." Hellen rolled her eyes and shook her head. "In Nikolaus's papers, she must have read one of his crazy theories about the Philosopher's Stone, the one that says that the third stone tablet Moses is supposed to have received from God has to be replaced in the Ark of the Covenant to activate its power. Or some hocus-pocus nonsense like that."

"There's nothing hocus-pocus about it, Ms. de Mey. We are standing in the country that has claimed for centuries to possess the real Ark of the Covenant. Now, the Ethiopians want to make the rest of the world believe that it's in Aksum. They even built a special building just to house it. But we happen to know that they've taken some inspiration from the Americans—the aliens aren't really in Area 51, after all. They're actually somewhere else, somewhere nobody suspects them to be, in a place nobody knows anything about."

She had turned away from Tom and now moved slowly over to where Abebe Abiye was sitting. She crouched in front of him. "And they are guarded by people that no one would recognize as guards."

She took out her pistol, placed it under Abiye's chin and pushed upward. Both of them rose to their feet.

"Why do you think I would reveal anything to you? Like my brothers, I am willing to die for it."

"You? Oh, yes, I believe you. But are you prepared to sacrifice innocent lives for it?" Ossana swung the gun to the left, aiming at Hellen's head.

"All right. You win." Tom tossed the remote detonator aside and positioned himself between Ossana and Hellen and Abiye. He handed Ossana the stone. "We'll help you find it," he said, and he turned back and nodded encouragingly at Hellen and Abiye.

"Tom, you old softie! You're so easily manipulated. To think that I get to be on the other side when the great Tom Wagner screws up," Noah said, deliberately mispronouncing Tom's last name. He said it as a German would —"Vahg-ner"—knowing how much Tom hated that. "I never in my wildest dreams thought I'd see this day."

He rolled over to Ossana and she handed him the stone. "Today you'll see for yourselves that the stone and the Ark are no myth." Noah suddenly raised his gun and shot Abebe Abiye.

Hellen screamed, but Ossana only rolled her eyes in irritation and said, "Now what was the point of that?"

Hellen caught Abiye as he stumbled and tried to support him as he collapsed. She knelt beside the dying man and pressed on the wound, trying in vain to stop the bleeding.

"I wanted to know if he was telling the truth. And I have to say, it looks as if he was," Noah replied coldly.

Hellen held the Abiye in her arms as he breathed his last. In the meantime, Ossana had gone to one of her soldiers and whispered something in his ear. He and another soldier left the church.

Tom looked at Hellen with admiration and let out an audible sigh. "I wanted to try and save you," he said to Noah, though his eyes stayed on Hellen. He couldn't bear to look at Noah now. "I thought you'd just strayed from the path. But now I see that you've blown up every bridge you've crossed. What happened to you?" He took a deep breath. "We'll meet again, Noah," he growled. No specific threat was needed to make clear what would happen when they did.

"Since the day I woke up in the hospital and the doctors told me I'd be stuck in this thing forever"—Noah's voice broke and he slapped against the armrests of his wheelchair angrily—"I've wanted my revenge. But I learned to wait. I learned to put on my brave-little-boy face until the opportunity came to make you pay for your incompetence."

"Enough!" Ossana snapped. "We have more important things to do, and Mr. Wagner still has a few lives he'd like to save." Moments later the two soldiers returned. They were carrying a large flight case, upon which lay a small silver suitcase. They set the flight case down on the church floor, and one soldier took the smaller case and stepped aside. The other crouched, opened the flight case and removed a very strange-looking piece of equipment.

74

THE ROCK CHURCHES OF LALIBELA, ETHIOPIA

Vittoria cared little for her own life, but the twelve priests imprisoned in Bet Amanuel were running out of time. The water was rising relentlessly and their lives were in her hands. Somehow, she had to get out of the helicopter. Just then, someone hammered on the cockpit window and her heart leapt into her throat. Two soldiers were standing outside the cargo hatch, about to open it up.

"You got that special gear in the back?" the soldier asked the pilot. Vittoria's panic grew. Her hands trembling, she took aim at the door.

"It's in the other chopper. I'll give you a hand," the pilot said, and he got out and went with the two soldiers to the second helicopter.

Now or never. Vittoria slipped the carrying straps of the bag she'd found over her shoulders, carrying it like a backpack. She jumped silently down from the cargo bay and pulled the sliding door closed behind her as gently as she could. Pistol at the ready, she crouched beside the helicopter, waiting and watching the men. The two soldiers seemed to have found what they were looking for. Carrying a large flight case with a smaller case on top of it, they jogged back up to the church of Bet Giyorgis.

Now what could that be? Vittoria thought. She waited until the pilot was back in the cockpit and the coast was clear, then hurried to the artificial ravine and followed it. She rounded a corner and suddenly pulled up short. In front of her, face down in the water, lay the motionless body of a soldier. She exhaled sharply, then bent down and searched the body, but she had little hope of finding anything useful. Tom—who else?—had done a thorough job.

She marched on through the flooded ravine, soaked to the skin, wading through the now knee-high water. Her training had certainly toughened her, but she could feel herself slowly but surely reaching her limits. But she could not allow herself to give up. The water might be up to her knees, but it had to be up to the priests' necks by now. Tom had once told her how it felt to be about to drown . . . she had to pull herself together now and do her job. She took a cell phone from her jacket and studied a stored satellite image of the church complex. She quickly found her position—she was right where she needed to be. Here, on the other side of the wall of rock in front of her and surrounding this group of churches, was the churchyard, with water still pouring into it.

Moments later she was standing at the point where the wall to the churchyard was thinnest. She slipped the bag off her back and zipped it open. From inside, she took out a large block of C4 explosive and pressed it into a crack in the wall. Then she twisted the detonator deep into the clay-like mass and activated it. With the remote trigger in her hand, she moved away. She needed cover, and found it behind a rock on a small embankment. She extended the antenna on the remote, lifted the protective cap covering the trigger, scrunched her eyes together and flipped the toggle switch.

Nothing happened.

Suddenly, the deactivated detonator fell onto the embankment beside her and she felt the barrel of a gun jammed against her neck.

75

BET GIYORGIS, LALIBELA, ETHIOPIA

The device looked like a cross between a robotic lawn mower and a Mars rover. One of the soldiers set it down in a corner of the church. Then he took the touchscreen remote control, activated both devices and handed the remote to Noah.

"Ground-penetrating radar. If there's anything down there, I'll find it," Noah said, and the scanner began to move. It was not an easy job, however: the peculiarities of the church's construction made the floor very uneven.

The second soldier opened the smaller case for Ossana. It contained a slim folder and the other two sections of the stone. Ossana removed a sheet of paper from the folder and the soldier turned to Noah, who placed the third stone piece inside the case. Overhead, lightning flashed, followed instantly by the crash and rumble of thunder. For a moment everyone held their breath. Noah coughed. Tom and Hellen abruptly realized that there was more to this than mere hocus-pocus. This was deadly serious.

The sheet of paper in her hand, Ossana turned and faced Tom and Hellen.

"Palffy was obsessed with the Library of Alexandria and the Philosopher's Stone. Twenty years ago, purely by chance, he managed to get his hands on this document, and recognized the ankh—the cross of life and the symbol of the Library—right away.

Hellen nodded. She recalled that Palffy had once mentioned it to her.

"But even with all his knowledge and contacts, he couldn't decipher it. It was written in an unknown language. As we learned later from Noah, there were three brothers, the Negozis. The second brother, the one who gave part of the stone to the Americans, was caught by the Nazis and taken to a concentration camp in Poland, but he wanted to send a message to his brother in Rome about his mission. So he wrote him this letter secretly, using a coded language the three brothers had developed for themselves as children, and shortly before his death he asked a Russian soldier during the liberation of the camp to pass it on. The Russian apparently didn't understand much of what the Italian said to him, so he simply took the envelope with him; after the war it ended up in a box in his attic."

Ossana paused, and a smile crossed her face.

"Sixty years later, the Russian's grandson found the letter, but he had no idea what to do with it. So he put it on eBay, to at least try to make a few dollars from it. Palffy saw it and bought it. That letter was what led us to the Smithsonian archive. Unfortunately, we did not know that the Americans had moved their piece of the stone elsewhere in the meantime."

Ossana smiled and shrugged. She waited a moment for Tom and Hellen to digest what she had just told them. Then she lifted up the page in her hand. "This is the last piece of the puzzle. If you'd do me the honor of reading the marked passage?"

She handed the page to Hellen, who took it reluctantly and read aloud: "The thirteenth church hides the secret. The thirteenth cross is the key."

"In the letter, however, there is no mention of where the third brother had taken the stone." Ossana went over to Abebe Abiye's body. "But that, Ms. de Mey, is something that you were kind enough to reveal to us in Washington." She tore open the man's blood-soaked kaftan and took a chain from around his neck. The pendant was a small Lalibela cross.

"Ossana," Noah interrupted. "I've found it!" He rolled to her and held up the remote control. On the display was a grainy image of a passageway directly beneath their feet. But where was the entrance?

The soldiers began to roll the carpets aside. Ossana went down on her knees and ran her fingers over the floor. Tom and Hellen were also curious. Ossana discovered a gap in the floor, at first glance no more than a crack in the rock. Hellen's mind automatically returned to the antiquated punch card that Scott had given Tom to help them get into the archive below the Washington Memorial. She also remembered that, just a short while earlier, she had been holding a Lalibela cross more than eighteen inches long in her hand. Without a word, she returned to the curtained room. One of the soldiers blocked her path, but a nod from Ossana and he stepped aside.

"Hellen? What are you doing?" Tom asked, surprised at her sudden participation.

"The necklace reminded me of something in Washington. I want to see if I'm right." She came back carrying the large cross, which she handed to Ossana, and began to pull down the cloths covering the walls. Behind them, two ropes appeared, one on the northern side and one on the southern side of the church. The ropes passed through an iron loop in the center of the ceiling and had been fed from there out through similar loops, to hang behind the curtains on the walls. Below the center loop, an iron hook was attached to the end of each rope.

Ossana and Tom gradually began to understand. Ossana and Hellen lowered the hooks, and Tom hung the Lalibela cross upside down from the hooks. The decorative flourishes on the suspended cross resembled the barbs on a fishhook. Hellen released her rope a little, and with a push from Tom, the cross disappeared perfectly into the gap Ossana had found in the floor.

"Turn the rope a little," Hellen told Tom, and the cross dropped a little deeper. Then Hellen jerked on the rope and the cross caught in the gap. "I could use a little help," she said.

"Help her, damn it!" Noah barked.

Three of the soldiers immediately went to the ropes and pulled on them together. Hellen stepped clear and, with the others, gazed intently at the gap where the ropes disappeared into the floor.

With a grating noise, a stone plate about three feet square rose slowly out of the floor. The soldiers hauled on the ropes with all their might, and the plate lifted clear of the floor. Tom's eyes followed the ropes upward, to where they met in the center of the ceiling. The shape that of the church was cruciform, and Tom suddenly realized something. "X marks the spot," he said to himself, and smiled. When he looked back at those around him, he saw only eager faces. Beneath the stone cover, a narrow passage had appeared.

"The path to the thirteenth church . . ." Ossana murmured.

". . . and the Holy of Holies," Noah said, finishing her sentence.

Ossana went first, then two of the soldiers lifted Noah down after her. Tom and Hellen looked at one another, then followed Noah into the passage.

76

BENEATH BET GIYORGIS, LALIBELA, ETHIOPIA

The passage gradually sloped downward, opening into a large artificial cavern after about fifty yards. Ossana and Noah were already inside when Tom and Hellen entered, closely followed by three soldiers.

The domed cavern was twenty yards across and about fifteen feet high in the center. In the middle of the floor stood an altar. A clever arrangement of mirror-polished metal plates reflected light from the outside through a small, innocuous shaft, directly onto the altar. The last plate, the one that reflected the light directly onto the altar, was mounted atop a large rectangular stone block that stood by the wall directly opposite where Ossana and the others had entered. Ossana moved off to the left, around the altar, while Noah slowly rolled toward it.

The altar was large and reddish and had been carved from a single, polished stone block. On top of it stood an object covered with a blue cloth. Two points protruded upward beneath the cloth, and on the sides of the object, left and right, were two long horizontal poles. No one dared to breathe. No rain, no storm, no movement—only silence, so quiet that those inside could almost hear their own heartbeats.

Hellen tried to take a step toward the altar, but Ossana raised her hand and the soldiers held her back.

Ossana, in awe, moved very slowly now, circling the altar. Finally, she grasped a corner of the cloth and pulled. Dust swirled into the air, making the entire cavern shine with a golden, almost divine light. The glittering dust particles whirled and danced in the air, lending the scene a touch of magic. Noah was breathing hard, staring in reverence at the golden masterpiece. It more than lived up to its description in the Bible; it was more beautiful than he could have dreamed. On the pedestal before them gleamed the Ark of the Covenant. On the *kapporet*, the "mercy seat"—the lid that covered the Ark—the two points beneath the cloth were now revealed as two cherubim, the ancestors of the angels. They spread their wings protectively over the top of the lid.

Noah stared at the Ark with glassy eyes. He had finally reached his goal.

"Open it," he said to Ossana.

She waved two soldiers over. They shouldered their weapons, took up positions on opposite sides of the Ark, grasped the lid and . . . hesitated. Naturally. Everyone there knew the scene from *Raiders of the Lost Ark*. They remembered what had happened to the Nazis' faces as soon as they opened the Ark.

Tom and Hellen shared a grin when they saw the soldiers hesitate. But then they went ahead and obeyed Ossana's order, lifting the *kapporet* clear of the case beneath.

And nothing happened.

"So much for Hollywood," said Ossana, shaking her head at the twinge of panic on the faces of her soldiers. Relieved, they set the lid down carefully on the cavern floor and stepped aside.

Noah opened the small case he had on his lap, and Ossana removed the first section of the stone to lay it inside the Ark. Noah's dream was about to become reality.

"Wait!" Tom cried unexpectedly. "Shouldn't someone say something? To mark the moment?" He looked around. "I mean, something as big as this—you know, the beginning of the end—deserves a little respect and recognition."

"Wagner, just for once, shut your goddamned mouth!" Noah barked. He turned to Ossana. "Go on, put the stone inside," he said.

"Just saying . . ." Tom murmured when Hellen glared at him.

Ossana carefully placed each piece of the stone into the Ark. Holding her breath, she stepped away again. Noah's excitement was indescribable, Tom and Hellen looked at each other with anticipation, and the soldiers edged back toward the walls. Noah's gaze was fixed on the Ark. He knew from legend that the pieces of the stone had to be placed in the Ark of the Covenant to unfold its power. He had studied the Scriptures countless times after Ossana had approached him with her plan. He had doubted at first, but then he had read through Palffy's documents: the sources were unequivocal. There were also numerous historical accounts of the power of the stone, stories that could be traced back to Joshua himself. And now, the three pieces of the Philosopher's Stone lay within the Ark of the Covenant. Its healing force was about to unfold once again.

But absolutely nothing happened.

Noah was confused, and began to get nervous.

"Maybe we have to close it again?" Ossana suggested. She moved again around the Ark and the same two soldiers lifted the *kapporet* back into place. Everyone was looking around the cavern as if they expected lightning to strike, lights to flash or the actual hand of God to appear.

Noah looked at Ossana. Seconds ticked by, and still nothing happened. From one second to the next, Noah's anger grew.

The Philosopher's Stone had triggered natural disasters, had made the old popes rich, had decided the outcome of battles and wars, and had produced more than one miracle in the name of the Catholic Church. But now Noah was utterly bewildered. The pieces of the stone had been lying in the Ark of the Covenant for a minute or more, and nothing had happened at all.

Suddenly, a burst of diabolical laughter echoed through the domed cavern. Mystification spread through the cavern. Most of those present knew that voice very well indeed.

"J'adore quand un plan marche!"

From behind the stone block opposite the entrance, François Cloutard stepped into the open.

"And for you, Noah, because I know that you have no talent for my beautiful native tongue, once more for the record: I love it when a plan comes together! *Connard!*"

77

THE ROCK CHURCHES OF LALIBELA, ETHIOPIA

Vittoria did not move even a millimeter. If she gave the man behind her even half an excuse to pull the trigger, she knew he would not hesitate for a second.

Her mind was racing. Was Tom still alive? What about Hellen and Abiye? What about the priests? Would they all drown because she had failed?

"On your feet. Slowly," said the man behind her grimly. Vittoria raised her hands beside her head and slowly stood up.

"Please don't shoot me," she whimpered helplessly, trying to lull the man into letting his guard down. For a brief second, the man got careless. He underestimated Vittoria, and he was standing much closer than he should have been. When she was almost upright, she spun around in a flash, jolting the mercenary's rifle to one side and grabbing hold of it. A shot rang out. She yanked the rifle toward herself, and the soldier, already surprised, lost his balance. Vittoria's knee shot up and hit him hard in the groin.

The man groaned and dropped to his knees, his face twisted in pain. Vittoria launched a right hook at his temple, putting him out of the fight for the moment. She snatched the detonator and ran along the embankment, but the soldier was back on his feet faster than she'd expected. Shots whistled past Vittoria's head, but the pain and the falling rain made it difficult for the man to aim accurately. Angrily, he clambered to his feet and went after her.

As she ran, Vittoria dropped the detonator and the remote trigger into her pocket and took out the pistol she'd taken from the chopper. She had to stop her pursuer, and she made a do-or-die decision. She would only get one shot. She slowed her pace slightly, turned and dropped to one knee in a single motion. Quickly, calmly, she took aim. The surprised soldier tried to raise his rifle, but Vittoria's bullet took him down in an instant. If there was one thing she'd excelled at in her training, it was target practice.

Trembling now, she lowered her gun and saw the body lying motionless on the muddy embankment. The next thing she knew, a searing pain flashed through her right shoulder. She turned around and saw another soldier, this one standing at the top of the rocky plateau. He fired a second time, but the bullet flew wide, and Vittoria was on the move again. Her shoulder burned like fire, but her mind was on the drowning priests. Failure was not an option!

The water at the bottom of the embankment was up to her knees as she splashed in a zigzag toward where the embankment narrowed into the artificial ravine, back to where she had placed the C4. Her face contorted with pain, she fished out the detonator as she ran. Bullets whipped into the water to her left and right. When she reached the C4, she threw herself flat against the opposite wall. Shots rained down from above, but the wall curved back just enough to keep her out of the line of fire. The bullets missed her by a hair's breadth.

During a lull in the firing, she darted forward and jammed the detonator back into the explosive, quickly activating it, then she took off along the wall at a run. This time, she wasted no time—no more than ten yards away, she flipped the trigger. The shock wave picked her up and flung her forward and she landed face down in the water. Boulders flew through the air, and as if from a broken dam the water poured out of the churchyard into the outer ravine. It took only moments before most of the water had flowed out of the interior of the church and the churchyard.

Vittoria struggled to her feet. Her first instinct was to take cover again, but she saw that the explosion had caused the soldier above to fall into the ravine, and he had been killed by a falling boulder. She ran into the churchyard, kicked the wedges out from under the door and tore it open. Eleven exhausted, sodden priests emerged from the dark church one by one. Weakened, some coughing, they supported each other as they came out, hardly able to believe they were still alive. The priests, Tesfaye among them, thanked Vittoria profusely. She sat down on some low steps next to the church, exhausted and in pain, but overjoyed.

78

BENEATH BET GIYORGIS, LALIBELA, ETHIOPIA

François Cloutard's entrance had been grand, and the expressions on the faces now looking at him were priceless. He carried an old Luger in his hand and held it steady, pointed at Ossana's head.

The two soldiers on the left and right sides of the room raised their weapons, but Cloutard had not come alone. Marcello and Giuliano also emerged from behind the block, Kalashnikovs at the ready.

"So, we meet again," Cloutard said to Ossana airily.

"Everyone stay perfectly calm," Ossana said loudly. "If anyone starts shooting now we'll all end up in body bags, and I don't think anyone wants that. I think we can sort this out like professionals."

"What took you so long?" asked Tom and immediately answered his own question: "You wanted to show off, didn't you?" Cloutard shrugged and smiled a little self-consciously.

The third soldier, the one behind Tom and Hellen, pressed his gun to the back of Tom's head.

"*Tu me connais.* I like a little drama."

Noah was on the brink of tears. What had happened? He spun his wheelchair around to look at Tom.

"Nobody move," Cloutard called out.

"Everybody stop!" Ossana barked, and the two soldiers by the wall, who had been edging slowly toward the exit, came to an abrupt halt.

"What the fuck have you done?" Noah hissed. He stared into Tom's face with a mixture of rage and disbelief.

"You're not the only ones who can make plans," Tom said with a touch of mockery. "After that little fiasco in Washington, where you turned out to be a backstabbing psychopath and all-around asshole, I called Cloutard and we figured it out. He flew here a few hours before we did. With a little assist from the Vatican, we contacted the local clergy and replaced the real Ark with a duplicate."

"A duplicate?!" Noah yelped, and the cleft between his eyes deepened.

"Oh, you didn't know?" Hellen said. "You should do better research. Every church in Ethiopia has a duplicate of the Ark of the Covenant. A building isn't a church if it doesn't have one. The *real* one is far away, and very safe."

Noah's face froze, as did Ossana's.

"And just in case it wasn't already clear: you're all under arrest," Tom shouted.

Noah laughed out loud and the soldier behind Tom jabbed his rifle barrel harder into the back of his head.

Suddenly a radio crackled to life, but all that came from it was static. Everyone turned toward the entrance, where the sound had come from. A moment later, the first bullet flew, then all hell broke loose. Marcello gunned down the soldier on the left and Giuliano shot the man on the right, then they both took cover behind the stone block. Quick as a cobra, Ossana grabbed Cloutard's gun hand and punched him in the nose with her right fist. He fell to the cavern floor, and Ossana threw herself on top of him.

Automatic fire whistled over Noah's head and ricocheted off the stone block hiding Marcello and Giuliano. Tom moved as fast as Ossana: he dropped and slammed his elbow into the groin of the man behind him, then grabbed the soldier's rifle and pulled down, hurling the man over his shoulder. A blur of punches left the man unconscious, and Tom had his rifle.

He jumped up and spun around, rifle at the ready, but stopped himself just in time.

Noah sat with his back to the entrance, facing the cavern. Behind him was the soldier whose arrival a few moments earlier had triggered the chaos. The man had his rifle pointed straight at Tom. Marcello and Giuliano now rushed to Cloutard's aid, and together they overpowered Ossana. Cloutard held his bleeding nose. He still had the Luger and he trained it on Ossana again, freeing up Marcello and Giuliano, who took aim at Noah and the soldier at the entrance.

In the turmoil Noah had managed to drag Hellen onto his lap, and now had one arm around her neck as his pistol dug into her temple. Hellen let out a stifled scream.

"Stop!" Tom shouted furiously, his rifle trained on Noah. "It's over, Noah. Let her go," he said, his voice hard and unwavering.

Noah had quickly realized the hopelessness of the situation. His dream had been destroyed. All he could do now was save his life.

"Get me out of here," he hissed at the soldier behind him. Marcello and Giuliano edged forward as soon as Noah's wheelchair began to roll. Seeing them move, Noah squeezed Hellen's neck harder. She was struggling even to breath now, and her eyes radiated panic.

"Stay where you are. Let him go," Tom commanded Cloutard's confederates. He looked deep into Hellen's terrified eyes, trying to make her understand: *you're not going to die here. I promise you that.* The soldier dragged Noah's wheelchair backwards into the passage. Noah held Hellen in an iron grip and dragged her with him. Tom followed as they disappeared into the passage, his rifle still at his shoulder.

"Noah, what are you doing?" Ossana screamed. She was back on her feet again, standing in front of Cloutard with her hands in the air.

"What did you expect?" said Cloutard, in a muffled, nasal voice. "He betrayed us, too." He pinched his nose with his free hand to stop the bleeding.

"You can't just leave me behind," Ossana screamed down the tunnel after Noah and the soldier.

"We'll come back for you. I promise," Noah shouted back.

A moment later, Hellen came stumbling back into the cavern. Behind her, a grenade rolled down the passage.

"Take cover!" she screamed. Tom spotted the danger instantly. He threw the rifle aside, grabbed Hellen and dragged her behind the altar on which the duplicate Ark stood. Cloutard threw himself on top of Ossana, and the two mafiosi took cover behind the stone block again.

A deafening explosion shook the entire cavern, collapsing the entrance to the long passage. The shockwave swept the Ark off the altar; it flew over Ossana and Cloutard and slammed into the stone block.

As the smoke and dust settled, they began to gather themselves. Tom was the first on his feet again. He helped Hellen up and made sure she wasn't injured.

"Get off me," Ossana snapped at Cloutard, who merely smiled as he got to his feet.

"Just like old times," he said, patting the dust from his suit. "But a simple 'thank-you' was too much to ask, even then." He ignored Ossana's outstretched hand.

Still lying on the floor, Ossana unexpectedly let out a cruel burst of laughter and looked up at Tom. "We're trapped. Now your priests are going to drown like rats. It looks like we're going to be here for a while," she said.

Marcello and Giuliano pulled Ossana to her feet and cable-tied her hands behind her back.

Tom looked at his watch, and laughed confidently back at her. "They should be drying off about now. I don't think Vittoria would have had too many problems sorting that out."

Suddenly, in the distance, they heard a muffled explosion.

"Correction. *Now* they should be safe," Tom said, and his smile widened. "And now, for the record: you're under arrest."

Ossana only glowered.

With Cloutard's help, Tom hoisted the Ark back onto its altar and replaced the lid.

"Thank God that was only a replica," he said as he inspected the Ark. It had suffered some damage, certainly, but was still in one piece.

"If Noah only knew that he went straight past the *real* Ark of the Covenant just a few minutes ago . . ." Hellen said and shook her head. She gathered up the three stone fragments— miraculously, they seemed no more damaged than before—and replaced them in the small suitcase.

"How do you think you're going to get out of here?" Ossana asked. She was their prisoner but she still acted as if she had the upper hand.

"How do you think I got in, *ma chérie*?" Cloutard said with a wink, clearly enjoying the chance to exact a little revenge on Ossana. "Follow me, *mes amis!*" He laughed wholeheartedly and disappeared through an unobtrusive gap in the wall behind the stone block.

79

ARLINGTON NATIONAL CEMETERY, VIRGINIA, USA

"Typical funeral weather," Tom said to Hellen as they climbed out of the car and opened their umbrellas. It was chilly for May; the wind was blowing hard, slinging the rain almost horizontally across the cemetery hill. Arlington National Cemetery lies to the southwest of Washington D.C., separated from it by the Potomac River. To the southeast it borders on the grounds of the Pentagon. The cemetery itself is characterized by its white gravestones, equally spaced, row on row, that cover the gently rolling hills. Each year more than five thousand funerals take place at the cemetery, and three state funerals have been held there: for Presidents William Howard Taft and John F. Kennedy, and also for General John J. Pershing. Admiral Scott T. Wagner's funeral was kept small, as he had requested in his will. Only a few of his close friends—among them Tom, Cloutard and Hellen—and a small contingent of Navy personnel were present. And, of course, the president of the United States with his Secret Service detail. The eulogy was delivered by the president himself.

"I had no idea your uncle was a Medal of Honor recipient," Hellen whispered when the president had finished his speech.

"Neither did I," Tom admitted. "Uncle Scott kept his cards close to his chest."

"That seems to run in the family," Hellen replied. She laid her hand on Tom's arm in consolation and smiled at him.

When the Navy chaplain had finished his service, seven sailors stepped forward and fired a three-volley salute in honor of their fallen comrade. Afterward, the flag, which had been held above the coffin during the chaplain's ceremony by the eight members of the coffin team, was folded into the traditional triangle. The coffin team was accompanied by a trumpeter who played "Taps". The flag was then handed over to Tom, accompanied by salutes.

After Tom had received the condolences of those present, one of the Secret Service men came to him. "The president would like a word, sir," the man said politely, pointing in the direction of a small stand of trees where the president was chatting with a Navy admiral. Cloutard and Hellen looked at Tom in surprise. Tom screwed his mouth to one side and followed the Secret Service man.

"Mister Wagner, I'd like once again to express my condolences," the president said. "The loss of Admiral Wagner is a loss for all Americans. He did a tremendous amount for our country, and he was never one to talk up his achievements."

"Thank you, sir," Tom said. "That certainly sounds like my uncle."

"Let's walk for a minute," the president said, and he stepped away without waiting. Tom followed, and two Secret Service men shadowed them at a discreet distance.

"I'm not going to beat around the bush. I've read your file."

"My file?" Tom said, raising his eyebrows, although even as he said it he realized that the CIA would have a file on every one of his uncle's family members and friends.

"You've been right where you need to be more than once. That thing with the diamond in Vienna, then that incident in Barcelona last year, and now the recovery of the . . ." he paused ". . . the artifact. You're good. Even by our standards, you're an outstanding operative, one I'd rather see fighting for me than against me."

"Sir, with all due respect, I'm afraid I don't know what you mean."

"I would like you to take your uncle's place. I'd like you to work for the CIA, reporting directly to me."

Tom stopped walking. He wasn't sure he'd heard right. "I doubt I'm a particularly suitable candidate for the CIA, Mr. President."

"That's where we disagree, Mr. Wagner. I need people able to think a little outside the proverbial box." He gave Tom a wink. "And I think you fall into that category."

"Thank you, sir, but this comes as quite a surprise."

"Oh, I'm aware of that. What I have in mind is not your typical CIA agent role. The kind of assignments I'd want you for don't come up often. That means, for now, that nothing will change for you. I'll be in touch personally the minute something comes up."

Tom had no idea exactly what the president meant, but there was only one thing to say: "Thank you, sir. I'm honored."

"There's one condition, Mr. Wagner."

Tom looked at the president inquiringly.

"No one, and I mean absolutely no one, can know that you work for me and the CIA. It doesn't matter how close you are to that person, you have to maintain absolute secrecy about our agreement. Can you assure me of that?"

Tom swallowed and glanced back over his shoulder to where Hellen and Cloutard were talking and waiting for him. Things between Hellen and himself were only just starting to thaw, and now he was supposed to keep this secret to himself? Would he have to lie to her? Was it worth it? The president snapped him out of his gloomy thoughts.

"Mr. Wagner?"

Tom cleared his throat. "My apologies, sir. You can count on me, of course," he said, although he had a very bad feeling in the pit of his stomach as he spoke.

They had reached the president's car. "You'll be hearing from me," the president said as he climbed into his limousine. Tom waited until the convoy had departed before he returned to Hellen and Cloutard.

Hellen looked at him. "Everything okay? What did the president want?" she asked.

"Just to pass on his condolences in person," said Tom. He knew already that he wouldn't be able to keep the secret for long.

80

A CONFERENCE ROOM ON THE 26TH
FLOOR, VIENNA INTERNATIONAL CENTER,
VIENNA, AUSTRIA

Hellen knew this conference room only too well. It was here that Count Palffy had first asked her to work for Blue Shield.

"I've never been to the UNO City before," said Tom, peering out over the Danube toward the Kahlenberg. "It's not exactly pretty from the outside."

"*Très moche*," Cloutard murmured—ugly as sin. He clearly did not feel very at home in the sparsely furnished conference room. Luxury and style were more to his taste than bland offices, break rooms, and conference facilities with musty-smelling air conditioning.

"It's just how they built things in the seventies," Hellen said.

Cloutard shook his head and drank a mouthful of coffee from the cup that he'd just been served. He grimaced.

"This must be the only bad coffee in Vienna. *Terriblement!*" he complained loudly, just as his cell phone pinged. He looked at the display.

Thank you. The operation was successful. My daughter is already recovering. I owe you. Farid.

Cloutard smiled.

"What are we even doing here?" Tom asked.

"You're here to hear my proposal," a voice said. All three, who had been gazing out the window, turned in unison to see Hellen's mother enter the conference room, with a small stack of files in her arms.

"Proposal?" Hellen said, instantly on guard. "What kind of 'proposal' is this, Mother?"

Tom had already met Hellen's mother several times. He decided to just take a seat and stay in the background for the moment. Cloutard did the same—he could see certain parallels between Mrs. de Mey and his own mother. Best not to say anything. Only Hellen remained standing, kicking her right foot back and forth nervously.

"Before I get to that, I have some important news. The Egyptian authorities have turned up some information about the man Tom shot in self-defense in the museum."

Hellen looked first at her mother, then at Tom.

"Arno?"

"That's not his real name, I'm afraid. The Egyptians have checked with Interpol, the Germans and MI6 and have uncovered quite a lot about him. Dozens of false identities, a list of crimes and a definite connection to AF."

Hellen's mother paused and looked at her daughter. "When it comes to men, Hellen, your choices leave a lot to be desired. You've never been much good at picking them."

Hellen did not know what to say to that. Her emotions were rioting. She had loved Arno, but with all that had happened she had hardly had any time to deal with his death. At first, she had ignored the fact that Tom had been forced to fire in self-defense. She had also ignored the possibility that Arno had not found his way into her life by chance. Now everything made a little more sense, but she would still need some time to work through it. She gave Tom a quick glance, which he studiously ignored. Hellen decided not to ask any further questions. She looked ruefully at Tom, formed an inaudible "Sorry" with her lips and lowered her eyes. It was time to stop torturing herself about Arno . . . or whatever his name was.

"Well, then. On to the real reason I wanted to talk to you."

Theresia de Mey tossed three files onto the conference table.

Tom already knew what the documents were: most likely reports about his escapades in recent years.

"You've done good work," Mrs. de Mey said, looking from face to face. "You're a rather unorthodox team, admittedly, and you have even more unorthodox methods, but your success speaks for itself."

She tossed another file onto the table. Hellen raised her eyebrows.

"Mother, where did you get that? That's Nikolaus's file."

"Which one?" Tom asked.

"Count Nikolaus Palffy III, in his capacity as president of Blue Shield and as my predecessor, put this file together," Hellen's mother said. "It contains a long list of mythical and historical objects, archeological phenomena and lost treasures that are a little on the exotic side."

"As exotic as the Philosopher's Stone?" said Cloutard, although he already knew the answer.

"*Absolutement*, Monsieur Cloutard," Theresia de Mey replied.

Hellen had picked up the file; she now sat down at the conference table and began to go through it. "This is incomplete. I saw this file about a year ago, at the UNESCO conference in Vienna. There was a lot more in it then."

"We know," her mother said. "The actual file was stolen from Palffy's house. This is an older version of it." Tom could already see where this was going. Hellen too, it seemed.

"Mother, please don't tell me you want us to track down the artifacts and treasures Nikolaus collected in that file and find them for Blue Shield."

Hellen's mother smiled and said nothing.

"Never!" Hellen said. "You're a terrible boss. There's no way I'm going to work with you breathing down my neck the whole time."

Tom laid a calming hand on Hellen's arm. "Let's just listen to what your mother has to say."

"Yes. You can still be outraged after that," Cloutard added.

"Monsieur Cloutard has kindly diverted a large sum of money from AF."

Cloutard smiled, though he looked to be in some pain. Tom and Hellen could not hide their amazement.

"Noah also lied to us about that," Cloutard said. "The money he showed us did not come from Mossad. It came from a black account operated by AF, which I then ... appropriated."

"Confiscated would be the more correct formulation, Monsieur. And in consultation with the UN, UNESCO, the Vatican and the G8 countries, I have now obtained permission to keep that money for Blue Shield."

Tom, Hellen and Cloutard looked at each other. One could almost hear their jaws drop.

"What? The whole 50 million?" Hellen said.

Hellen's mother nodded. Just then, the door opened and Vittoria Arcano came in, her right arm still in a sling. Her smile at Tom lasted just a little too long, which did not please Hellen at all.

"Signorina Arcano has drawn up the contracts. They are very generous."

343

Cloutard flipped through the pages. *"Vraiment généreux,"* he said.

"Maybe if you are paid well enough, you won't have to go breaking into museums or cleaning out strangers' bank accounts," Theresia said pointedly to Cloutard.

Hellen was still not thrilled, but neither was she blind to the opportunities her mother's offer opened up. This was like the Holy Grail of archaeological research: virtually bottomless funds and free rein to go in search of humankind's greatest myths. She hated to admit it, but it sounded tempting.

Hellen's mother still had a stern eye on Cloutard. "Monsieur, I tell you this. If you want to be part of this team, then you will have to stick to the rules."

"He will. I'll make him," said Tom, and he whacked Cloutard between his shoulder blades harder than necessary, then hugged him.

"What has become of Ossana since we handed her over to the authorities in Ethiopia?" Cloutard asked, wanting to change the subject.

"Ossana is to be extradited to the United States. She must have a lot of useful information about AF, and considering the Americans' interrogation methods, she'll no doubt be telling them this and that before long," Hellen's mother said coolly.

Cloutard grimaced. As much as he wanted revenge on Ossana, he was no fan of waterboarding or other "enhanced interrogation" techniques. He sympathized with her.

"So Ossana's out of the picture," said Tom. "But I have the feeling we'll cross paths with Noah again."

Hellen nodded. "He was obsessed. He's not about to give up."

"Back to business." Hellen's mother drew their attention to the folders Vittoria had brought in. "You can sleep on it, of course," she said casually.

"But not too long," Vittoria added. "The first assignment is already lined up." She drummed her fingernails meaningfully against the cover of another file.

Tom, Hellen and Cloutard looked at each other. Then, together, they nodded. Each signed the contract in front of them, and Vittoria handed them the file with their first mission.

———

— THE END —

OF „THE LIBRARY OF THE KINGS"

Tom Wagner will return in:

„THE INVISIBLE CITY"

THE INVISIBLE CITY

TURN THE PAGE AND READ THE NEXT TOM WAGNER ADVENTURE!

CHAPTER 1
VIENNA AND BERLIN, 1976

The shrill scream of the telephone startled Arthur Julius Prey from sleep. He leaped out of bed and ran to the tiny office he kept in his Vienna apartment fast enough to stop it from ringing a second time. No need to wake his wife or daughter at this ungodly hour. As a freelance reporter, getting a call in the middle of the night did not necessarily mean the end of the world, but it usually didn't bode well. More often than not, a call like this would entail a long journey abroad and, to the chagrin of Wilhelmine and Maria, his wife and daughter, often to a crisis region steeped in danger.

He picked up the receiver and heard a young woman's voice say, "This is the long-distance operator in Berlin. You have a call from East Berlin. Please stay on the line."

East Berlin? He did not know anybody in Berlin, East or West. There was a buzz on the line, then a clicking sound.

"Arthur? Is that you?"

Arthur's eyes widened as he recognized his old friend's voice.

"Artjom! What is it? What are you doing in East Berlin?"

"Arthur, I need your help," the man said in his heavy Russian accent.

As he listened to what his friend had to say, a few framed photographs standing on the bookshelf beside his desk caught Arthur's eye. One showed himself and Artjom together. It had been taken on the most dangerous and terrifying mission of his career. With youthful exuberance, driven by a moral compass molded in the 1960s and inspired by Eddie Adams's Pulitzer Prize-winning photograph of the summary execution of a Vietcong prisoner by a South Vietnamese police chief in February 1968, Arthur had joined the Associated Press—and just six months later found himself smack in the middle of the Vietnam War.

After slogging through weeks of hardship and misery, Arthur had witnessed a bombing raid while on a day's R&R in Saigon. He had gone to the aid of a young girl hurt in a blast but had been taken by surprise by another explosion and was injured himself. Father Lazarev had given him first aid and saved the lives of both Arthur and the young girl. He had not moved from their bedsides in the hospital. An experience like that forges a bond, and they had been close friends ever since.

A year earlier, Arthur had finally found the time to visit the man who had saved his life. Through contacts, he had managed to travel to the Soviet Union and, more importantly, to get out again safely. While there, he had spent a few weeks in a small village east of Moscow. There, in a crumbling wooden church beside a small lake, the second photo that held a place of honor on Arthur's bookshelf had been taken.

Twenty-four hours after the call from his friend, Arthur found himself walking along Friedrichstrasse in Berlin.

He stopped to look at the Berlin Wall and the famous square in front of it, with its white wooden hut: Checkpoint Charlie. Just behind the hut began the narrow no-man's-land that separated East and West. Since 1961, gray cement, barbed wire and armored vehicles had tainted the day-to-day views confronting Berlin's inhabitants. The windows of the buildings that stood alongside the wall were all bricked up, but graffiti added a little color to the bleakness, at least on the western side. Many refugees seeking freedom beyond the walls had died in that bordering strip of land. Those who tried to flee from East to West were shot without mercy.

Arthur looked at the time, turned away and went down the next narrow side street. He had to be at the meeting point on time.

It was late, and the streets around the border crossing were deserted. Arthur strode quickly down the alley before turning again. They had arranged to meet at the next intersection. Eleven p.m. on the dot, not one minute later, his friend had said. He looked at his watch: 10:54. He was alone. The air was cold and damp, and he felt a chill creeping into his bones. An uneasy feeling slowly grew in his belly. On the opposite side of the dimly lit street, a drunk staggered out of a bar and swayed along the sidewalk. Arthur paced anxiously. The few minutes felt like an eternity. Then an old VW T1 microbus turned slowly around a corner and rolled toward him. Arthur looked in from the passenger side when the van rolled to a stop.

"Get in the back. Come on, quick," hissed the man at the wheel, looking around nervously.

Arthur hesitated, but did as he was told. He looked around, opened the rear door and climbed into the windowless microbus. Hardly had he sat down when the man turned around and held out a black cloth sack.

"Put this on," the man said. Surprised, Arthur took the sack. *What have I gotten myself into here?* he wondered as he pulled the sack over his head. The driver hit the gas.

CHAPTER 2

CHURCH OF OUR LADY OF KAZAN, LAKE SVETLOYAR, NEAR NIZHNY NOVGOROD, RUSSIA. PRESENT DAY.

Two men scouted the grounds around the church, before finally approaching it from different directions. They took up posts at the entrance of the church, in the pale light of the moon.

Lake Svetloyar looked small, but it was far deeper than one would expect from its size. The moon shone brightly, reflected in the calm surface of the lake. The church, built entirely of wood, had stood on the shore of the lake for almost a century, and in the silvery glow of the moonlight it looked almost unnaturally mystical.

The two guards seemed bored, but they were professional enough to take their jobs seriously. The clothes they wore seemed inherently unsuited to their surroundings: they were dressed in suits, specially tailored to conceal the contours that pistols and shoulder holsters usually made. Only one paved road led to and from the church, connecting it to the Voskresensky district. Reaching the church meant crossing an old, ramshackle-looking bridge. A third guard had been posted there.

As he did every evening, the priest knelt before the altar of the small church and thanked God for choosing him. He thought of the many guardians before him who had dedicated their lives to preserving the secret—a secret that indeed meant little to most of the world outside, but meant everything to the people there. Only a few knew the legend, and even fewer knew about the treasures, both material and spiritual, that he had dedicated his life to protecting—as many before him had done.

The breeze whistled lightly through the cracks in the wooden walls of the church. There was never a moment of absolute silence here. Something was always creaking or cracking or squeaking somewhere, so the priest did not look up when he heard noises from outside, in front of the entrance. It was probably one of the brown bears that frequented the area and which he saw almost daily, he thought. But he knew that he was safe inside the church. The guards had been hired on the advice of his son.

The priest was starting to think that his time was growing short. He was approaching his eighty-fifth birthday, and God alone knew how much longer he would be among the living. He felt healthy and energetic, but he knew that could change very quickly at his age. He would make the preparations he needed to make. A successor needed to be found as soon as possible.

Outside, four men in camouflage appeared, as if from nowhere. Equipped with night vision equipment and with MP5 submachine guns at the ready, they crept quietly toward the church, doing their best to conceal themselves in the shadows cast by the bright moon. One of the guards saw them instantly, but was too slow. He had no time either to shoot or sound an alarm. A bullet between the eyes and he was dead before his body hit the ground.

As the other guard turned to see what had happened, he too was eliminated.

The coast was clear.

Want to know what happens next?

THE INVISIBLE CITY

(A Tom Wagner Adventure 3)

A vanished civilization. A diabolical trap. A mystical treasure.

Tom Wagner, archaeologist Hellen de Mey and gentleman crook Francois Cloutard are about to embark on their first official assignment from Blue Shield – but when Tom receives an urgent call from the Vatican, things start to move quickly:

With the help of the Patriarch of the Russian Orthodox Church, they discover clues to an age-old myth: the Russian Atlantis. And a murderous race to find an ancient, long-lost relic leads them from Cuba to the Russian hinterlands.

What mystical treasure lies buried beneath Nizhny Novgorod? Who laid the evil trap? And what does it all have to do with Tom's grandfather?

Click here or open link:
https://robertsmaclay.com/3-tw

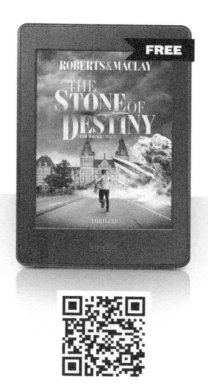

THE TOM WAGNER SERIES

THE STONE OF DESTINY

(Tom Wagner Prequel)

A dark secret of the Habsburg Empire. A treasure believed to be lost long time ago. A breathless hunt into the past.

The thriller "The Stone of Destiny" leads Tom Wagner and Hellen de Mey into the dark past of the Habsburgs and to a treasure that seems to have been lost for a long time.

The breathless hunt goes through half of Europe and the surprise at the end is not missing: A conspiracy that began in the last days of the First World War reaches up to the present day!

Free Download!
Click here or open link:
https://robertsmaclay.com/start-free

———

THE SACRED WEAPON

(A Tom Wagner Adventure 1)

A demonic plan. A mysterious power. An extraordinary team.

The Notre Dame fire, the theft of the Shroud of Turin and a terrorist attack on the legendary Meteora monasteries are just the beginning. Fear has gripped Europe.

Stolen relics, a mysterious power with a demonic plan and allies with questionable allegiances: Tom Wagner is in a race against time, trying to prevent a disaster that could tear Europe down to its foundations. And there's no one he can trust...

Click here or open link:
https://robertsmaclay.com/1-tw

———

THE LIBRARY OF THE KINGS

(A Tom Wagner Adventure 2)

Hidden wisdom. A relic of unbelievable power. A race against time.

Ancient legends, devilish plans, startling plot twists, breathtaking action and a dash of humor: *Library of the Kings* is gripping entertainment – a Hollywood blockbuster in book form.

When clues to the long-lost Library of Alexandria surface, ex-Cobra officer Tom Wagner and archaeologist Hellen de Mey aren't the only ones on the hunt for its vanished secrets. A sinister power is plotting in the background, and nothing is as it seems. And the dark secret hidden in the Library threatens all of humanity.

Click here or open link:
https://robertsmaclay.com/2-tw

———

THE INVISIBLE CITY

(A Tom Wagner Adventure 3)

A vanished civilization. A diabolical trap. A mystical treasure.

Tom Wagner, archaeologist Hellen de Mey and gentleman crook Francois Cloutard are about to embark on their first official assignment from Blue Shield – but when Tom receives an urgent call from the Vatican, things start to move quickly:

With the help of the Patriarch of the Russian Orthodox Church, they discover clues to an age-old myth: the Russian Atlantis. And a murderous race to find an ancient, long-lost relic leads them from Cuba to the Russian hinterlands.

What mystical treasure lies buried beneath Nizhny Novgorod? Who laid the evil trap? And what does it all have to do with Tom's grandfather?

Click here or open link:

———

THE GOLDEN PATH

(A Tom Wagner Adventure 4)

The greatest treasure of mankind. An international intrigue. A cruel revelation.

Now a special unit for Blue Shield, Tom and his team are on a search for the legendary El Dorado. But, as usual, things don't go as planned.

The team gets separated and is – literally – forced to fight a battle on multiple fronts: Hellen and Cloutard make discoveries that overturn the familiar story of El Dorado's gold.

Meanwhile, the President of the United States has tasked Tom with keeping a dangerous substance out of the hands of terrorists.

Click here or open link:
https://robertsmaclay.com/4-tw

———

THE CHRONICLE OF THE ROUND TABLE

(A Tom Wagner Adventure 5)

The first secret society of mankind. Artifacts of inestimable power. A race you cannot win.

The events turn upside down: Tom Wagner is missing. Hellen's father has turned up and a hot lead is waiting for the Blue Shield team: The legendary Chronicle of the Round Table.

What does the Chronicles of the Round Table of King Arthur say? Must the history around Avalon and Camelot be rewritten? Where is Tom and who is pulling the strings?

Click here or open link:
https://robertsmaclay.com/5-tw

————

THE CHALICE OF ETERNITY

(A Tom Wagner Adventure 6)

The greatest mystery in the world. False friends. All-powerful adversaries.

The Chronicle of the Round Table has been found and Tom Wagner, Hellen de Mey and François Cloutard face their greatest challenge yet: The search for the Holy Grail.

But their adventure does not lead them to the time of the Templars and the Crusades, but much further back into mankind's history. And the hunt into the past is a journey of no return. From Egypt to Vienna, from Abu Dhabi to Valencia, from Monaco to Macao, the hunt is on for the greatest myth of mankind. And in the end, there's a phenomenal surprise for everyone.

Click here or open link:

https://robertsmaclay.com/6-tw

————

THE SWORD OF REVELATION

(A Tom Wagner Adventure 7)

A false lead. A bitter truth. This time, it's all or nothing.

Hellen's mother is dying and only a miracle can save her...but for that, the team needs to locate mysterious and long-lost artifacts.

At the same time, their struggle with the terrorist organization Absolute Freedom reaches its climax: what is the group's true, diabolical plan? Who is pulling the strings behind this worldwide conspiracy?

The Sword of Revelation completes the circle: all questions are answered, all the loose ends woven into a revelation for our heroes — and for all the fans of the Tom Wagner adventures!

Click here or open link:

https://robertsmaclay.com/tw-7

THRILLED READER REVIEWS

"Suspense and entertainment! I've read a lot of books like this one; some better, some worse. This is one of the best books in this genre I've ever read. I'm really looking forward to a good sequel. "

———

"I just couldn't put this book down. Full of surprising plot twists, humor, and action! "

———

"An explosive combination of Robert Langdon, James Bond & Indiana Jones"

———

"Good build-up of tension; I was always wondering what happens next. Toward the end, where the story gets more and more complex and constantly changes scenes, I was on the edge of my seat"

———

"Great! I read all three books in one sitting. Dan Brown better watch his back."

———

"The best thing about it is the basic premise, a story with historical background knowledge scattered throughout the book–never too much at one time and always supporting the plot"

————

"Entertaining and action-packed! The carefully thought-out story has a clear plotline, but there are a couple of unexpected twists as well. I really enjoyed it. The sections of the book are tailored to maximize the suspense, they don't waste any time with unimportant details. The chapters are short and compact–perfect for a half-hour commute or at night before turning out the lights. Recommended to all lovers of the genre and anyone interested in getting to know it better. I'll definitely read the sequel."

————

"Anyone who likes reading Dan Brown, James Rollins and Preston & Child needs to get this book."

————

"An exciting build-up, interesting and historically significant settings, surprising plot twists in the right places."

ABOUT THE AUTHORS
ROBERTS & MACLAY

Roberts & Maclay have known each other for over 25 years, are good friends and have worked together on various projects.

The fact that they are now also writing thrillers together is less coincidence than fate. Talking shop about films, TV series and suspense novels has always been one of their favorite pastimes.

———

M.C. Roberts is the pen name of an successful entrepreneur and blogger. Adventure stories have always been his passion: after recording a number of superhero audiobooks on his father's old tape recorder as a six-year-old, he postponed his dream of writing novels for almost 40 years, and worked as a marketing director, editor-in-chief, DJ, opera critic, communication coach, blogger, online marketer and author of trade books...but in the end, the call of adventure was too strong to ignore.

———

R.F. Maclay is the pen name of an outstanding graphic designer and advertising filmmaker. His international career began as an electrician's apprentice, but he quickly realized that he was destined to work creatively. His family and friends were skeptical at first...but now, 20 years later, the passionate, self-taught graphic designer and filmmaker has delighted record labels, brand-name products and tech companies with his work, as well as making a name for himself as a commercial filmmaker and illustrator. He's also a walking encyclopedia of film and television series.

www.RobertsMaclay.com

Printed in Great Britain
by Amazon

26021558R00209